D1051340

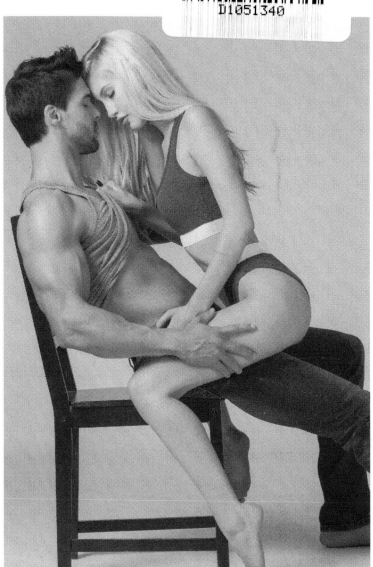

FIGHTING FOR EVERYTHING

A WARRIOR FIGHT CLUB NOVEL

LAURA KAYE

Fighting for Everything

FIRST EDITION May 2018

FIGHTING FOR EVERYTHING © Laura Kaye.

ALL RIGHTS RESERVED.

7298 6903 7/18

The characters and events portrayed in this book are fictional and/or are used fictiously and are solely the product of the author's imagination. Any similarity to persons living or dead, places, businesses, events, or locales is purely coincidental.

Cover Design and Photography by Sara Eirew

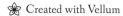 Created with Vellum

READ HARD WITH LAURA KAYE

Warrior Fight Club Series
FIGHTING FOR EVERYTHING
FIGHTING FOR WHAT'S HIS - August 7, 2018
FIGHTING THE FIRE - Fall 2018
WORTH FIGHTING FOR - March 2019

Blasphemy Series
HARD TO SERVE
BOUND TO SUBMIT
MASTERING HER SENSES
EYES ON YOU
THEIRS TO TAKE
ON HIS KNEES

Raven Riders Series
HARD AS STEEL
RIDE HARD
RIDE ROUGH
RIDE WILD

RIDE DIRTY

Hard Ink Series
HARD AS IT GETS
HARD AS YOU CAN
HARD TO HOLD ON TO
HARD TO COME BY
HARD TO BE GOOD
HARD TO LET GO
HARD AS STEEL
HARD EVER AFTER
HARD TO SERVE

Hearts in Darkness Duet
HEARTS IN DARKNESS
LOVE IN THE LIGHT

Heroes Series
HER FORBIDDEN HERO
ONE NIGHT WITH A HERO

Stand Alone Titles
DARE TO RESIST
JUST GOTTA SAY

Join Laura's VIP Readers for Exclusives & More!

THE WARRIOR FIGHT CLUB SERIES

This fight club has one rule:
you must be a veteran...

FIGHTING FOR EVERYTHING
FIGHTING FOR WHAT'S HIS - AUGUST 7, 2018
FIGHTING THE FIRE - FALL 2018
WORTH FIGHTING FOR - MARCH 2019

To Lea Nolan, my sister from another mother,
Thanks for always inspiring me!

CHAPTER ONE

Noah Cortez was burning in his skin. The fire was all in his mind, of course, like a war that raged inside himself. Razing everything he'd once been and turning the landscape unrecognizable. And yet, here he stood, making small talk over burgers and dogs at his parents' annual Memorial Day barbecue. His first one since he'd been discharged from the Marine Corps.

Joining the party had been a mistake. Just like he knew it would be. Because Noah sure as hell didn't feel like he had anything to celebrate, least of all himself. He was trying his best to hold his shit together, but every time one of his parents' friends thanked him for his service he kinda wanted to puke. Or punch someone. And since neither was socially acceptable, he'd retreated to the edge of the party. More observer than participant.

Which sounded a helluva lot like his life right now.

Because Noah was lost.

Johnson. Kendrick. Martinez. Fender. Smythe. Khan. Stein...

He concentrated on the names of his fallen buddies from the Marine Corps. Those were the men who deserved to be memorialized, and they were also the single best reminder of why Noah should be grateful to be alive. Because he knew he *should* be.

"Noah? Hey, Noah, you all right?"

Blinking out of the thoughts, Noah found his father and brother Josh looking at him with *that expression.* The one that said he'd totally checked out again, that they were worried about him, and that they knew he wasn't all there. Not anymore.

Partial deafness and blindness from an IED explosion and brain injury did that to a man. Among other things.

Noah's gut clenched and he tried to subtly shift his stance to put his good right ear closer to the conversation. "Yeah, sure," he said, taking a swig of his beer. He'd been holding it so long it had gone warm.

His dad nodded, his gray eyes scanning Noah's face and not missing a thing. Despite the fact that Elias Cortez was not his biological father, his stepdad had been able to read Noah almost from the very beginning, when he'd been a seven-year-old still grieving over the loss of his father in a car accident two years before. Inability to fake it in front of the man—in front of anyone, really—was one of the reasons Noah preferred being alone these days. "Was just wondering what time you can get into your new place on Saturday," his dad asked louder.

"Rental office opens at nine," Noah said, the gaze of his good right eye drifting over his dad's shoulder to the colorful lanterns strung up around the big backyard. The sun was setting, making them glow against the surrounding woods. "I don't have a lot to move, though, so it shouldn't take long."

He'd gone right from college graduation to five years in the Corps, so he'd never had time to accumulate much. In the seven months since he'd been medically discharged, he'd been living in his parents' basement in Alexandria, Virginia. Trying to figure out what to do with his life. Going to physical therapy and doctors' appointments to try to get his body working again.

Occasionally seeing the shrink to get his head screwed back on right. The latter was a losing proposition, for sure. At least, that's how it felt.

His dad nodded. "We're giving you the furniture downstairs."

Noah smothered the frustration that had built over months of his parents worrying about him. Like he couldn't take care of himself. Like he wasn't a grown-ass man with a healthy savings account and a body that was mostly able despite the fact it didn't work like it had before. He knew they meant well. But what they didn't know was that their good intentions were feeding into how bad he already felt about himself. Not that he really needed much help in that department. "Don't have to do that. I can get what I need."

His father smirked and arched a brow. "Your mother insists. Take it up with her if you want to register a complaint."

"Better just take it," Josh said, grinning. Two years older, his brother reminded Noah so much of the man he used to be that it was sometimes hard to be around him now. Big smile, wicked sense of humor, glass-half-full outlook, and his whole life planned out to the last letter. He was an associate in a law firm with a growing book of business and the respect of everyone who knew him.

"Hey, babe," Josh's fiancé Maria said, coming up to stand beside him. She threaded her arm through his. "Ready to grab some food?"

Josh kissed her temple, his nose nuzzling against her wavy black hair. "Absolutely. Wanna join?" Josh asked, looking from their father to Noah.

"I'll be there in a minute," Dad said, clapping Noah on the shoulder. "Gonna go help your mother."

Noah shrugged. "I'm good for now." He tried to give them a smile, but wasn't sure it came off.

As Noah watched the couple walk away, something squeezed inside him. Because there was *another* thing that Josh had that Noah didn't, *and wouldn't*—a relationship with a good woman who loved him. Josh and Maria were engaged to be married in August, and Noah was happy for them. He really was. At least, he tried to be. But he hated how Josh's happiness made him feel even worse about himself.

Despite agreeing to be the best man at his brother's wedding, Noah was rocking some not-so-healthy feelings about the whole thing. Resentment that his brother's life seemed to be falling into place so easily. Jealousy that the guy had things Noah wasn't sure he'd ever find, now. Because what woman would want a man so twisted up inside that on some level he resented his own brother's happiness?

Worse, Noah wasn't just jealous and resentful, as if those weren't soul-sucking enough.

He was angry. Irrationally so. At Josh having what he didn't. At Josh being whole while Noah was so damn broken. At... everything. Noah gripped the bottle in his hands so tight he thought it might crack. At least the glass slicing into his palm would give him something else to think about.

And then he found himself *really* wishing the glass would do its worst—because right at that moment, the thing he'd been most dreading at this party happened.

Kristina Moore stepped out from the back door of his parents' house onto the wide wooden deck.

And, God, with her long blond hair, bright blue eyes, warm peaches-and-cream skin, and pale pink dress flowing almost to the ground around those generous curves, she was such a lovely fucking vision that it made his chest ache. She'd always been pretty, but now she seemed to have come into her own. Kristina was more outgoing, more confident, more independent than she'd been when he'd left for the Marines. And it was so fucking sexy.

That sexiness also confused the hell out of Noah. Because Kristina was his best friend. Had been since his family had moved into this neighborhood after his mom and stepdad married, since they'd been kids riding bikes and camping in the backyard and having movie nights in one another's basements. While he'd been overseas, the steady stream of care packages she'd sent and their regular email exchanges and Skype sessions had helped him beat away the worst of the homesickness. She was two years younger than Noah, but the difference had never mattered. They'd clicked on grief over their fathers and so many other things...

Kristina scanned the crowd, and he knew she was looking for him. Just like always. Just like old times. When hanging out together was a given. Only, the Noah standing in the growing darkness wasn't the man she used to know.

When Kristina spotted him hanging at the edge of the party, her whole face brightened. And, man, if that wasn't a kick in the gut. Because as much as a part of Noah wanted to see her, talk to her, hang with her, he also *didn't*. Because if she realized just how fucked up he'd become, just how much like her old man he was, he didn't think he could stomach seeing the pity in her eyes.

Or the disappointment. Or the fear. And she knew him too damn well.

It was why he'd been avoiding her since he got home. At some point he was going to break, and he didn't want to do it in her presence.

Kristina cut through the party and came right up to him, the dress flowing behind her. "Hey, you," she said, a warm, sexy grin on her face. Without a moment of hesitation, she pressed her body against him and wrapped her arms around his neck, hugging him tight.

He couldn't keep his muscles from bracing against the touch, against the way her full breasts crushed against his chest and her soft hair caressed his neck. "Hey," Noah managed. God, she smelled like sweet vanilla cream. Her heat soaked into him and warmed places that felt so very cold. He was so unused to feeling anything good that he started to harden.

Which showed just how messed up he was. Because how many times over the years had they joked about being squarely and happily in the friend zone? *Dos amigos.* Best buds. Best friends. *Without* benefits. The one time they'd given kissing a try when she was about fourteen it had felt so weird they'd laughed about it for the rest of the night.

Noah valued their friendship down into his very soul, because it was quite likely the most meaningful relationship with a woman he'd ever had. Maybe the most meaningful relationship he had, period. No one knew him like Kristina did. Now, given the ugliness inside him, he hoped no one else ever did.

Before he chased more of that pleasurable goodness by grinding his erection against her, Noah stepped backward out of the circle of her arms, shrugging her off more blatantly than he'd intended. The flash of hurt and confusion in her eyes cut him down deep, but this was Kristina, for Christ's sake. Not someone to get off on. Not someone to disappoint. And not someone to scare, either.

Tension and stress made his muscles go taut, and a shakiness bloomed inside his gut. Behind both eyes, a headache throbbed, and a distant ringing sound played deep within his good ear.

God, not now.

Whenever something stressed him out these days, anxiety

needled its way through him and ambushed his central nervous system like a damn insurgent. Noah hated it.

"So, guess what?" she said, a smile coming back to her lips.

"What?" Noah said, restlessness flooding through him. His gaze pinged around the yard, identifying escape routes. Prickles ran down his spine.

"I got the job at the Art Factory for the summer. So I get to teach poetry and short story workshops and I'll only have to teach one block of regular summer school," she said, her voice so full of excitement, of life. Kristina taught middle school language arts, but she'd also published some of her poetry and stories in literary magazines.

"That's great," Noah said, fisting his hands against the sensation of his fingertips going numb. Judging by how her expression dimmed, his reaction had disappointed her. *He'd* disappointed her. Just like he knew he would. "Really. Good for you," he added, but it came out breathy and unconvincing because his chest had gone tight.

He needed to get away before he ended up having a full-blown panic attack in front of all these people. In front of Kristina. In front of his parents and brother. In front of all these strangers. Embarrassing himself and ruining everyone's night. But if he could just leave and get himself together for a few minutes, then maybe he could come back and act like a normal human being.

Sometimes, he really fucking wished he'd had a limb blown off, or that the injuries to the left side of his face hadn't healed so well. Then at least he'd have an obvious reason for struggling to readjust to civilian life. Then people would look at him and just *know* what his fucking problem was.

Kristina hugged herself, her arms pushing the mounds of her breasts together under the low V-neck of her dress. "Yeah, so—"

"I, uh..." Noah tore his gaze away from her cleavage and swallowed hard. "Gotta...go...," he said, not even sure of the words coming out of his mouth. And then he pushed past her and headed toward the house, not turning back when Kristina called his name.

No doubt disappointing her one more time.

CHAPTER TWO

Kristina stared at Noah's back and wondered what the hell just happened.

The distant, sullen man who couldn't be bothered to be interested in or spend five minutes with her was not the Noah she'd known most of her life. Tonight wasn't the first time since he'd come home from the Marines that he'd acted weird around her. And weirdness was something they'd *never* had between them, not in all the years she'd known him, not when they'd confessed things to one another they would never otherwise say, and not even when they'd dated other people and shared the juicy details.

For a long moment, she stood at the edge of the party and debated, and then she decided—she wasn't letting it go this time.

Her gut told her Noah needed her.

Making her way through the other partygoers, she headed toward the deck, intent on confronting Noah about what was going on with him once and for all. Because that's what best friends did—that's what *they'd* always done.

Growing up, Kristina had always clammed up whenever her father's schizophrenia worsened—and Noah knew her well enough to know her silence and withdrawal meant something was bothering her. Every time, he worked to draw it out of her no matter how much she resisted. He'd always been relentless about it, knowing she needed to let it out even when she hadn't wanted to face just how troubled her father was—and that he might never get better.

Noah needed Kristina to be that relentless now. Her gaze followed him as he disappeared inside the house.

For a lot of reasons, she'd been holding back since he'd gotten home from the military. Because he'd been upset about being discharged. Because he'd earned the right to feel anger at no longer being able to do what he loved. Because after everything he'd been through, he'd needed time to heal without her jumping on him.

Well, not *jumping* on him. Because, even though Noah was totally freaking jumpable, they were just friends.

Actually, *just friends* didn't begin to do them justice. They were so much more than friends. Kindred spirits, maybe.

Kristina jogged up the steps and nearly ran into Mr. Cortez as he came out of the back door, his hands full of bags of buns for the burgers and dogs.

"Ah, there you are," he said wearing that big open smile that all the Cortez men had. Well, Noah *used* to have it. Had she seen him smile even once since he'd been home? "How are you doing, Kristina?" He gave her a one-armed hug.

"Summer's almost here, Mr. Cortez, so I couldn't be better," she said, giving him a wink. Truth be told, she loved being a teacher, so she didn't spend the school year wishing for June's summer dismissal to arrive. But she appreciated the extra time summer gave her to concentrate on her writing, which was harder to come by when she had papers and homework assignments and course preps needing her attention at nights and on the weekends. Teaching was one of those jobs where, no matter how much you worked, there was always something else you could be doing.

Mr. Cortez laughed. "I bet. Make sure you get something to eat," he said, gesturing to the bags of buns. "We made enough food for the entire neighborhood."

"I will," Kristina said, giving him a smile and then slipping inside the Cortez's big, warm kitchen. Mr. and Mrs. Cortez were both amazing cooks. Kristina had many fond memories of watching the couple in the kitchen, of spending time with what she'd sometimes wished was *her* happy family, of meals filled with laughter and conversation, rather than the tension and awkwardness that had often filled her home.

Searching for Noah, Kristina peered into the family room, then the living room. No luck. In the hall, she opened the door to the basement where he'd been living the past few months. "Noah?"

All was quiet.

She jogged halfway down to where the wall gave way to a railed bannister and peered into the open rec room. A pool table sat at one end and a big, comfy seating area and TV filled the other. "Noah, are you down here?" she called again.

Despite the lack of response, she continued down and crossed the room to the mostly closed door in the back corner— Noah's bedroom since he'd returned just before last Christmas. God, Kristina had thought she'd received the best Christmas present *ever*—Noah home safe and sound.

Well, mostly sound, anyway. An IED blast had taken the hearing and most of his vision on his left side, and he'd struggled with bad migraines and equilibrium problems when he'd first returned. But he was home and he was *alive*, and having him back again had made it feel like she could finally breathe after years of knowing he was in danger every second of every day.

She knocked softly. "Hey Noah, it's me."

All she heard was a long exhale of breath, but it was enough.

Why hadn't he answered her? Her stomach clenched as she pushed open the door far enough to see Noah standing in the dark doorway to his bathroom, his back against the door jamb, his arms crossed, and his head hanging on his big shoulders.

She didn't need to ask if he was okay, because he was radiating *not okay* loud and clear. Kristina walked right up to him. "What's going on?" she asked. Dim light from the rec room filtered over him, allowing her to just make out the tight clench of his square jaw, the narrowed cast of his dark brown eyes, the harsh set of his beautiful mouth.

Wait. What? Where had *that* come from?

Noah shook his head, forcing Kristina to drop the ridiculous line of thought.

She stepped closer so that she could look more directly into his eyes. "Come on, Noah. It's me." She ached for him to open up, but what she noticed even more was the low buzz rushing through her body. From how close she stood to all his taut hardness. It wasn't like she was just noticing that Noah was hot, like, *dayum* hot, but nearly five years in the Marines had matured him and built hard muscle that hadn't been there before. And clearly her *body* was just noticing, probably because they hadn't had the chance to spend much time together since he'd gotten back.

"Kristina," he said, his voice so low it was nearly a whisper, or a plea. He leaned his forehead against hers. It was such a sweet, needful gesture that Kristina's chest seized.

"First, I'm hugging you. Then we're talking, buddy," she said, wrapping her arms around his big shoulders and planting her cheek against his chest. The embrace wasn't unusual—they'd always been affectionate with each other. She'd lay against him while they watched a movie or he'd sling an arm over her shoulders while they were out together. When things were bad with her dad, he'd hold her when she finally gave into her grief about it and cried. That's how they'd always been.

He embraced her right back and leaned his face against her hair.

After a long moment, Kristina pulled away—

Noah wouldn't let her go. His grip on her tightened, and he held her fast against him. Was he breathing faster? Was he trembling?

Against her belly, he hardened.

Kristina's breath caught in her throat. Noah was aroused... by her? Or just, like, in her general vicinity? Or...? She swallowed hard as her thoughts flew.

As they stood there, suspended in the dark, stolen moment, the air around them flashed hot and closed in, narrowing the world to all the places their bodies touched. His erection grew, pressing against her with more insistence.

And holy shit. He was big. Like, *big*.

Heat bloomed over her skin everywhere and she held herself perfectly still. Because this was different. This was *not* friendly. This was more.

A strange tension wrapped around them, and it scared and attracted Kristina in equal measure. She shuddered out a breath as her body came to life against his. Her breathing quickened, her nipples peaked, her core clenched.

Noah made a noise in the back of his throat like a moan, and his arms tightened around her, pulling their bodies totally flush.

Kristina's breath caught at the hard press of his erection *and* at the shocking arousal it unleashed in her.

This is Noah. This is Noah. This is Noah.

But it didn't seem to matter to her body. The soft cotton of her dress became heavy and irritating against her skin, and all she wanted was for it to be *off*. So he could be all over her. This sudden, intoxicating need was brand new to her—in general and certainly with Noah. She wasn't a virgin, but she'd never felt with another man the kind of desire rocketing through her just then. And all they'd done was touch.

Why was this happening?

Her hips shifted without her meaning to do it, and it made her belly grind against all that long hardness.

Noah hissed in her ear. His fingertips dug into her back... and then wandered, one hand pressing low against her hip, one skimming up her neck into her hair. Holding her tight. Bringing her closer.

She was half sure she was imagining that they were locked inside this raging bubble of attraction, except that his heart thundered beneath where her head rested, his breathing had gone rough, and his skin felt every bit as feverish as hers.

She had to stop this...whatever this was.

Tilting her head back, the words were on the tip of her tongue. Her eyes locked with his, and even in the dimness she could see that they were blazing hot and almost predatory in their directness. It stole her capacity to speak, because she was unequivocally sure he'd never looked at her like that. Need roared off of him and through her, spiking her arousal so hard and fast that she became wet between her legs.

From just a look.

Heart pounding like a bass drum, Kristina swallowed hard. What would she do if he kissed her? One kissing experiment aside, she'd never had to ask that in regard to him. Another question followed close behind: what would she do if he *didn't*?

He didn't give her the space to debate. His hand fisted in the back of her hair. The roughness licked flames through her and sent her heart into a sprint. And then he was guiding her head, bringing them together, bringing his face closer and closer to hers. His gaze dropped to her lips, and a shaky breath caressed her skin.

Noah kissed her.

The first press of his lips against hers was soft and sweet, and she thought she might shatter from the shock of sensation just that light touch delivered. The one that made her want to forget who he was and what he was to her and climb him like a tree.

This is Noah. This is Noah. This is Noah.

Kristina had never wanted anything like this with him. Never *before*. But now that she'd had a taste, it was like she'd never eaten a meal in her life. His lips skated over hers, and she moaned at the unexpected goodness of it.

And it was like the sound burst some dam inside him. On an answering groan, he planted both hands in her hair and kissed her harder than she'd ever been kissed in her life. His mouth claimed, his tongue penetrated, his body grinded against hers. He pushed her against the opposite side of the door frame, pinning her there with all his muscled strength.

It was stunning. It was glorious. It was so wrong.

This is Noah. This is—

So freaking good.

The kiss felt like he was feasting on her, like he'd been *starving* for her and finally let himself have a taste. His desire was thrilling. His rough intensity was breath-stealing. His need fueled hers. Against his chest, her nipples ached to be tugged and sucked. She clenched her thighs together, dying for relief from the inferno he'd ignited inside her. She sucked hard on his tongue and ran her hands up the corded muscles of his biceps to grasp his thick shoulders, trying to anchor herself against the storm his desire had unleashed in both of them.

Her brain tried to remind her why she'd come down here, that she'd wanted to confront Noah—*her best friend, Noah,* but then his hands skimmed down her body—over her breasts, her belly, to her hips—and his clutching, urgent touch chased the thoughts away.

Later. There'd be time for talk, for thought, for consequences...later.

Because there wasn't a chance in hell she was pulling away from what he was giving her. Not when she'd never felt anything like it before. Not when she hadn't even known her body was capable of feeling this way. Not when he'd been the one to open her eyes to how she *could* feel.

With the right man.

Except he isn't—

Later.

Tongue stroking and twining with hers, his hands squeezed her hips, his fingers digging in to her ass. The thin cotton of her dress and the thinner satin of her panties allowed his heat to reach her skin, setting her on fire everywhere. And then his hands palmed her ass and hauled her even tighter against him.

On tiptoes, Kristina's head fell back on a moan. She ground her hips against his, needing more. More of his touch. More of him against her. More of the hard press of that delicious ridge in his jeans. More of Noah everywhere.

She could hardly believe she was thinking this way about *Noah*, but as he ran kisses and small nips down her throat, all she could do was grasp the back of his head and hold him there, urging him on.

God, how far was she willing to go here?

Because her mind already had her naked and underneath him—

He pulled her off the wall and walked her toward the bed. He separated from her long enough to reach over and give the door a hard push. It clicked shut, encasing them in darkness. And then Noah was right back on her. Kissing her. Touching her. Lowering her to the mattress and climbing on top of her.

Why wasn't he saying anything? Why wasn't she?

Part of her thought she should slow this down and see if he was really okay taking them where they were going. But *damn* was it hard to think when his knees pushed her thighs apart and his hips settled between her legs. His weight covering her felt obscenely good. "God, Noah," she moaned. Kristina's thighs spread wider as she drew them up and her knees fell open.

"Fuck," he rasped, attacking her mouth again. His hips circled against hers, giving her the hard friction she was so desperate for. "Feels good. God, it feels good." He kissed along her throat to her shoulder, and then he pulled aside the straps to her dress and bra.

Kristina moaned as his lips and fingers followed the fabric's retreat, until Noah's breath caressed her breast and his lips dragged across her nipple. She arched at the goodness of him licking her, flicking at her, sucking her. Her hands flew to his dark hair, loving that it was long enough that she could fist and pull.

Noah moved to the other side and bared her there, too. And then he was sucking hard on one nipple while he teased and tugged at the other. Each touch, each lick, each bite flashed through her and pooled liquid heat between her thighs. She used the leverage of her heels against the bed to rock herself against him—

Pop. Pop-pop-pop. Pop. Pop. Boom.

Noah was off her in a flash.

In the dim light thrown by the LED screen of his alarm clock, she saw him tumble in a quick and controlled move into a crouching position on the far side of the bedside table.

Boom. Boom. Pop-pop-pop.

Heart thundering in her throat at the confusing suddenness of his movements, Kristina couldn't figure out what the hell was going on. "Uh, what are you doing?"

No answer. The fireworks display that the Harlows always put on at their big riverfront house seemed even louder against his silence.

She frowned. "Noah?" Scooting to the edge of the bed, Kristina tugged her dress back into place. Sheer bewilderment pushed every other reaction away as she leaned over and fumbled for the lamp on the nightstand.

Light illuminated the room, coming from right above where Noah remained crouched.

And it was like he didn't even notice. Like he didn't see it. Or her.

Like he wasn't there at all.

CHAPTER THREE

THE FIREFIGHT RAGED AROUND NOAH. He crouched at the edge of a building and peered around the corner, automatic weapon in hand, trigger finger at the ready. A bombed-out car, half-hidden passageways between the buildings, and high rooftops gave their enemies plenty of places to hide down the seemingly empty street.

Pop-pop-pop.

Noah pulled back. God, he had a bad feeling about this. Where was the fucking shooter?

He looked around the corner again... The image before him went shimmery, a strange light shining through the landscape.

What the hell? Was he experiencing haloes now? The visual disturbances happened sometimes when he looked at bright lights.

Wait. That didn't make sense.

Squeezing his eyes shut tight, Noah shook his head.

He blinked his eyes open again to find Kristina kneeling in front of him, golden light spilling over her. His first thought was that she was in danger. But then his brain registered the room surrounding her—surrounding them.

His room. At home. In Alexandria.

Where the fuck had *that* come from? He'd had a lot of issues since returning stateside, but he'd never before been sucked into a memory like that. He might as well have blacked out. Jesus, it had been so real it was like he'd really been there. He flinched against another explosion of fireworks.

Humiliation flooded through Noah fast and hot. Anger followed close behind. He gulped for air.

"What just happened?" Kristina asked. And damn if her cheeks weren't still flushed from...

Fuck. From how Noah had kissed her, touched her, ground himself against her. Chasing something good. Something beautiful. Something that would help him escape all the ugliness inside him.

Boom-boom-boom. Noah's breath caught in his throat and he flinched. The fucking fireworks. The sound had pulled him right back into Iraq, and there had been absolutely nothing conscious about it. Still wasn't, judging by the sweat trickling down his back, the paranoia burning through his mind, and the triple-timing beat of his heart against his sternum. His mouth was like a desert, and he couldn't manage to form words around the panic seizing his body.

Kristina crawled closer and reached her hand toward him. "It's me, Noah."

He recoiled, his back coming up hard against the corner of the room. "Don't," he choked out. Sadness carved worry lines onto her pretty face, and he was certain he couldn't loathe himself more than he did just then. For long minutes, they sat there. Facing off. Both of them trapped in the awkwardness his delusions had created.

Finally, the fireworks boomed in a symphony of explosions, big bangs, smaller pops, and crackling, whistling noises combining in what had to be the finale. But it was like the fireworks were hyperlinked to sounds and sights and even smells from his past. Buddies crying out. Spilled blood. Torn bodies. Burned flesh. Noah's heart was going to beat right the fuck out of his chest. He was sure of it.

Silence.

Well, all except for the rasping pants of his attempts at breathing. Christ, it sounded like he'd just finished a thirty-mile hump with a sixty-pound pack on his back.

Actually, he'd never sounded this bad after one of those.

Pressure against the top of his sneaker. Kristina's hand rested there, trying to reach him, trying to comfort him. But all he felt was soul-scorching humiliation. He *knew* he'd lose it in front of her. He hadn't known when or how or why, but the very fact of it had been all but certain. Now he'd done it. And she was looking at him like his head might start doing three-sixties as he spoke in tongues.

He couldn't *stand* it.

"Go," he rasped, shaking now from anger as much as from the residuals of the panic attack. Or whatever the hell it had been.

"What? No." She scooted closer, her hands going to his drawn-up knees. "Tell me what's going on, Noah. Talk to me. I want to help—"

"You *can't*," he bit out on a quick shake of his head. God, the closer she got, the less air there was in the room. And, ah, hell, the fact that he'd been all over her right before he'd fallen to pieces just made it that much worse. He'd just felt *so* bad and she'd felt *so* good and he'd broken and given in to the sheer *need* to feel better. Just for a little while.

What an asshole he was to use her that way. His best friend.

And then the fireworks. They'd been over for what felt like

several long minutes, but his body didn't seem to be unwinding one damn bit.

"I'm not leaving." She met him glare for glare, and he could see her digging in.

"Should," he managed.

She shook her head and ignored him entirely. "Was it the fireworks?"

Noah heaved a shuddering breath. She wasn't going to back off. Part of him loved her for that, because he would've done the same thing if their positions had been reversed. But their situations weren't the same. Because he hadn't weathered a lifetime of living with a father who had a habit of deciding he no longer needed his meds, which would lead to a sometimes months-long episode of troubling or even dangerous behavior that sometimes resulted in the police being called to assist in an involuntary hospital admission. But even when he was on his meds, Mr. Moore sometimes believed he was an undercover agent involved in covert investigations, investigations he'd actually pursue when he was out in public—though he only made admissions quite that revealing when he was doing worse.

Damn if Noah didn't now have a helluva lot more insight into what Mr. Moore might've been facing all these years. It wasn't the man's fault that he perceived the world differently, and it wasn't Noah's either. He knew that. But that didn't mean either of them were always easy for the others in their lives to handle. And the last thing Noah ever wanted to do was burden Kristina with his *own* mental health issues. She had enough to deal with.

And he was hanging on by a very thin thread.

"Kris," he managed, hands fisting against his thighs.

"Sshh," she said. "Just breathe for a minute." She rose in a flourish of pink cotton, disappeared into his bathroom, and returned a moment later with a cup of water. "See if this will help."

Hating the feeling that she was nursing him, he accepted the cup in his hand, knowing he wouldn't be able to hold it steady even as a little water sloshed over the rim. Noah sucked half of it down in one greedy gulp. It eased his throat and cooled the hottest edge of the fire inside his chest.

"Thank you," he whispered, his head dropping back against the wall. He closed his eyes and wished he could will the whole world away.

"Have you had panic attacks like this before?"

Noah kept his eyes closed and clamped down on the knee-jerk reaction to snap at her. He was going to have to give her just enough to get her to back off, wasn't he? Fine. He'd go with the basics he gave his family.

"Have had panic attacks before. Normal consequence of the TBI, apparently," he said, referring to the traumatic brain injury caused by an IED blast that had taken out a lot of his unit and stolen half of his hearing and sight.

The real shit of the situation was that the wiring in his brain was so fucked up not just because of that one blast, but also because he'd experienced dozens of blasts over the course of his military career. Maybe even more than a hundred. And it turned out that blast waves played punching bag with your brain coming and going and had a cumulative effect his neurologists said they were just starting to fully understand.

Which was apparently why the hit he'd taken had fucked him up as bad as it did. It'd been the final straw that had broken the already-beat-up camel's back.

All that was a real bitch to learn after the fact for someone who'd served in the 2nd Combat Engineer Battalion, which handled anything and everything having to do with explosives—

breaching doors and roofs, ordnance disposal, demolitions, minefield construction, and sweeping operations, to name a few.

He gulped more water. "Never this bad before, but it's also the first time I've heard fireworks since I've been back."

If he never heard them again, it would be too soon.

"And the fireworks...sounded like...shooting?" she asked carefully.

Noah lifted his head, guilt and embarrassment swamping his gut. "Look, I didn't mean to freak you out. Especially given..." His gaze flickered to the bed.

"Don't apologize, Noah. It's not your fault," Kristina said. "I only care that you're okay. Are you at least...talking to someone about this?"

He nodded. "I got a guy." And a bad habit of canceling appointments, but she didn't need to know that. Problem was that the more he talked about all of it, the more the nightmares plagued him. And the last thing he wanted to do was waste his or the doc's time by quietly staring at the carpet in the guy's office for an hour a week. Being forced to talk didn't help.

Which was why he needed to get out of this conversation right now.

"You can always talk to me, you know. I'm still the same old Kristina, and you're still the same old Noah. Just like before," she said. The smile on her face was so damn pretty...and hopeful.

He couldn't bring himself to dash that hope, but he had none to give. "Right," Noah said. "Thanks. I'm good. Actually, I think maybe taking a shower might help chill me out."

"Yeah? That sounds like a good idea," she said. They rose off the ground, and hell if he didn't have to keep a hand against the wall to maintain his balance. Panic attacks and anxiety did shit for his equilibrium problems. "I could grab us some food and bring it down for when you're out—"

"*No.* I mean, nah, I'm tired. I, uh, just wanna crash," he said, forcing a false ease into his voice he didn't feel at all. He'd be lucky to sleep. And what sleep he did get would likely leave him wrung out and exhausted. But Kristina didn't need to know any of that, either.

"Oh. Right. Sure." She smoothed her hands over the front of her dress, like she didn't know what else to do with herself. "Well, whoa—" She took a step back and almost tripped over a pillow that had been knocked on the floor. Kristina caught herself on the edge of the bed and chuckled. "That could've been bad." She picked it up and tossed it against the headboard.

Noah gazed from the pillow to her. "Sorry. And, uh, about that," he said, glancing to the bed again. "I probably shouldn't have... I mean, before, when I, uh, kissed you and..." Goddamnit, was it hot in this room or was he in the process of internally combusting? "I think...maybe..."

"It was just a crazy accident," Kristina said, saving him from his apparent inability to string together a coherent sentence. "Heat of the moment." She smiled.

"Yeah. Heat of the moment." A gut check said it was more than that, but none of his checks and balances were working too good these days, now were they.

"Don't worry about it," she said, giving him a wink.

"Okay. Won't happen again, ma'am," he said, making a weak effort to inject some humor.

"Dude, you're the geezer in this friendship, so drop the *ma'am* crap." Kristina pushed onto her tiptoes and gave him a strictly platonic peck on the cheek.

Friendship. Right. Good, at least they were on the same page.

She walked around the foot of the bed and stopped with her hand on the doorknob. "Sure you're okay? I wouldn't mind hanging awhile."

"I'm good," he said, forcing a smile, forcing himself to stay together for just a few more seconds.

"Okey dokey," she said, disappointment plain in the cast of her eyes. "Gimme a call tomorrow."

"Yup."

Kristina slipped out the door and closed it behind her.

Noah released a long breath and braced his hands against his knees. The room seemed cold and the silence loud without Kristina there. And he didn't want to examine that too closely. Or, really, anything that'd happened in this room during the last...hell...he didn't even know how long he'd been with her.

On autopilot, Noah tore off his clothes, locked himself in the bathroom, and turned on the shower water. Not wanting to meet his own gaze, he kept his eyes off the mirror while he waited for the water to warm, and then he stepped in, closed the shower curtain, and rested his hands against the white tile as the hot water sprayed down onto his head.

A sob clawed up from deep inside his chest. Shit, no. If he let that sucker free—

No, goddamnit.

Noah raked his fingers into his hair and pulled against the pressure building up inside him. He'd already lost it. He'd already lost it enough today. No more. *No more.*

Except the pressure just grew and grew and fucking grew—

Noah whirled and punched the wall. Hard. White tile cracked and crumbled under the blow. The destruction...was fucking freeing. He punched again. And again.

And, damn it all to hell, it was like someone had pressed a release valve. He sagged against the side wall and stared at the damage he'd done at the back of the shower. Fuck.

He felt guilty about that. He really did. And he was going to have to get it fixed quick so he didn't have to explain it to his parents.

But it also didn't escape his notice that despite fucking up that wall—and the knuckles on his right hand—he could breathe again. He didn't feel good, but it was still the best he'd felt in days.

CHAPTER FOUR

THURSDAY CAME AND WENT, and still Kristina didn't hear from Noah. She'd texted and called him. Nothing. And it was stressing her out on so many levels.

Sitting in her car in the parking lot at school, the air conditioning slowly but surely cooling the late May air, her thoughts raced.

First, his panic attack. What if he'd had more? What if he was holed up in his room and fighting against them on his own? Kristina had witnessed her dad having plenty of panic attacks over the years, so she knew how they could make a person feel exhausted and in despair, isolated and alone.

Second, his overall mental health. After a lifetime of living with someone who suffered from mental illness, she knew that panic attacks could be just one part of a larger picture. So she'd spent last night ignoring end-of-term papers that needed grading and researching veterans and fireworks online. Her reading led her beyond panic attacks to PTSD, blast-injury symptoms, depression, and the terrifying statistics of how many veterans with untreated conditions like these committed suicide every day.

Twenty-two. Twenty-two veterans *every day*. How was that even possible?

Not that she had any reason to believe Noah was struggling that badly, but that didn't stop her chest from aching every time she thought about all she'd read.

Third, their make-out session. Was he avoiding her now because they'd kissed? Or was that her projecting her own confusion onto him? Because Kristina *was* confused. By what had happened. By her reaction to it. And by the series of dreams she'd been having all week that played out every filthy-hot scenario of what might've happened if those fireworks hadn't gone off.

She'd masturbated to those memories and imaginings. Twice. She'd had orgasms thinking about Noah. *Noah.*

That wasn't weird at all. Nope.

Oh, God, it's so weird! Kristina dropped her forehead against the steering wheel.

At some point, she was going to have to spill about her make-out session to her best friend from college, Kate Arnold. But for today, there was only one way to know the answers to any of the questions swirling around her brain. Talking to Noah. Since he wasn't answering his phone or her texts, that left Kristina only one solution.

She threw the silver Honda Civic into reverse, backed out of her parking space, and made her way to the Cortez house.

Twenty minutes later, she pulled off the George Washington Memorial Parkway that led out to historic Mount Vernon and onto the narrow roads of her old neighborhood. Neither she nor her parents lived here anymore, her parents having moved to Philadelphia while she was in college so her mom could take a new job, but Noah's family still lived in the same house that she'd half grown up in. As she pulled into the big gravel circular drive in front of the two-story brick house, Kristina once again felt like she was coming home.

Noah's dark green Ford Explorer sat in the driveway. Perfect.

When knocking failed to bring an answer, Kristina found the spare key under the middle flowerpot where it had lived for at least fifteen years. She unlocked the door, returned the key, and stepped inside. She almost called out, "Honey, I'm home," but after what had happened between them the other night, maybe that wouldn't be funny?

That she had to even give it a second thought represented all the issues their kissing raised in a nutshell.

"Noah? It's me," she said instead.

She poked through the first floor but found everything quiet and empty, so she headed downstairs. Running water told her the shower was on.

No problem. She'd just wait for him to be done and then she'd let him know that she was there. She sat on the big leather couch and flipped through social media on her phone. And tried like hell to ignore all thoughts of Noah in the shower. Naked. Wet. Muscles glistening.

Stop it, Kristina! Right.

She flicked through her Facebook newsfeed. Read the new comments about her summer workshop position. Liked a video about cats jumping in and out of boxes. Congratulated a friend announcing a promotion.

The water turned off.

Noah is wet and naked and getting out of the shower now.
Ack! Stop it!

She could be normal. Just like she'd been for the previous nineteen years that she'd known him. Determined, she pushed off the couch and crossed to his bedroom door. It sat a few inches ajar, so into the opening she called, "Noah, it's Kristina. Just didn't want to scare you by being out here."

The click of a door opening. "Kristina?"

She chuckled at the surprised tone of his voice. "Yup. Get decent and get your butt out here," she said.

The bedroom door whipped open, and there stood Noah dripping wet holding a white towel around his hips. So close she could've reached out and tugged it off. "Everything okay?" he asked, his brows set into a deep frown.

"Uh...what?" she asked, her gaze stuck on his abdomen. He had the hint of a six pack. Since when did Noah have a six pack? Her gaze raked upward. And he had a tattoo on his left arm where his biceps reached his shoulder. The Marine Corps eagle-globe-anchor symbol in stark black.

"I asked if you were okay," he said, a weird tone in his voice. Maybe because she was standing there slack-jawed and drooling? Crap.

She tore her eyes away from his body and finally looked at his face. Water droplets ran from his hair. They continued down his neck to the warm, olive skin of his chest. She wanted to lick him dry. When had Noah Cortez become so freaking hot? Her *friend* Noah Cortez.

Kristina cleared her throat. "Yeah. Yes. Definitely. More than okay."

"Then why are you here?" He raked a hand through his hair, making his muscles move in all sorts of fascinating ways. "Not, of course, that I'm not glad to see you."

She forced her gaze to stay locked with his dark brown eyes. "I'm here because you've been avoiding me. So I'm making sure you can't avoid me anymore. I want Seven Guys and you're coming with me." Her use of the nickname eked a small smile from him. Five Guys was their favorite burger joint, and always had been. Add Ben and Jerry to those five and you got seven... It had made sense when she was sixteen, anyway. And they needed some old-time normalcy right about now. At least she did. "So, uh, go get decent."

Before I tackle you to the ground and make us both wet.

"Yeah, okay. I guess I could eat," he finally said.

Good. Because she wasn't giving him a choice.

Five minutes later, he walked back out in a dark gray T-shirt and a pair of jeans that hung low on his hips. Kristina rose and nearly fumbled her phone, but finally managed to pull herself together. "Mind if I use your bathroom real quick?" she asked, stepping toward his bedroom door.

"Course not," he said as she disappeared into his room. "Oh, uh, wait. It might be better if you go upstairs."

"I can't wait," she called as she flipped on the bathroom light. "I'll be quick."

She closed the door...and it was like bathing in Noah. The heat of his shower still hung in the air along with the same clean-soap scent she'd inhaled off his skin when they'd kissed. She did her business then stepped to the sink to wash her hands. Glancing in the mirror, Kristina did a double take. At a big hole in the shower tiles.

What in the world? She walked closer and leaned in enough to reach out and touch the broken edge, her thoughts whirling.

She dried her hands, retreated from the bathroom, and found Noah sitting on the coffee table, elbows braced on his knees and head looking down. One hand cupped around the other. And that's when she knew. "You punched the wall?"

His hands went lax and slipped apart, revealing purple bruising and red cuts all over the knuckles of his right hand.

"Why?" she asked, working hard to keep her voice normal, casual. Even though she didn't feel that way inside.

"I needed to," he said. And nothing more.

That didn't begin to satisfy her, but something squeezed in

her belly, telling her that if she pushed, he was going to shut down. Even more than he was already doing. "Okay, well...you ready?" she asked. "Because I skipped lunch and I'm starving."

He finally looked up, and it was like he was assessing her. Assessing whether he should really believe that she was going to let it lie. "I'm good to go," he said.

"Good." Kristina made for the steps. "Then move your ass, Cortez. Because Mama needs a bacon cheeseburger. Stat."

"HUNGRY?" Noah asked as Kristina polished off her burger. The meal had been filled with small talk about her day, the summer workshops she'd be teaching, and Josh's wedding plans, and even a little of their normal banter. Her apparent willingness to stick to comfortable subjects allowed him to relax.

She scowled at him as she took a drink of her soda. "You know, you're not funny." She eyed his food. "You going to finish those—"

He pushed the rest of his fries toward her, earning a big smile. Noah wasn't sure he'd ever finished all of his own French fries in Kristina Moore's presence. Not that he minded. "Ice cream?" he asked when she was done.

"Hells yeah," Kristina said. "How can you have Seven Guys without Ben and Jerry?"

"You can't. Obviously," he said, carrying their tray to the garbage can. Noah could still picture Kristina sitting in the Ben & Jerry's shop explaining what Seven Guys was when she'd been maybe sixteen or seventeen. Sixteen, probably, since it was the summer before he left for college. Kristina's hair had been in a high ponytail and she'd had on a pale blue tank top and the necklace he'd bought her for her sixteenth birthday. It had "Best Friend" etched into a heart that hung through one of the loops of an infinity charm. She'd gotten chocolate-chocolate-chip ice cream and had smacked him on the arm for not telling her she had a smudge of chocolate on her cheek. God, he could picture her as clearly as if he were remembering yesterday.

"Precisely," she said, opening the door onto the busy street.

Noah followed her out and tried really damn hard not to study the way the short skirt she wore hugged her heart-shaped ass. The ass he'd held in his hands when he'd—

"You game to walk down?" she asked, turning to him.

His eyes snapped to her face. "Yeah, sure." He fell in beside her, putting his good ear closest to her as they started down King Street into the red-brick charm of the heart of Old Town. "Do you still have that necklace I gave you when you turned sixteen?"

Kristina's smile was immediate. "Of course. What made you think of that?"

Shrugging, Noah looked straight ahead as they crossed a street. He wasn't sure what had resurrected the memory, all he knew was that Kristina had been on his mind non-stop all week. Ever since he'd held her, kissed her, felt all her soft curves sprawled beneath him. She'd felt so right there, so good. And then he'd ruined it when the damn fireworks went off.

Then again, maybe he hadn't ruined anything. Maybe he'd *saved* them by getting knocked on his ass before burying himself deep inside her and changing their relationship forever.

Because that's where they'd been heading.

Problem was, he couldn't stop thinking about what might've happened if he'd had just a little more time with her... And his body was strung tight imagining it. So tight that he was glad she hadn't let herself into his bathroom while he'd been showering, or she might've heard him groaning her name as he stroked himself to orgasm. Like a damn teenager. It hadn't been the first time this week either.

"Oh, I meant to ask you the other day. I replaced my desk last summer, but I kept the old one. It's pretty plain, just oak. Need it for your new place?" Kristina asked.

"At this rate, all of you are going to save me from furniture shopping at all. Mom gave me the furniture downstairs. Josh and Maria are giving me their kitchen table so they have room for a new one, and now this."

"Is that a yes?" she asked, eyebrow arched.

Noah rolled his eyes. He'd given up on fighting everyone's desire to help him. His discomfort with it had more to do with his own bullshit anyway. "Sure."

"Good. Besides, no furniture shopping means you should be a very, very happy man," she said, chuckling.

"Yeah, I should," he said. The words hung heavily in the air, fraught with additional meaning he hadn't meant to give them. "I, uh, could come by Saturday and grab it. I'll have the truck all day."

"Okay," she said. "What else do you still need? Do you have kitchen stuff? Plates, cups, spatulas...?"

"Spatulas? How much cooking do you think I plan to do?"

"Dude, if spatulas are your threshold for cooking, I'm guessing not much." She bumped into his side and smirked.

Noah gave a small smile and shook his head. "Fine. I guess I need a spatula. I *can* cook eggs, after all."

"Aw, look at you go." Kristina winked at him, and her playfulness made him feel lighter than he had in months. He missed this. Maybe he'd been wrong to stay away from her, especially now that she'd seen him at his worst. "So, whenever you're done Saturday, come grab me and my desk, and then we'll go shopping for house stuff."

"Ooh, sounds thrilling." He gave her a droll stare and tried not to react to the idea of grabbing her.

She laughed, infusing him with more of that lightness.

"Don't be such a boy. Anyway, if anyone can make house stuff thrilling, it's me, baby."

Of that, he had no doubt. Kristina had a knack for making the mundane and everyday special and fun.

He wanted this—her—back in his life.

Which meant, somehow, he needed to put Kristina back in the strictly friends box.

Having lost so much over the past months, he knew he couldn't stomach one more loss. Especially not of his best friend. And though she didn't seem to be acting differently toward him, *he* was looking differently at her. Noticing her ass, the curve of her calf in the sling-back heels, all that soft, soft hair flowing around her shoulders in the early summer breeze.

Noah had always thought Kristina was pretty, and had routinely told her when he didn't think a guy was good enough for her. Because she deserved the best. But he'd never before been distracted by her looks or sexually attracted to her, and now that he'd touched her, some part of him didn't want to stop.

But it had to stop.

They paused at an intersection and waited for the light, then started across.

Tires screeched. A horn blared. And Noah turned just in time to see a car barreling straight for them.

CHAPTER FIVE

Noah grabbed Kristina by the shoulders and hauled her back as an asshole left turner careened by, yelling at them out his window. The car had passed so close that Noah didn't know how it'd missed her.

"Oh, my God," Kristina said in a breathless, shaky voice. She turned the rest of the way into his chest, and her being against him was the only thing that kept him from barreling down the street after the sonofabitch. "He would've run me over if it weren't for you."

Heat shot through Noah's veins, equal parts adrenaline and rage. And damn his imperfect vision, because he hadn't been able to catch the license plate. But Kristina was all that mattered.

"Come on," he said, keeping her tucked tight against his chest and guiding her the rest of the way across. Her pulse was racing so hard he could feel it beating beneath her warm skin.

"You all okay?" an older woman asked.

Noah scanned around them enough to see that more than a few people had witnessed what'd happened. He nodded to the lady. "Yes, ma'am. Thank you for asking." She gave them a worried smile and continued down the sidewalk.

"I'm okay," Kristina said, her voice shaky.

"I know, but come over here for a minute," he said. "I've got you." He pulled her behind the column of an office building, wanting to give her a little privacy to react to what'd just happened. No doubt her adrenaline was pumping as much as his, and maybe more, and he knew exactly how the let-down of all those chemicals could screw with your emotions.

She held up her right hand, the back of which was swelling and promised to bruise. A cut marred one busted knuckle. "We match now," she said in a strained voice.

"Fuck," Noah said, seething. "*Fuck.* I didn't realize he clipped you. Can you make a fist?"

Hand visibly shaking, she curled her fingers and hissed. "Yeah. It hurts, but I think I can. Can you just...would you just...hold me?"

She didn't have to ask, because just then, he wanted nothing more.

Careful of her hand, Noah hugged her tight against his chest and breathed in her trademark vanilla cream scent. Goddamn that asshole. Fantasies ran through his mind. Of seeing that car again. Pulling the sack of shit out through his window. Introducing the guy's head to the front grill to see how he liked it. Repeatedly.

"I'm okay," Kristina whispered after a few minutes. "Just shaking. I'll be okay."

"Of course you will. Just take a minute, then we'll get you cleaned up." Truth be told, Noah wasn't in any rush for her to move. Because that bullshit had rattled him. Five years in the military had taught him that it was always worse to see a buddy hurt or even in harm's way than to find yourself there. And the same had been true just then. This could've been so much worse...

No. He wasn't even letting himself imagine.

After a long moment, she lifted her head and looked up at him with wet eyelashes that just about broke his fucking heart. "If you hadn't pulled me out of the way, I would've really been hurt."

Noah thumbed away the wetness below her eyes. "I didn't react fast enough," he said, gently cupping her hand where it rested on his chest. Hell, if the car had come at them from the left side, he might not have reacted at all. A thought that did absolutely nothing to help the anger and frustration roaring through him.

"Stop that. You did too." Her expression was earnest and so damn vulnerable.

Heaving a breath, Noah eyed the bruises blooming on her knuckles. "We should take you to the ER."

"What? No way. I don't need all that. It's just some bruises." She blinked the tears away, visibly pulling herself together as he watched.

"Kristina—"

"Noah, really. I'd go if I thought I needed to. Would you go?" She arched a brow.

He thought about lying, but she knew the truth. "Okay, but I'm a stubborn asshole."

Her laughter melted away some of the anger inside of him. "Can I quote you on that?" She nudged him.

He sighed, but he wasn't feeling playful about her having gotten hurt. "Fine, but we're at least getting you some ice," Noah said as he slipped the beat-up fingers of his right hand into the uninjured fingers on her left. Just a few doors down the street, they ducked into a fast-food restaurant. At the counter,

Noah pointed to Kristina's hand and said, "My friend was just hit by a car. Would you be able to give us a bag of ice?"

Overhearing his question, an older man came up to the counter from the back of the restaurant. "I'm the manager here, and I'm happy to help. Do you need some bandages? I have a first-aid kit."

Noah nodded. "We'd really appreciate that." He squeezed Kristina's hand, not caring at all about the ache doing so set off in his own.

The man led them to a tiny office with a desk, file cabinet, and two chairs. He pulled the red and white kit out of a drawer and opened it on the desk. "I'll go get some ice."

"Thank you," Kristina said. She blew out a still-shaky breath and sank into a chair.

Noah sorted through the kit and pulled out an antiseptic wipe, some antibiotic ointment, and a few bandages that looked like they might be the right size. "This might sting a little," he said, holding the wipe over her hand.

"It's okay," she said.

Nodding, he wiped at the bloody cut on her knuckle. A flash of the gunshot wound through Kendrick's hand. Noah frowned and blinked the image away. When that cut was clean, he moved to a smaller one he hadn't seen on the outside of her pinkie. A little trickle blood lined her whole finger. Stein's severed leg, the result of a landmine.

Noah gritted his teeth. What the hell? Now the simple sight of a little blood was gonna fuck with his head? "You okay?" he bit out more harshly than he intended.

"Yeah," she said. "Are you?"

"I'm pissed off." He heaved a breath and worked to box up his bullshit.

"Me, too. I haven't had my Ben & Jerry's yet. It's a travesty of justice to get between a woman and her chocolate."

Noah smirked at her and applied the ointment, though talking seemed to have blocked out the surfacing of anymore memories. And damn if he didn't get the feeling that *she* was trying to make *him* feel better.

The manager returned with the ice and settled the bag on the desk. "Can I get you anything else? Should I call an ambulance?"

"No. Thank you, sir," Kristina said. "I think it's just bruised, but I'll keep an eye on it. I really appreciate your helping me, though."

"Of course. With all the pedestrians, you'd think people would drive more carefully down here," he said, shaking his head and watching Noah over his shoulder. The man was perfectly harmless and obviously a good person, but Noah's instincts did not love the guy hovering on his six. At all.

"Do you have a business card?" Kristina asked as Noah wrapped bandages around her hand. "I'd like to send a letter of appreciation."

The man pulled a card from his wallet. "I appreciate the thought, miss, but that really isn't necessary."

"Not everyone would've been this kind, Mr. Johnson," she said, glancing at the card.

He gave a nod. "Just leave the kit here when you're done. I'll put it away later." He left again.

"All done," Noah said. He gently applied tape to hold the bandage in place, but with the way the back of her hand was swelling, there wasn't any safe place to press. Sonofabitch. He couldn't believe this had happened to her. And on his watch.

"You're taking really good care of me, Noah. Thank you."

"I will *always* take care of you," he bit out. And then he realized what he said, and just how vehemently he'd said it. And damn if it hadn't sounded a whole lot more than *friendly*. He chanced a glance at Kristina, and it was clear that she'd registered something in his tone, too. He threw away the trash and sat against the edge of the desk. "Why don't you sit with the ice for a few minutes?"

Kristina rose and stood right in front of him, her pretty eyes even with his given how he was leaning. "I don't need to sit," she said in a low voice, her gaze boring into his.

"Well, I need you to sit. So sit."

Her eyebrow went up. Just the one.

Under other circumstances it might've made him laugh. Could she ever just fucking listen to him? But he was wound so tight over witnessing her getting hurt, over the idea that it could've been so much worse, over seeing her spilled blood, that it was all he could do not to redecorate Mr. Johnson's office along the lines of his shower. He was nearly vibrating with pent-up frustration.

And now Kristina was boxing him in, observing him too closely, not giving him an out.

"Here's the part where I'm gonna say 'thank you,' and you're going to say 'you're welcome.' Ready? Thank you for protecting me and taking care of me, Noah." Her expression was expectant, and not a little amused.

Something about her playfulness wound him a notch tighter. Because he wasn't playing. His gaze dropped from her eyes to her full pink lips, and desire sucker-punched him so hard he nearly gasped. "Does your mouth hurt?" he rasped.

"Why would my—"

Noah was on her in a flash. Hand cupping the side of her face, arm hauling her tight up against him, mouth claiming hers on a deep, needful, soul-healing kiss. Kristina's muscles braced in surprise, but then she melted against him, going soft and pliant against all his hardness. And he was hard. So hard, so on edge, so in need of release, that he could've spun her around, lifted her onto the desk, and buried himself deep right here and right now.

He needed to be more gentle with her, but the need roaring through him wouldn't allow him to slow down or back off. And her eager responsiveness didn't help, either.

Her good hand fisted in his hair, her mouth sucked maddeningly at his tongue, and her body writhed against his erection. And goddamn the noises she was making, because the desperate moans and little mewls of need were hot as *fuck*, every one stroking his cock and making him harder.

Instinct told Noah that Kristina wouldn't hinder him playing out his little fantasy on the desk.

Except she was hurt. And they were in a fucking sub shop. Annnd, he couldn't forget about what was behind door number three—they were supposed to be Just. Friends.

"Shit," he rasped. "I did it again."

She grasped at his face. "Yes, thank you for that, too. Keep doing it." Kristina went in for another kiss. This time, her tongue penetrated him, like she wanted to fight him for control. And hell if that didn't set off all kinds of heat inside him.

He flipped them around and pinned her to the desk, nearly leaning her backwards over it. The position brought his hard-on flush with that sweet, hot spot between her legs. She cried out and tried to grind against him, but his weight and her skirt kept her pinned tight.

Hurt. Sub shop. Friends.

"Shit, wait." He stepped back, putting space between them. Because he didn't think he'd have the strength to resist a third time. Especially when she stared at him with such abject fucking need, her cheeks flush with desire, her hair mussed from his hands, her luscious breasts heaving under that clingy V-neck top. "You're hurt."

"And?" Kristina asked.

Noah glared. "Kristina, I'm kinda on the edge here, if you can't tell."

She slipped up onto the desk and spread her legs, just the little bit the skirt allowed.

But it was so much like his fucking fantasy that he had to close his eyes. "Get. Down."

"Noah—"

"Please," he rasped.

Her heels clicked against the floor.

Noah chanced a glance. Back on her feet again. "Grab your ice and let's go. Fucking sub shop." He left out the door before he changed his mind.

Out on the street, the sun still shined over the summer evening. Kristina sighed and started back the way they came.

"Where are you going?" Noah asked.

"Oh," Kristina said, turning. "Um, I figured home?"

Home had privacy. Home had a bed. Home seemed...very, very bad right now. "Ice cream's this way," he said, pointing in the other direction. "Unless your hand hurts too much?"

"Pfft," she said, rolling her eyes. "On my death bed, I will want chocolate in any and every form. Remember that."

Oh, for fuck's sake. "Don't joke about that right now. So, you still game or what?" he asked, her attempt at humor not helping him unwind. Not one bit.

"I guess," she said, eyeballing him like she could see all the things he thought but didn't say. "Just didn't think you would be."

Noah came close, and leaned down so he could meet her eye to eye. "You want chocolate. I want to give you what you want. Simple as."

THE WORDS HUNG THERE, and Kristina blinked up at him as innocently as she could. Because she definitely had wants. And, right or wrong, they didn't involve anyone named Ben or Jerry. "*Anything* I wan—"

"I swear to God, Kristina, if you finish that sentence..." He planted his hands on his hips and glared.

She was pretty sure she was supposed to be intimidated right now. Except, all his aggressiveness was doing funny things to her. She'd never seen Noah like this before, and it was making her want to challenge him. Making her want him to lose control. Making her yearn for him to come at her with all that pent-up angst.

Friends. Friends. We're just friends.

Yeah. Friends whose kisses alone made her wet. Crap.

"Fine, get me ice cream," she finally said, trying not to pout as she adjusted the ice against the back of her hand. Kristina couldn't believe she'd been hit by that idiot. If Noah hadn't been there...if he hadn't seen what was happening and pulled her out of the way... She shook her head and peered under the ice. Around the bandages, her puffy skin was turning purple.

They started walking. "How's it feeling?" Noah asked, his tone less intense than it'd been a minute ago.

"Probably a lot like yours did after you punched the wall," she said. She peered up at him, eyebrow arched. Maybe she shouldn't have gone there, but *damnit*, just how many things between them were going to be off the table? "Except you didn't have me to take care of you after."

"I'm glad you weren't there," he said, but then he took the sharp edge off the words by taking her good hand in his.

"I want to take care of you too, you know. That's what friends do for each other," she said, realizing she had her own pent-up frustration that needed venting. Not just of the sexual kind, either, though that was definitely there. Because, holy hell, the way Noah had claimed her in that office had been one of the most incredible moments of her life. Even now, her lips still tingled from his rough, demanding kisses. Kristina had been so lust-drunk that she would've welcomed Noah between her thighs right there on sweet Mr. Johnson's desk.

But there was also her pent-up worry for Noah. Pent-up disappointment in all the times she'd been sure he was avoiding her. Pent-up concern that, even now, he was still holding her at a distance. Despite the fact that he was holding her hand.

Noah didn't answer her, and they fell quiet as they walked down the hill to the bottom of King Street. The warmth of his big hand around hers offered a nice distraction from the throb of her other hand. The ice had helped, as would some Ibuprofen when she got home, though she was pretty sure the best pain reliever would be the one she couldn't have—Noah finishing what he'd started. Twice, now. Because she hadn't even been able to feel the pain in her hand when he'd been kissing her.

Kristina paused when they finally reached the Ben & Jerry's store. "This bag is starting to leak everywhere. I'm gonna chuck it. I can put more on later if I need to."

"I'll take it," Noah said. He retreated down the sidewalk to the nearest trash can, and Kristina tried really hard not to stare at his ass as he went. But the guy did all kinds of justice to a pair of jeans. And she was horny as hell after her second make-out session of the week with him. And even more confused.

Why did this keep happening? And would it really be such a problem if they let it go even further? Because it was clear there was something between them. Something more than what had ever been there before.

Inside, they got in line and stared up at the board of flavors. "What are you getting?" she asked.

"Cookie dough," he said.

Kristina smiled up at him. "I think you've gotten that every time we've ever been here."

He cocked a playful eyebrow, and it eased the strange tension between them. "Then why did you ask?"

She bumped into him and rolled her eyes. "Because maybe at some point you'll want to try something new. Smart ass."

The line moved, and Kristina moved with it. Standing right behind her, Noah said, "But what if I tried something new and didn't like it as much? What if I tried something new and it messed up my old favorite? Because I couldn't live without my old favorite."

Kristina's heart suddenly slammed against her breastbone.

There was no way Noah was talking about chocolate chip cookie dough ice cream right now. Was there? It sure as hell didn't feel that way. She went to turn, but Noah planted his hands on her shoulders, keeping her facing forward. Facing away.

"Um," she said, struggling to respond with all his muscled heat pressed against her back. "But trying something new doesn't mean you have to give up your old favorite, does it? It would just give you something new to have in addition."

What exactly was she advocating here? That they should explore the crazy sexual tension pinging between them and see where it led? That they should give in, just once, just to get it out of their system? Or that they give friends with benefits a try? This was all so unexpected that she honestly wasn't sure.

"Can I help you?" the girl behind the counter asked, smiling at Kristina.

"Oh. Uh. Yes." Kristina scanned the tubs of ice cream displayed in the case. "Can I please have a sugar cone with Chocolate Therapy and Hazed and Confused?" She gave a rueful chuckle as the girl worked on her cone. Those two ice creams summed up her state of mind pretty good just then.

"What's so funny?" Noah asked.

"I think the ice cream's talking to me," Kristina said, finally peering over her shoulder to look at him. And Noah's expression made her laugh. "Don't worry, it's a temporary condition."

Noah ordered his cone, and then they were out on the street again. The sun hung lower in the sky now, stretching the shadows across the ground.

"I haven't been down here in a long time," Noah said. "Years."

"Wanna walk over to the waterfront?" she asked. He nodded, and they crossed the street to the brick-paved promenade that fronted the Potomac River. The breeze off the water kicked up runaway strands of her hair. "For the record, holding an ice cream cone in my left hand is very weird. It's throwing off my ice cream mojo."

"You have ice cream mojo?"

Kristina chuckled. "Not right now I don't." She shifted the cone to her right hand, but trying to curl her fingers around it was awkward with the bandages and felt a little like someone had taken a hammer to the back of her hand. She stuck out her bottom lip.

Noah almost managed a small smile, but the effort made his expression look sad. "I'm sorry you got hurt. Wish it had been me instead."

The fury that lanced through Kristina took her by surprise. She whirled on him. "Don't *ever* say something like that again, Noah. You've been hurt enough for a lifetime. Imagine what it was like knowing my best friend had been blown up and lay all alone fighting for his life in a hospital half a world away. I would've given *anything* for that not to have happened to you. Even now that you're doing better, I would still give anything to be able to take it all back for you. So don't think for a minute that I'd ever want you to get hurt in my place. I would give you my eye and my ear if I could."

Tears pricked at the backs of her eyes, but she was so overwhelmed with emotion for him that she couldn't hold all this in. Not anymore. Damn, she hadn't even realized just how much she'd been bottling up all these months.

Peering down at her, Noah's brown eyes blazed. "Kristina," he said, voice strained.

She blew out a long breath, suddenly afraid of what he might say. Because she wasn't sure whether she wanted him to fight for their friendship, or fight for something more. "Forget it. I'm just upset over my hand. And my messed-up ice cream mojo."

Noah shook his head. For a long moment, they just stared at each other, and then he finally spoke. "You're...you're a good friend. The best. I'm sorry I said that."

His words unleashed a sinking feeling in Kristina's belly, revealing more about what she hoped he might want than she was maybe ready to admit. But she forced a happy face and said, "I feel the same way about you. No matter what."

CHAPTER SIX

Noah's weight pressed Kristina into the soft bedding, and she loved the feeling of him on top of her. His kisses were feverish and rough, his tongue plundering her mouth until she could barely breathe, his stubble rasping against her chin and cheeks and neck. She wouldn't have changed a thing about any of it.

He worked kisses down her throat to her chest, shedding her clothing piece by piece as he moved. A hot thrill shot through her when his chin scratched against the soft skin of her belly, soothing, wet kisses following close behind. She spread her thighs to make way for his big shoulders, her whole body trembling at the promise of what Noah was about to do.

He stared up her body, dark eyes hot with intensity. "I will *always* take care of you," he bit out.

"I know," Kristina whispered, her hand stroking his hair.

Noah lowered his mouth to her core, and Kristina lifted her hips, dying for that first touch, for his mouth to devour her.

Oh, please please please...

Kristina whimpered. Her eyes blinked open. And she almost cried.

Despite the very real arousal flooding through her, Kristina was alone in her bedroom. No Noah. No about-to-be-amazing orgasm. No fantasy come true.

Breathing harder than normal, she curled onto her side and drew up her knees. The LED screen of her alarm clock read 6:05. So much for sleeping in on a Saturday morning.

Now she was awake *and* horny over a man she wasn't supposed to want. If she didn't live in an apartment building with close neighbors on every side, Kristina would've been tempted to scream in frustration.

Part of her almost wished Noah had never kissed her last Monday night, because then maybe she wouldn't be feeling this constant, impossible yearning for him now. No other man had ever driven her to such great distraction, and no man had ever invaded her dreams this way. It made her wonder if any other man ever would.

Or ever had before.

She thought back over her past relationships. About six months after Noah had left for the Marines during her junior year of college, there'd been Brent, who was a year older and had already been accepted for graduate school at Cambridge University in the UK. Kristina had always known she had no intentions of following him out of the country, but they'd had a lot of sex that spring semester. Because she'd known it was inevitable, her sadness at his departure hadn't lasted that long.

Half-way through her senior year, she'd had what she'd then thought was a hot fling with a guy named Carter, a sophomore frat brother with a penchant for making out and having sex in places where they might get caught—a classroom after hours, the student newspaper offices, a bathroom during a party, his Jeep up at the lake. He'd been fun and she'd felt kinda daring being with him, but it had never gone deeper than that. And with all those quickies, she'd faked more than a few orgasms to keep him from feeling bad when she couldn't get there fast enough.

Then there'd been John, who she'd met at a bar while out with some work friends one Friday night. John had been...nice. A few years older. Steady job as a patent officer. Handsome enough. And they'd both enjoyed trying out new restaurants. But his kisses had left her...underwhelmed. There was nothing wrong with him, but then he'd said he thought they should just be friends because he didn't see them going anywhere. Her ego had been a little bruised, but truth be told, she hadn't been upset. Not really.

There'd been other dates with other guys—some she'd met on her own, some her friend Kate had set her up with—but nothing she'd ever thought had the potential to turn into something more, something lasting, something like...the kind of connection she had with Noah.

Even before they ever kissed.

Kristina pushed the covers off and sat up in her bed as a sinking feeling curled into her stomach.

All this time, she thought she'd really been out there. Dating. Searching. Giving happily ever after a genuine, honest try. But looking back now, all of those relationships seemed pale and shallow compared to what she had with Noah—in general and just this past week.

Was it possible that...*she'd* been the problem in all those relationships? The reason they hadn't been deeper, more fulfilling, longer lasting? Was it possible...could it be...that she'd been holding back? Or holding everyone else up to the same relationship standards she had with her best friend? The deep, longtime knowledge, including some of the most private, hurtful parts of herself and her family. The unconditional acceptance. The inherent trust. The natural way they clicked, no special effort required.

Kristina's gaze scanned over her dresser, jam-packed with some of her favorite framed photographs. There was one with her father holding her when she'd been an infant. It was her favorite picture of him because his eyes were clear, open, and free of the shadows cast by the mental illness that would get worse as she got older. There was one of her posing with her mom in front of her very first car, a small, red Saturn. There was another with her high school besties at graduation, all of them in their caps and gowns. And there was a dual frame with her and Kate in it—on one side, a picture in their dorm room freshman year; on the other, a picture from their senior week vacation at the beach.

But most of the rest were with or of Noah Cortez.

Kristina pushed out of bed and crossed to the dresser. Morning sunlight from the nearby window fell on the portrait of him in his Marine dress blues. So freaking handsome. There was one of them together in front of the Cortez Christmas tree when he'd been home on leave the year before he'd been discharged. Another was of *his* high school graduation, him in his gown, her in his cap. She'd been so crushed that she wouldn't see him in school anymore as she had for so many years. Another was from before the high school Homecoming dance her freshman and his junior year, posing in the Cortez backyard before they caught up with the big group of friends with whom they were going.

Kristina picked up a frame from the Magic Kingdom at Disneyworld. She'd gone with Noah and his family for a vacation in Florida when she'd been in eighth grade. It had all been sudden and unexpected, and Kristina later learned her mother had made it happen to protect her from knowing that her dad had hurt himself.

Vacations. Dances. Holidays. Pictures of hanging out and goofing off.

Noah. Noah. Noah. Noah.

Would any other man ever measure up to him?

Why had she never before asked this question?

And did either of those even matter if he—they—thought they should remain just friends? Because she got his concerns about messing up the incredible thing they had. She really did.

Returning the frame to the dresser, Kristina sighed. These were not questions that could be answered without some serious caffeine on board.

She flicked through social media while she drank her coffee and ate a blueberry yogurt, her mind circling around this whole situation. She opened up her text messages and began typing.

I need girl time. You around this weekend? She shot the text to Kate.

A few minutes later, Kristina got back, *Absolutely! Tomorrow night work?*

Kristina smiled as she typed her reply. *Yes. Dinner at The Grill?*

Yes. Cya soon!

Feeling a little better, Kristina finished her breakfast, showered, and dressed. Popping some Ibuprofen, she decided to skip the bandages on her hand. She opened and closed her fist a few times and found that she was able to do so much more easily today. Aside from a dull ache beneath her knuckles, her hand seemed okayish. At this point, it looked worse than it felt.

Noah would be over in the afternoon to get her desk and take her shopping, so she wanted to use the morning to pick up a housewarming gift for him. She hadn't been sure what to get until they'd teased about spatulas, and now she had a fun idea that would hopefully make him laugh. Because Noah needed more laughter in his life right now.

The truth of that unleashed an uncomfortable pressure inside her chest.

As Kristina retrieved her purse from the kitchen counter, a packet of blue papers fluttered to the floor—the informational flyer she'd grabbed last night when she'd stopped into the Art Factory to fill out employment forms. She hadn't known they offered a whole program of therapeutic classes specifically for veterans—in pretty much every form of creative expression, but given the large veteran community in Northern Virginia, she wasn't surprised.

On impulse, she'd grabbed the packet for Noah. No doubt he was going to laugh his ass off at her for even suggesting he consider taking an art class, of all things, but her gut told her he needed some sort of outlet for everything he was dealing with.

The hole in the wall of his shower seemed to prove that.

Maybe art could provide that outlet for him the way it did for her. She retrieved the pages and placed them back on the counter.

An hour later, she was pushing a cart around the kitchen section at IKEA. She turned into the utensils aisle and...bingo. She grabbed the superheroes spatula set off the hook. It had four spatulas, and the flat parts were made out of the heads of the Hulk, Spiderman, Ironman, and Captain America. Kristina chuckled as she dropped them in the cart. What other fun guy stuff could she find?

A set of slotted spoons with eyeball- and moustache-shaped holes. A pair of wooden spoons that had drumstick tips on one end. A cheese grater shaped like an electric guitar. A measuring cup and spoon set that, when all stacked together, looked like the Star Wars robot, R2D2. An Army man bottle cap opener. A pizza cutter shaped like a unicycle being ridden by a monkey.

Kristina grinned, totally digging Sweden's sense of humor.

Next, she found a kitchen knife set—instead of a traditional square wooden block to store them, it had a circular block with a plastic man tied to it spread-eagle. When resting in the block, the knives appeared to have been thrown into it, circus-performer style. Next to that she found a rectangular cutting board that read, "DANGER: MEN COOKING." Kristina chuckled as she dropped those into the cart.

She rounded to the next aisle and laughed out loud. Salt-and-pepper shakers. Lots of them. Humping pigs. An old man sitting on a toilet. A dog and a fire hydrant. A bent-over gnome whose naked butt cheeks were the shakers.

That one was kinda disturbing, actually.

Further down the display, Kristina found the perfect set—ninjas, one black, one white, only their eyeballs showing under their ninja get-ups.

Okay, she totally hadn't set out to buy this much, but now she was having too much fun to stop, especially when she imagined Noah's reaction to each thing. Not to mention, but who could possibly choose between superhero spatulas and ninja salt-and-paper shakers?

Not her, that was for sure. Besides, she'd do or buy just another anything to make Noah smile.

Back home again, she made a turkey sandwich for lunch and settled down to wrap everything. Which was harder than it sounded. Some people—like her mother—could wrap presents beautifully. Square, flat edges to the paper, hidden seams, tightly tied ribbon.

And then there was Kristina. Whose attempts at wrapping paper always seemed to make it look like she'd balled the paper around the item and layered enough tape on it to make it hold together.

This was why she usually put everything in a gift bag with tissue paper. Seriously, gift bags were the greatest invention in modern history.

Or maybe that was computers. Whatever.

The point was, she didn't want to use gift bags here because she wanted Noah to have the fun of tearing everything open. The anticipation of doing more than pulling a folded piece of loose tissue out of a bag to find his present.

But as she sat on her living room carpet looking at the literal mountain of kitchen supplies she'd bought, she was rethinking the wisdom of her plan. At least she'd bought a few extra rolls of tape from the gift wrap aisle.

She fortified herself with a few bites of her sandwich and chips, and then picked an easy, normal-shaped item to start. The cutting board. Really. How hard could *that* be to wrap?

She rolled out a big sheet of paper and laid the cutting board on it, then cut off a piece that looked big enough to wrap around it. She frowned at the cut, which was about as straight as a wet noodle. No worries. She could hide that. Besides, she could hardly be blamed when her hand was still so achy. All true. Except, when she wrapped the two sides around the board to meet in the middle, the paper was too short on the bottom half of the board.

"Freaking wrapping paper," she muttered as she cut another small piece off the roll and taped it to the board. She wrapped the paper around it again. "There," she said proudly. Her patchwork filled the gap perfectly. Holding the paper in place with one hand, she eyed the tape dispenser.

This was where things got tricky. Leaning over, she held the paper with her elbow so she'd have two hands to get a piece of tape—which promptly got all crinkly and stuck together. She flicked it away and got another. It applied nice and flat to the paper.

"Ha!" She threw her arms into the air in victory, then celebrated by polishing off the rest of her sandwich.

Now, for the ends. Kristina grabbed the loose paper on one ended and folded it over the board. Five pieces of tape later and that end was secured. Same on the other end and—bam! Done.

Kristina lifted the package and frowned. The ends looked like rolled-up newspaper. She turned it over. Oh. Apparently, she hadn't pulled the paper taut either. It was all bubbled and loose.

"So what," she said, setting it aside. The paper had a bacon design. Who was going to notice if the bacon was flat and square? Right?

An hour later, Kristina has two cuts on her fingers from the tape dispenser, a sheered-off fingernail from the scissors, and a steady ache in her hurt hand. Which all spoke to why she taught language arts and not *art* art. And why all her bulletin board decorations came pre-made from the dollar store. Her worst eighth-grade artist was better than her. By a lot.

Still, the pile of presents looked *spectacular*. Her best wrapping job ever.

As she placed all the packages into a huge blue gift bag that would make them easier to carry, her phone buzzed.

Just finished lunch with Dad and Josh. What time should I come over?

Noah.

Ha. Look at that. Perfect timing. *I'm ready for you to come now*, Kristina replied. She popped a chip into her mouth—and choked on a laugh when what she'd written sank in. Oh, she was ready for him to come all right. As long as she came, too.

God, she was hopeless. She dropped her head into her hand and chuckled.

"Well, let's see what you make of that, Cortez," she muttered. And then she couldn't stop staring at her phone and wondering if he'd take the bait.

CHAPTER SEVEN

I'M ready for you to come now.

Clearly, Noah was a goddamn pervert, because his dick had an interpretation of that text message he was a hundred percent sure Kristina didn't mean.

Trying something new doesn't mean you have to give up your old favorite, does it? It would just give you something new to have in addition...

Kristina's voice answering a question he never should've asked had been haunting him for the past two days. Given her inviting response, maybe he should reduce his certainty on the meaning of that text to ninety-nine percent. Because he *really* didn't need to be thinking that she was flirting with him, teasing him, egging him on like a bullfighter with a red fucking flag.

After his father and Josh left his new apartment, Noah had half a mind to break in his shower before he went to see Kristina to ensure his tongue didn't end up down her throat again. *Be there in about 30,* Noah finally replied.

"This is gonna be a nice place," his dad said, pulling Noah from his thoughts. His father tore down a box and threw it on a pile by the door for recycling. Furniture aside, Noah didn't have that much stuff, so getting him in and settled hadn't taken very long.

Noah looked around the open-concept living/dining/kitchen area of the small apartment. Miles of white walls and bare hardwood floors gave it no personality whatsoever, but despite the fact that he was twenty-seven years old, it was the first place he could truly call his own. So Noah didn't mind all that blank slate too much.

Blank slate.

Without the Marines shaping his life and giving it purpose, that pretty much described how he felt about himself, too. What was he going to be now that the Corps was in his rear-view mirror?

"Yeah," Noah said, dragging a hand through his hair and doing his best to push the deep thoughts away. "And, uh, just think how much longer your food will last without me or Josh in the house." He tossed the dirty paper plates and napkins inside the pizza box and set it with the other empty boxes.

"Speak for yourself, little brother," Josh said, patting his stomach. "Today's carb-overload aside, I've been busting my butt to make sure I look all svelte for my tux."

"Dude, tell me you're not dieting," Noah said, arching a brow. Truth be told, his brother had put on some weight over the past year or two, but he looked so damn happy all the time that Noah hadn't really given it much thought.

Josh laughed. "Well, I might've gotten the looks, but you got the metabolism genes. And I have a job that plants my ass in a chair for twelve hours a day."

Noah smirked. "Hate to tell you, but I got the looks genes, too."

Josh flipped him the finger as their dad said, "Well, neither of you got a single iota of common sense, so..." They laughed and the teasing started all over again.

His dad joked with them, but the humor didn't quite reach the man's eyes. Not when they both knew that Noah's appetite hadn't been what it used to be. Not since he got discharged. Not since his equilibrium problems, which the docs said might never go away, often had his stomach toying with the idea of tossing his cookies. Not since losing so much of who he was and what he thought he'd be left him with a hollowness inside that no amount of food would ever be able to fill.

Hell, he'd probably eaten more Thursday night with Kristina than in the whole past week combined...

And wasn't that realization a kick in the ass he didn't want to examine too closely.

"If you don't need anything else, I should fly," Josh said. "Wedding is three months from today and Maria has a to-do list a mile long."

"No, I'm good," Noah said. "I appreciate the help when you're so busy."

"Wouldn't have it any other way," Josh said, clasping Noah's hand and pulling him in for a quick hug.

Noah knew that was true. Josh had always been there for him, which meant—Noah's bullshit aside—he needed to man up and do the same. "Let me know how I can help with the wedding stuff," Noah said. "You know I'm free right now. Put me to work if you need me."

"Yeah?" Josh asked, smiling. The surprise in his voice told Noah everything he needed to know about how good he'd been doing by his brother. "I will."

Fifteen minutes later, they'd cleared out the empty boxes and his dad and brother were gone. Noah took a quick cold shower and shot over to Kristina's apartment in the moving truck.

The last time he saw her, he'd been about two seconds away from burying himself between her legs. Today, he was going to make sure they moved squarely back into the friend zone. Things were getting too intense, too warped, too...different between them. And that seemed dangerous for both of them, because he wouldn't be able to stand doing anything to hurt her, and hurt was all he had to give right now.

Maybe that was just how it was going to be for him. Permanently.

As he turned the truck into the long lot in front of the grouping of garden-style apartment buildings in her complex, Noah knew he needed some basic rules to get through the day with Kristina.

So, okay. No kissing. No hugging. No touching. No suggestive questions cloaked in conversations about ice cream. No fucking sub shops. In short, nothing that might lead to him fighting the basic, primal instinct to get inside Kristina Moore.

Busted-up body aside, at the core he was a goddamned U.S. Marine. And always would be. He'd looked death in the face and laughed. More than once. Even with a damaged eye and ear, he should be able to handle one twenty-five-year-old grade-school teacher on his own terms.

For fuck's sake.

Noah took a deep breath as he knocked on her door.

"Hey!" Kristina said with a big smile as the door flew open. "I was beginning to wonder if I was gonna have to send out a search party."

What. The fuck. Was she wearing.

Roughly cut-off white denim shorts that were so short the pockets poked out the bottom. He forced his gaze away from the apex of her thighs, where hanging threads made his fingers itch to brush them away—or unravel them altogether. A loose, worn blue halter top with a plunging neckline and skinny straps covered a breast-hugging white tank that lay beneath. Lacey blue bra straps peeked out at her shoulders. Layers of beads trailed almost mesmerizingly over her breasts and circled her ankle and wrist.

And her hair. Oh, her hair was a sexed-up dream. The mass of blond curls and waves hung flirtatiously off to one side, swept back off of her face. Noah fisted his hands against the urge to bury his fingers in all that silken blond and pull her in...

No. There will be no burying of fingers or anything else. Remember the goddamn rules.

"Nope, I'm here," he said.

Kristina nodded, her eyebrow arched. "Well come on in, master of the obvious."

Smirking, Noah pushed by her—without touching—and glanced around her apartment. His gaze landed on a huge blue gift bag on the coffee table.

"I have goodies for you," Kristina said, scurrying past him. Holy hell, the denim was just as short in the rear. Her thighs looked so smooth and soft. Touchable.

"Oh, yeah?" Noah said, dragging his gaze away.

"Yep." She grabbed the gift bag's handles and turned to him wearing the most exuberant smile. It brightened her whole face, and it made her so damn pretty. "I am about to be your favorite person ever."

The words did funny things to his chest. "You already are my favorite person." It was true. All of the recent weirdness between them aside, no one had ever *gotten* him the way Kristina did. Even not really understanding the full extent of what he was dealing with right now, she still got him in ways no one else did.

"I know. But now I'm taking my awesomeness to a whole new level." She held the bag out toward him.

He accepted it into his hands, surprised at how heavy it was. "What's this for?"

Kristina rolled her eyes. "Just open it."

"Now?" As much as he appreciated the gesture, he didn't deserve presents. Least of all from her, who he'd been purposely avoiding for most of the last seven months.

She gave him a droll stare. "No, next Thursday. Yes, *now*. Come sit."

He joined her on the couch and placed the bag between his legs on the floor. He pressed his lips together as he pulled the first package out of the bag. It was...the worst wrapped gift he'd ever seen. Really, a total vintage Kristina job. "So, you're getting better," he said, giving her the side eye.

Her gaze narrowed. "Shut up. I did good this time."

"Let me see your fingers," he said, because somehow she always gave herself paper cuts when she attempted to wrap a gift.

She stuffed them between her thighs, which eked a smile out of him. "Uh huh. That's what I thought."

"My awesomeness is escalating in direct proportion to your suckiness," she said, outright scowling.

He grabbed the wrist of her uninjured hand and tugged it, forgetting that there was supposed to be no touching until *after* his fingers had brushed the silky skin of her thigh. She wore two Band-Aids on her fingers. "Aw, look. You risked your life. For me."

Kristina dove for the present, nearly wrestling it out of his hands. Things went downhill from there, because his instinctive response was to hold it away from her, which caused her to half-fall across his lap. And then she was laughing and yelling at him and climbing up his body, bracing herself on his chest as she reached for the package in his outstretched hand.

Against his utter best interest, sheer competitiveness kicked in. Determined to keep her from getting the prize, Noah's arm banded around her lower back. His grip plastered her front to his and trapped her breasts right at his eye level. Right at his mouth level.

Heat roared through his body and his cock was hard in an instant. He wanted to plunge his tongue in her lush cleavage and suck those beautiful full breasts into his mouth.

"I'm never giving you a present again, Cortez. Give it back," she said.

"No," he growled, breathing her scent in from up close. God, he was drowning in her. He *wanted* to drown in her.

What the hell am I doing?

Shaking his head, Noah lowered his arm and let Kristina grab the present. When she jerked back, he let her go, and she ended up kneeling right next to him. Breathing hard, she glared at him, but the humor was plain on her face.

"If you want this, you'll repeat after me: Kristina is the best gift-wrapper ever and I will never make fun of her wrapping again."

Releasing a shaky breath, Noah nodded and dropped his hands into his lap to hide his hard-on. "Kristina is the best gift-wrapper ever and I will never make fun of her wrapping again."

Her lips twisted. "You gave in way too easy to that. Very suspicious."

Nope. Not suspicious. Self-preservation. Because so far Noah's plan to follow a few basic rules was totally FUBAR. For fuck's sake.

He held out his hand and shrugged. "I want the loot."

Smirking, she handed it back to him and crossed her arms, the gesture plumping her cleavage.

Noah tore his gaze away. "Beautiful job, Kristina. Truly."

"That's what I'm talking about," she said, somewhat mollified.

He tore off the god-awful bacon paper—who even *knew* they made bacon paper?—and chuckled. "These are awesome," he said, examining the heads of the superheroes closer. "You got me spatulas."

She grinned. "Happy housewarming."

"You didn't have to do this," he said, moving on to the next package. Ninja salt shakers. "I am going to have the coolest kitchen ever."

"You totally are. We might have to have joint custody of a few things in this bag."

"You can come visit any time you want. How 'bout that?" Noah said.

"Well, that's just a given," she said.

"Of course it is. Speaking of which..." He pushed his fingers into his front jeans pocket. "I have a present for you." Noah held out a brass key on a plain ring. "Since I have one to your place, I figured you should have one to mine."

She grabbed it and smirked at him. "You just want me to come let you in the eight hundred times you'll manage to lock yourself out."

Noah nodded and chuckled. "Pretty much," he said, going for the next present in the bag.

He pulled a unicycle-riding monkey pizza cutter from the knot of wrapping paper, which tempted another chuckle from him. In fact, the whole bag of gifts had him smiling more than he could last recall doing.

And it just emphasized the point—Kristina got him like no one else did. She knew what he needed and how to make him feel better without pressing him to talk, without worrying over him, without making him feel like he couldn't take care of himself. And even though that meant she realized that he wasn't doing that damn great, the way she'd chosen to deal with it meant a lot to him.

This. *This* was why Noah could never chance harming his relationship with Kristina.

Which meant the damn rules were back in effect. For good.

CHAPTER EIGHT

Seven hours later, Kristina and Noah collapsed on his leather couch, shopping bags piled on the coffee table and sitting on the floor in front of them.

"I'm in a shopping coma," Noah said in a flat voice.

Kristina laughed. It *had* been a long day, but it had also been nice spending so much time with Noah. They'd laughed, talked, and just been together. Without any weirdness or tension. Just like old times. And after the dream that had woken her and the realizations she'd made about her relationship history, Kristina was really glad for that. "You were a trooper."

"I was. I deserve a gold star." He yawned.

"Or a cookie." Kristina grinned at him.

His eyes lit up. "You bought cookies?"

Laughing, Kristina shook her head. "Unfortunately, no. A metaphorical cookie."

"Can't eat no metaphorical cookie," he groused.

"How can you be hungry?" They'd capped off their shopping trip with a huge dinner at their favorite Mexican restaurant.

"Since when do you have to be hungry to eat a cookie?" His

eyebrow arched, and it made her laugh. It was really freaking good to see Noah like this again. Relaxed. Talkative. Playful. Part of her had worried he'd lost this part of himself when he'd lost so much else.

"Well, I suppose that's true." Kristina rose from the couch on a chuckle. "Come on. Let's get to work. Why don't you start washing your new kitchen stuff and I'll find your laundry room and wash your new bedding so you can have it for later. Then I can help you dry and figure out where you want things in the kitchen."

"The sheets are new. Why do they need to be washed?" he asked, standing.

Kristina grimaced. "Because they'll be all stiff and stuff. Besides, ew." She found the bags with his new sheets, comforter, and laundry detergent.

"If you say so." He shrugged.

"I don't know what you'd do without me," she said. "Honestly."

Noah busied himself grabbing a bunch of bags. "Me either," he murmured.

Something about his tone seemed more serious than she'd expected, and it almost made her reach out to hug him. But, aside from that moment on her couch earlier, Noah had been really hands-off today, and it made her think back to him saying he wouldn't be able to live without "his old favorite." Her. So she'd tried really hard all day to respect the physical distance he seemed to be trying to put back between them. Even though it made a part of her ache with want.

But if he couldn't handle anything more with her, then she couldn't either. Given how much she already cared for him—anything romantic she might be feeling aside—Noah could probably hurt her in ways none of those other men had even come close to being capable of.

"Laundry's in the basement?" she asked.

Noah nodded. "There's a jar of coins on my dresser."

"Cool beans," Kristina said, grabbing what she thought she'd need before heading out.

The laundry room was a big bright room with a half dozen washers on one side and the same number of dryers on the other. They'd totally lucked out because only two of the dryers were in use. She dropped the bags to the big table in the middle and removed the wrappers and tags from Noah's new stuff.

"Hey," came a deep male voice.

Kristina looked up to see a hot guy stride into the room and head toward the two rumbling dryers. He was tall and lean with wavy light brown hair and tattoos covering a lot of both arms and part of his neck. "Hey," she said.

He checked the clothing in both dryers and then reset them. Turning, he leaned against one of the machines and pulled his phone from the back pocket of a pair of worn black jeans.

She grabbed a big armful and made for one of the washers, stuffing as much in as the machine could handle.

"You new here?" the guy asked. "I saw people moving in this morning."

"That's my friend, Noah," she said with a smile. She grabbed the comforter to put in its own washer. "I'm just helping him get settled in."

"Must be a good friend to do his laundry on a Saturday night," the guy said, his smile flirtatious and kinda sexy. Well, this made doing laundry a lot more interesting.

"Since we were kids," she said. "I'll make him pay me back somehow."

"Yeah, I'd say he owes you big." Something about the shy grin he gave her unleashed a loop of butterflies in her belly.

When she got everything loaded up, she poured in the

detergent, inserted the quarters, and started each of the machines.

"So, do you live around here too, then?" he asked.

Kristina brushed all the loose trash into one of the big shopping bags. "My place is over near Shirlington. Not too far."

He nodded and gave her an appraising look, then he crossed to the table and held out his hand. "My name's Ethan."

She shook his hand and tried to restrain her inner squee at the interest this guy was showing. Close on the heels of that excited feeling was another: guilt. *What about Noah?*

The question almost sucker-punched Kristina in the stomach. Except...what about him should stop her from flirting back with a handsome stranger? It didn't matter how much Kristina liked Noah when he didn't like her back—not that way, anyway. "Kristina," she said with a smile.

He repeated her name like he was trying it out. She wasn't sure if it was his tattoos, or how the long strands of his hair fell across his eyes, or the way his jeans hung on those lean hips, but Ethan oozed sensuality.

He didn't stir the crazy arousal that Noah had brought out in her lately, but he was still nice to look at.

Frustrated, Kristina cut off the thought. She and Noah were friends. Just friends. And that's how he apparently wanted to keep it. They *both* did. Which meant, *hello Ethan.* "So we know why *I'm* doing laundry on a Saturday night, but how do *you* explain it?"

Ethan chuckled and crossed his arms. "Didn't get in from the bar until four in the morning, so the day didn't really start for me until about two this afternoon. And then I realized if I didn't do a little laundry before I head back out tonight, I'm gonna have nothing to wear to my parents' anniversary dinner tomorrow night."

Kristina smiled, enjoying how easy-going Ethan was. "Must've been a good night," she said, flirting back. Just a little.

He flicked his tongue against his bottom lip and grinned. "Not that good." He winked. "I bartend. Whenever I close it's that late before I get home."

"Aw, too bad," she said, grinning at him.

He chuckled again. "Yeah."

She threw the trash away and grabbed the bottle of detergent. A part of her was disappointed to have no reason to stay. But at some point, Noah would wonder what was taking her so long.

"Maybe you should let me take you out some time, and we could both have a better night."

Holy crap! "Better than doing laundry on a Saturday night seems like a pretty low bar," she teased.

He gave a sheepish grin and nodded, the expression on his face so cute—sweet, sexy, with just a little vulnerability thrown in for good measure. "Got me there. So...is that a no?"

She bit back a smile because she didn't think she was imagining the hopefulness on his face. Maybe Ethan was what she needed to get over all the turmoil Noah had set off inside her lately... "It's a maybe," she said, heart racing in her chest despite the cool façade she was trying to muster.

His expression brightened. "Yeah? Wanna trade numbers?" Her belly doing a loop-the-loop, they traded phones, and she entered her cell number into his. "How 'bout next Saturday night?" he said as he gave her back her phone. "I have off. We could do dinner or something. Whatever you like."

Kristina smiled because, clearly, this was the luckiest laundry room on the face of the planet. She debated for a long moment, and then decided—she had no reason to play it cool. "Okay," she said. "Text me and we'll work out the details."

Ethan grinned. "Better believe it."

Back upstairs, Kristina took a moment to do a little personal flail before she returned to Noah's apartment. Then, on a deep breath, she pushed through his door. "I'm back," she said.

Noah cussed up a storm and stripped his shirt over his head.

"And you're getting naked in the kitchen," she said, freezing just inside the doorway.

Scowling, he turned and wiped water off his neck and chest. "The damn sprayer has a leak and just squirted all out the side."

"Oops." Chuckling, Kristina dropped the laundry supplies on the breakfast bar and picked up a hand towel.

Noah chucked the shirt to the counter, and Kristina tried really hard not to ogle the movement of his muscles. His arms, his abs, his back. He was so fit it was almost mesmerizing.

"Be right back," he said, striding out of the room. A few minutes later, he returned wearing a white T-shirt.

"What's up with you?" he asked, eyes narrowing on her.

Shit, she'd been thinking about her conversation with Ethan again. Schooling her expression, she picked up a superhero to dry. "Nothing."

"Bullshit," he said, coming around to the sink again. He turned on the water and squirted soap into the running stream.

Stomach fluttering, she rolled her eyes. "I'm just standing here drying Captain America. What makes you think there's something going on?"

Noah braced his hands on the edge of the sink, making his shoulder muscles bunch in a rather delicious way. "For one, you're avoiding my question. For two, you look like you did that time you found out that Josh made out with Melanie Hart in the locker room."

Kristina rolled her eyes. "That was really good gossip."

"Uh huh, which is why I know you're sitting on something right now."

Crap. He wasn't going to let this drop, was he? Well, fine. It wasn't like he wouldn't find out at some point, right? And it wasn't like he'd care either. Because, just friends. Except, then why did her belly feel like she was riding a roller coaster?

"I have a date." She picked up the Hulk. *Wipe, wipe, wipe.*

"A date," he said. She nodded but kept her eyes on her task. "With who?"

"One of your neighbors." Next, she worked through the stack of new ceramic dishes he'd bought. *Wipe, wipe, wipe.* His gaze felt like the mid-day sun shining on her face.

"Since when?"

"About ten minutes ago?" She chanced a glance at Noah. Eyes narrowed. Jaw tight. Knuckles white where they gripped the sink.

He smacked his hand against the faucet lever, shutting off the water. "So, let me get this straight. You just agreed to go out on a date with a total stranger you met in my laundry room?"

Kristina sat aside the dry dish. "Yep."

"What the fuck are you thinking?"

She dropped all pretense of drying the dishes and tossed the towel onto the counter. "Uh, I'm thinking that a hot guy asked me out and that was nice and it seemed like it could be fun. Why is that a problem?"

Kristina did not love the ribbon of guilt curling into her belly. It wasn't like she'd done anything wrong. She was young and single and it was just a dinner date, for God's sake. Not to mention that Noah had made his position clear. They both had. On multiple occasions.

"You know nothing about this guy," he said, turning toward her and bracing his hands on his hips.

She rolled her eyes. "His name is Ethan and he's a bartender. Besides, that's kinda the point of a date. You know, you talk and get to know a person better."

Noah stalked closer, then closer still, anger and heat rolling off of him. His dark eyes blazed down at her. "I...why...why are you doing this?"

Kristina shook her head, absolutely bewildered. "Why does anyone go on a date?" She pushed off the counter and came right up in front of him. "The real question is, why are you flipping out about it?"

His jaw ticked and a war of emotions played out across his annoyingly handsome face.

"Huh?" She poked her finger into the hardness of his chest. "Why do you care if I go on a date?" It wasn't like they hadn't been totally open with one another about dating before. Because they always had, going way back.

Noah shook his head, his chest heaving, his nostrils flaring. His lips parted, and she hung on the edge of a precipice as she waited for him to answer. To say it was because he didn't want her to go out with someone else, to say it was because he wanted her for himself. Instead, he said nothing.

So...what? He didn't want her, but he didn't want anyone else to have her either? Screw that. "Right," she managed. "That's what I thought." A stinging sensation sprang up behind her eyes, and Kristina was suddenly sure she was going to cry. Stupid. So stupid. She hadn't accepted the date with Ethan to elicit a reaction from Noah, so she wasn't sure why the exchange with him was squeezing her chest so damn hard now.

She pushed by him, bee lining for her purse. She had to get out of here. Before one of them said or did something they'd regret.

"Where are you going?" Noah asked from behind her, the anger gone from his voice.

"Home. I'm tired," she said. As she picked up her purse, she saw the stapled flyer she'd grabbed for Noah at the Art Factory. She pulled it out, turned, and crossed the room to him. "I picked this up for you. Thought there might be something helpful, and maybe even fun." She shrugged. "I know it's probably not your thing, but..."

He took the papers without looking at them. "Kristina—"

"I gotta go." She turned for the door.

"Your car's not here."

She came to a stop and nearly groaned out loud. "I'll...uh, get an Uber."

"Fuck that. If you want to go home, I'm taking you." He came up behind her and settled his hand against her lower back.

The contact made her want to turn into him, wrap herself around him, and push him for more. For everything. Instead, she pulled away. "Okay," she whispered.

It was the longest car ride of her life. Quiet. Tense. Realllly awkward.

Kristina hated it.

And it made her realize that Noah had been right.

Their flirtation this week was dangerous. If it could lead to a moment like *this*, when they'd rarely shared a truly angry word in almost twenty years of friendship? Yeah, that was a problem.

Which meant Kristina had to lay her more-than-best-friend feelings for Noah Cortez aside once and for all.

CHAPTER NINE

SITTING at a table in the hip bistro the next night, Kristina was so glad she'd organized some girl time. She hadn't realized how much weirder things were gonna get with Noah, and therefore how much she'd need it.

"Here's to girls' night out," Kate said, lifting her Mojito glass. Kate had short brown hair, huge blue eyes, and warm olive skin, and had been one of Kristina's closest friends since they'd been freshman roommates in college.

"I'll drink to that," Kristina said, lifting her Mojito. She had a weakness for the strawberry-and-mint combination, and for the rock candy lollipop in the glass. They clinked drinks. For a few minutes, they engaged in high-level negotiations over appetizers and shared entrees, and then ordered.

"So, I have news," Kate said, waggling her eyebrows.

"Which is?" Kristina asked, chuckling at how Kate always made a show of her gossip.

Kate raised her glass, and her expression went solemn, serious. "I. Got me. Some big, fat D."

"Oh, my God," Kristina said with a laugh. She held up her

hand for a high-five. "I suppose congrats are in order? But also, spill!"

"You better believe it," Kate said. "Mama had three big ohs, too."

Kristina couldn't stop giggling as she held up her glass for another toast. "I'll definitely congratulate you on that." As horny as she'd been lately, she not only felt happy for her friend, but extremely envious. "So, who was this orgasm-giving god?"

"Oops," Kate said, grinning at the male waiter who of course chose that exact moment to arrive with their appetizers. The look on his face said he'd overheard their conversation.

Chuckling, Kate waited for the guy to leave and, as they devoured a plate of nachos, launched into a long and colorful story about a guy she'd met at the gym. Kristina was nearly crying as Kate recounted that she could tell he was hung because he regularly ran on the treadmill but didn't wear compression shorts. And things *moved*. A lot, apparently. So she'd introduced herself, they'd gone to lunch, and quickly thereafter ended up in bed.

"If I thought he was impressive when he was soft, it was *nothing* compared to when he was hard. I'm not even kidding," she said.

Annnd of course the waiter chose that moment to deliver their food—an artisan pizza and an entrée salad they were sharing.

"So what about you?" Kate asked around a bite of pizza. "Any exciting news?"

Kristina smiled, because she actually had news. For once. "Well. I have a date next weekend."

Kate almost spewed lettuce across the table. "You wench. How long have you been sitting on this?"

Laughing, Kristina took a bite of salad, and then said, "I met the guy last night." She recounted the story and described Ethan in vivid detail.

"Mmm. He sounds delish," Kate said.

"Yeah, he is," Kristina said.

Kate's gaze narrowed. "So why don't you seem more excited?"

"No, no. I am," she said, knowing before Kate even said anything that she wasn't going to believe her.

"Kris, I love ya and all, but I've seen you excited. And this ain't it."

Kristina's shoulders fell as she debated exactly what to say.

"Oh, no. I smell Noah Cortez on this story," Kate said, pointing at her with her fork.

"Yeah," Kristina said. "Okay, here's the short version of the story. Noah and I made out twice in the past week, both times accidentally, and then when Ethan asked me out, Noah flipped out. But that was after he insisted we go back to being just friends." She busied herself with a big bite of salad.

"How do you make out accidentally?" Kate asked, gaze narrowed.

On a sigh, Kristina launched into the longer version with all the gory details.

"Do you *want* to be more than just friends?" Kate finally asked.

Kristina set down her slice of pizza. "I don't know. On the one hand, I do, because no one has ever made me feel like Noah does. On the other hand, he's my oldest friend, and all the weirdness this week proves that we could really hurt our friendship if we tried for more and it didn't work out. That scares me. A lot. Not to mention that he's pulled back every time."

"But he's also the one who initiated both times. Right?" Kate asked. Kristina nodded. "And he freaked out over your date.

Clearly, he wants you. He just hasn't decided that he can have you."

"Maybe," Kristina said.

"Tell me this. Did you accept the date to make him jealous?"

"No," Kristina said immediately. "I did think of Noah when I was talking to Ethan, but only about the fact that since Noah wanted to remain friends, it wouldn't hurt to go out with Ethan. It never occurred to me that Noah would react so badly, because he'd been the one putting on the brakes."

They ate in silence for a long moment.

"Here's the thing," Kate finally said. "The reality is, you guys have already gone there whether you want to admit it or not. It's gonna be hard to take the sexy times out of your relationship now that they've already been there. You know I was always skeptical that you two could be so platonic."

Kristina sat back in her chair. "I know, but we were. Truly."

"So what changed?"

"He did," Kristina said without hesitation. "All his injuries, having to retire from the Corps. I get the feeling Noah's hurting a lot more than he's letting on. Given all that, maybe I'm the only one he feels like he can be himself around? I don't know."

"What about you?" Kate asked. "Have you changed, in regards to him?"

Kristina gave the question some thought, because she really hadn't asked that of herself before now.

Finally, she said, "I didn't think I had. But maybe...his pushing me away all these months, after being gone so long, made me want to be around him even more. And, physically, he's also changed a lot over the past few years—and it made me look at him more as a man and not just my best friend."

"You've changed too, you know," Kate said. "Physically, I mean. When we first met in college, you always covered your body up with oversized clothes. Now you're more confident. You wear things that flatter and show off your curves. Confidence is sexy. He's probably reacting to that, too."

Had she changed so much? Kristina hadn't thought so, but she couldn't deny that there was some truth to Kate's observation. "I guess so," she said. "I realized something else, too. I don't think I've been giving the guys I date a fair shot—"

"You don't. You compare them all to Noah." Kate raised her glass and took a drink.

Kristina nearly swallowed her tongue. "What? How did you...why do you..."

"Oh, honey. I could've told you that years ago," Kate said.

Kristina ate a big bite of pizza, giving her thoughts a moment to gel. How could it have been so blatant to Kate when Kristina had only just realized it for herself? "So, then, what should I do? Should I push Noah to try for more or stick with just friends?"

"I can't tell you that," Kate said, a sympathetic look on her face. "You gotta decide what would be harder to live with—not going for it and him eventually falling in love with someone else, or going for it and it changing things between you."

"Yeah," Kristina said, her stomach falling at the idea of either outcome. "The question is, how do I make that decision?" And did she have to make it *before* her date with Ethan?

A FLASH OF BRIGHT LIGHT. And then the blast hit Noah in the chest, lifting his innards and slamming them back down again. Voices echoed somewhere beyond the piercing ringing in his ears. His chest hurt. His back. His head. Like he'd just gotten kicked by a horse, if a horse had a foot that could cover his whole body.

Noah tried to push himself up, but the world was spinning. His eyes were blurry, flashing, totally fucked up. That ringing made him want to puke.

"Fender!" he called, though his tongue was thick in his mouth. With sand. With blood. The guy had been right next to him. Where was he? *"Fender!"*

Noah gasped and opened his eyes. For a long moment, the scene in his head was interwoven with the reality of his dark room. And then he was all there. In the quiet stillness of his bedroom, safe in Virginia.

Quiet except for his rasping breath.

Wetness on his face. Noah wiped at his forehead, his eyes, his ears. In a panic, he went for the light. His gaze went right to his hands.

Clear moisture covered his palms. Sweat.

Not blood. It wasn't blood.

Dull pain pulsed through Noah's skull. As he pushed out of bed, the room spun around him. The pain clamped down harder, heavier. Noah groaned and weaved through his bedroom door and into the bathroom. He lost the rest of the vision he had in his left eye as wavy lines appeared behind his right.

Fuck, migraine.

He'd had just enough time to complete that thought before he was heaving his guts into the toilet.

Not that there was much to heave. He'd eaten almost nothing yesterday, but that didn't stop his body from trying. When the nausea finally passed, he took some meds and dragged his ass back to bed, where he stayed for almost twenty-four hours until the pain finally released him from its prison.

Not that he ever truly got free.

When he could finally pull himself from bed, he was surprised to find it was early Tuesday morning. And he was equally surprised to find that he had no messages or missed calls from Kristina.

Fuck.

How are you? Not letting himself debate it, he let the text message fly her way.

In the kitchen, Noah stumbled through making the coffee, then half lay on the kitchen counter while he waited for it to brew. Slowly, the fragrant brown liquid filled the pot, and Noah grabbed a coffee cup from the cabinet. There was nothing special about the plain dark blue ceramic he'd picked out, except that it made him remember shopping with Kristina.

They'd had a good day together. Normal. Easy.

Then he'd gone and fucked it all up by getting jealous over her date.

And, holy hell, he'd been...disproportionately angry. The news of her date had just taken him by such surprise. And she'd looked so excited.

Like a fucking child, Noah had been *pissed* because he wasn't the one to make her look that way.

And then she'd called the guy hot. It was like Noah was a bomb and someone had clipped the red wire. He'd been all but ready to explode.

Right up until she announced she was leaving.

By then, it was too late. His shit had ruined their evening. And she'd rebuffed every one of his admittedly stilted efforts to get them talking again.

Noah poured the coffee and took a nice long sip.

All his anger had achieved was to piss Kristina off and alienate her. Because she was still going out with Ethan the Dickhead Neighbor, wasn't she?

He poured a bowl of cereal and sat heavily at the table. He hadn't eaten since dinner on Sunday and, despite his generally poor appetite, he was fucking starving.

Beneath his keys and wallet, Noah spied the course catalog Kristina had given him before she'd left on Saturday night. He'd given it a long enough glance after he dropped her off to see that it was a listing of art therapy courses—music, dance, theater, studio art, music, writing, and more.

It had only taken an additional two seconds for his brain to say *no fucking way.*

Noah sighed. He'd tried the therapist. Tried keeping it all bottled up inside. He'd tried it his way and was falling the fuck apart. Maybe it was time to try something else?

Giving the flyer a second look, he flipped through the pages between bites of frosted flakes.

Buzz.

Relief flooded through Noah's gut as he reached for his cell. Kristina. Finally. He thumbed on the screen.

Want to tell me about this hole in your shower? I'm standing here with a tile guy you scheduled...

Not Kristina. His father.

"Fuck," Noah said. With the migraine, he'd totally forgotten about the appointment he'd made. He'd meant to get up and over to his parents' place before they knew what was going on. "Fuck."

I'm sorry, he typed back. *I was trying to take care of it without bothering you.* He sent those messages and stared at the screen.

If Noah *didn't* explain that he'd forgotten because of the migraine, he'd just look like an inconsiderate asshole. If he did explain about the migraine, he'd have to admit he wasn't doing well to his father.

Rock, meet hard place.

Be right over, he texted. Then the truth trumped his need to make everyone think he was fine, just fine, thank you very much. *Had a shit migraine for the past two days and lost track of time. I'm sorry.*

Noah inhaled the rest of his cereal and threw on some clothes, and then he stood in front of his bathroom counter which held so many pill bottles it looked like a pharmacy had vomited all over it.

One by one, he downed the battery of meds he had. For depression. For anxiety. For his equilibrium issues. When he'd choked them all down, he collected his keys and wallet and then, without thinking too much about why, he grabbed the listing of courses, too. Ten minutes later, he pulled into his parents' driveway behind the contractor's service truck.

He found his father standing at the island in the kitchen, a cup of coffee in his hand and the newspaper spread out in front of him.

"Good morning," his dad said in what sounded like a neutral tone. But Noah knew that was really an invitation for him to come clean about the damage he'd done—and why he'd done it.

"I'm sorry," Noah said, bracing his hands on the far side of the island.

Dad pressed his lips together and gave Noah a sad look. "I don't care about the hole, Noah. I care about you. I saw the cuts on your hand and I let it go because it's clear you don't like being pushed to talk, but now that I know how it happened, I have to ask—"

"It was the fireworks." Noah dropped his gaze to the cook-top stove in between them. "At the Memorial Day party." He shrugged, searching for the words, and debating just how much to reveal. He didn't need to bring his fuck-up with Kristina into it, that much was for sure. "They set off a full-on flashback. I didn't know where I was. Actually, that's not true. I was *in* Iraq, only, I wasn't. Afterward, I lost it. I'm sorry."

His Dad came around the counter to stand right next to Noah. "I didn't even think of how the fireworks might affect you."

Noah chuffed out a laugh that held no humor whatsoever. "Me either."

His mind was so damn fucked, and the weight of it was just...too much to bear. He yearned for a release, just a way to lift a little of it from his shoulders, even if only for a short while.

"Talk to me, son."

Pressure clamped down on Noah's chest and a knot lodged in his throat. "I'm having flashbacks. Nightmares. Anxiety all the time."

"What does your therapist say?"

Noah shook his head. "Talking makes it worse."

His father's shoulders fell. "You're not going." It wasn't a question.

"Not for over a month," Noah whispered.

Sighing, Dad put his arm around Noah's shoulder. Every one of Noah's muscles braced against the urge to curl into his father's chest like he'd done when he was a little boy. "You need some way to let this out, Noah."

The echo of his own thoughts—his own yearning—brought a sharp, unexpected sting to the backs of Noah's eyes. Blinking fast, he nodded. "I know. Kristina gave me this." He pulled the rolled-up blue pages from the back pocket of his jeans and spread them out on the counter in front of them. "I was thinking...maybe...if I tried something that didn't make me talk..."

His dad leafed through the pages.

An embarrassed restlessness flooded through Noah as he waited for a reaction from one of the men he admired most in the world. "I mean, I don't know. It's probably stupid. I'm not an artist. And I don't really see how painting a picture could help—"

"Give it a try. Kristina could be on to something here." His dad looked up at him, his expression full of rock-solid support and encouragement. "Hell, give a couple a try until you find the right outlet. And stop beating yourself up." The older man cupped Noah's cheek in his big, calloused hand. "You've suffered a traumatic brain injury. The doctors said it'd be a while before you got to whatever your new normal is. Don't make that any harder on yourself than it already is."

A fast nod, and then Noah had to dash his fist against a little moisture at the corner of his eye. Damnit.

"Now, you good to hang while the tile guy finishes up? He didn't think it would take long to patch, but I should head out to work." His dad turned away to clean up his coffee and paper.

"Yeah, I'm good. And I'm covering the bill."

"Yes, you are." His dad winked as he gathered his things. "I'm always here for you, Noah."

Noah nodded. "Thanks. For everything."

"Yup. Lock up on your way out," his dad called as he headed down the hall.

All alone, Noah checked on the tile guy's progress and then settled at the island with the list of art therapy classes. He ruled the theater and writing classes out right off the bat. Both seemed too much like talking, one thing he knew for sure didn't work for him. Same for singing and songwriting classes. Next, he ruled out all the dancing classes. He just couldn't see himself taking a class called Soldiers Who Salsa. That mostly left various studio art classes, but since he knew next to nothing about art, he wasn't sure how to judge what he might like.

Part of the description of a class called War Graffiti caught his eye.

According to a recent CBS 60 Minutes story, when Vietnam veterans came back, it took 8 to 10 years before they succumbed to homelessness. Now, within a year of separation from the

Armed Forces, our warfighters are on the street, homeless. Though some of them are victims of our economy, these staggering statistics point to the increased occurrence of invisible wounds such as TBI and PTSD.

God, Noah didn't want that to be him.

Did these classes really help people so much?

He read on, and came to a class called Masks of War. It was aimed at active-duty service-members and veterans suffering from PTSD, TBI, and other psychological health concerns. Over the course of four Saturday mornings, they'd make masks that illustrated hidden feelings. That last part of the description made Noah grimace a little, but the masks sounded kinda cool. And it was only four classes. The instructor's bio listed him as a vet, too. Those parts sounded decent.

What the hell.

He carried the flyer into his parents' study and booted up the desktop computer. Before he gave himself the chance to second-guess it, he registered for the mask class.

When he was done, he found himself wanting to tell Kristina. He picked up his cell and found he had a text from her.

Okay. You?

Hmm. He knew Kristina-speak after all these years, and okay was not actually okay.

Which meant she was upset. And it was his fault.

Noah had to find a way to make things right between them. Pronto.

CHAPTER TEN

Kristina came out of school and stepped into the warm June sun. She felt restless and kinda down. And she didn't have to think too hard to figure out why.

The fight with Noah. And the fact that he hadn't bothered to call or text her until this morning.

The three days of silence had her repeatedly analyzing why she'd agreed to go out with Ethan. Maybe she *had* accepted to make Noah jealous? Maybe even unconsciously? Either way, she felt like crap about the silence that had been between them ever since.

Maybe she should pick up some dinner to take over to his place...

"Bye, Miss Moore," two girls from her fourth period class called, giggling and whispering conspiratorially between themselves.

"Bye, girls. Have a good night," she said, giving them a smile. Not even dinner and drinks with Kate on Sunday night had cheered her up. At least, not all the way. Because Kate's question had been weighing on her mind, and she still didn't have a good answer to it.

Kristina rounded the corner of the building and glanced toward the parking lot.

Noah.

Leaning against the driver's door to her car. He hadn't spotted her yet, so she took a minute to drink him in. He wore blue jeans and a plain black T-shirt and a pair of bad-ass black sunglasses. Together with his dark hair, he was tall, dark, and handsome personified.

Or maybe that should be tall, dark, and brooding.

Either way, it made her sigh with longing.

Noah finally glanced up and saw her standing there, so Kristina closed the distance between them. "What are you doing here, silly man?" she asked, hoping she sounded normal.

"Delivering a peace offering." He slid off his sunglasses and held out a small, dark blue cooler bag.

"A peace offering?" Relief curled into her belly. She hadn't been the only one worried about the tension between them then. Kristina smiled uncertainly as she accepted it from him and rested it on the hood of her car so she could unzip it. Four pints of Ben and Jerry's ice cream—Hazed and Confused, Americone Dream, Chocolate Therapy, and Chocolate Chip Cookie Dough, naturally. She laughed and warmth filled her chest. "Unnecessary but very appreciated."

Fingers just barely caressed the bottom of her chin, urging her to look up. "No. Very necessary. I was an asshole. And you were right to be pissed about that. I'm sorry."

His apology caught her off-guard. "I actually thought you were mad at me," she said.

He frowned. "Why would I be mad?"

She shrugged. "I don't know. I just thought...maybe...I'd been inconsiderate."

Noah shook his head. "You weren't. Not at all, Kristina. That was all me. And it's time I try to get my shit together."

Kristina studied his eyes, which somehow looked a little lighter despite the circles underneath. "Meaning?"

"I signed up for a class at your art school. For starters, I guess," he said, dropping his gaze.

"You did?" He nodded, looking a little uncomfortable. "That's so awesome!"

He kicked the toe of his shoe against the asphalt. "We'll see. Makes me feel a like a kid signing up for arts and crafts, but—" Noah shrugged. "—whatever. I'll give it a try. I gotta give *something* a try."

Kristina nodded, happiness and affection making her grin. She knew it couldn't be easy for a guy trained to kill you in fifty-two different ways to walk into an art therapy class, but everything on that flyer had been for active-duty or veterans, so he wouldn't be the only highly trained killer wielding a pen...or a paintbrush...or whatever. Speaking of which... "What class did you register for?"

He nudged the cooler. "Have a reverse dinner with me? And I'll tell you all about it."

"You got it," she said. "Hop in."

Twenty minutes later, they were finding a spot in the grass at Gravelly Point, a park along the Potomac River that sat right across a small inlet from the runway at Reagan International Airport. Picnicking in the park, the planes took off and landed right over your heads, making it a fun place to hang out, walk, or catch some rays. She and Noah had been going there for years.

Noah spread a blanket on the grass and they both sprawled out on their stomachs, which was a little awkward for Kristina in her pale blue jersey wrap dress, but the sun felt so good she didn't care.

"What do you want to start with?" Noah asked, unzipping the cooler. He reached in and produced a spoon, which he handed to her.

"Ooh, look at you, Boy Scout," Kristina said. "I'll start with some Chocolate Therapy. It's the last week of school, after all, and the kids are climbing the freaking walls."

Noah pulled out his old favorite and tugged off the lid. "I remember that. The last week of school always seemed so pointless. Exams were over. Grades were in. And yet we were still stuck in school."

"Pretty much," Kristina said, opening her pint. The ice packs in the cooler had mostly done their job, but the ice cream was just a little soft, making it easy to get a nice big scoop. "Mmm, this is so good." She swallowed and gestured with her spoon. "And I need the downtime so I can finish getting my course materials together for my short story class. Speaking of which, tell me about this class you're taking."

He poked around at his ice cream for a minute, and then finally said, "It's a mask-making workshop. Creating masks that illustrate veterans' hidden feelings." Sarcasm dripped from his tone, but she didn't give him a hard time about it.

Because the fact that he was trying made something squeeze in Kristina's chest. Concern. Affection. Pride. "That sounds like it could be cool."

"Yeah, I guess. Hopefully it's not too...touchy-feely."

"It'll be a classroom full of people just like you. You're probably not the only one for whom something like this is new." Kristina ate another bite and eyeballed Noah's reaction. Things seemed normal between them again. Relaxed. Relief could've melted her right into the warm blanket.

"That's true," Noah said.

"Oh, here comes a plane," Kristina said, pointing over Noah's shoulder.

Noah peered up at the sky to see—

His whole body went rigid. Kristina thought she imagined it at first. But as the airplane got closer, his arms flew over his head like he was shielding himself. The airplane was nearly overhead now, so low it felt like you could touch it, and the roar of the engines got louder and louder as it passed them by to land just across the water.

"Noah?" she said. No response. No wonder, between his hearing deficit and the plane.

She scooted closer, unsure whether to touch him, but absolutely certain that he needed her to help bring him back from wherever he'd gone. Laying right beside him, she gently rested her hand between his tense shoulder blades. Still no response.

With her lips close to his good ear, she said, "Noah, it's okay. You're not in—"

He pinned her. In a quick series of moves, he pushed her to her back and covered her upper body and face with his. "It'll be over soon. And then I'll get you out of here. Just hang on, man."

Kristina didn't even want to imagine the scene his mind was painting for him. She had to bring him back. "Noah. It's me, Kristina. You're okay. Everyone's okay."

But, oh God, over his shoulder she spied another plane coming in for a landing. Sometimes it was like that—lulls intermixed with one landing after another.

It was clear when Noah heard the second plane, because he jerked, his far-off gaze searching for the source of the low rumble. She could feel it in the ground on which she lay as much as hear it. "Fuck. Incoming."

She cupped his face in her hands. Her mind scrambled. On instinct she barked, "Cortez!" His eyes snapped toward her.

Kristina kissed him.

At first, he didn't respond. And then his lips moved softly, tentatively, like he wasn't sure. And then he was freaking devouring her.

His muscles went lax on a groan and he wrapped himself around her. His arms cradled her shoulders. His hands raked into her hair. All while his lips sucked and his tongue plundered and his teeth nipped.

"Fuck," he moaned as the plane passed directly overhead, the engine roar louder now. He shuddered out a breath that ghosted over her wet lips. "You saved me."

And she would keep on doing it, as long and as much as he needed her to do it. All the while, it was like she was caught in the center of a storm. Heat lashed her nipples and core. Concern tossed her belly. Emotion overwhelmed her like a waving crashing over her head.

She had no time to wonder whether this was a good idea. She couldn't let herself take the time to think, to debate, to weigh the pros and cons. She reacted on pure instinct—the instinct that said that Noah needed her to ground him in this world. Right here. Right now. And she was willing to do anything to bring him back to her.

"I'm sorry," he rasped, his lips claiming hers again and again. "So sorry."

She shook her head, her fingers plowing into his hair. "You're good. We're good." Needing him, too, she sucked on his tongue hard, and the strangled groan he unleashed was a heady thing. Hot and needy. Raw with emotion.

The plane's noise receded.

No part of Kristina wanted to give up Noah's kisses. And she knew they had a better than average chance of taking another hard left into awkward territory once this moment passed. But they had to leave before the next plane started in on its descent.

Pulling back and breathing hard, she held his face in her hands. "Let's get out of here."

Dark brown eyes searched hers, and even with the tension carving hard angles into his face, he was still the most gorgeous man she'd ever seen. He studied her a long moment, then gave a tight nod, his gaze skittering around them like he was looking to see if anyone else had noticed him.

Noah rose to his feet and looked toward the distant sky, wariness in his eyes. Kristina knew what he was looking for, which was why she had the cooler packed up and the blanket balled in her arms in mere seconds. She took his hand, and his fingers wrapped tightly around hers. Like maybe he still needed her to ground him. And she was totally okay with that.

Sitting in the driver's seat, she turned to him. "Come home with me and I'll cook dinner?"

He scowled out the windshield. "Barely had dessert."

"Have you ever known me to waste ice cream, Cortez?" She raised an eyebrow at him, hoping against hope that things wouldn't become awkward. "Now, you game?"

"Means you'd have to take me back to my car later," he gritted out.

The fact that he wasn't demanding she take him there now seemed like an admission that he still wasn't feeling quite right. Kristina shrugged. "Deal."

His only answer was a single tight nod.

The car ride home was quiet and tense. The only sound was the brushing of Noah's jeans against the center console as he bounced his foot. Kristina wasn't sure what to say to make him feel better, so instead she played things normal by singing along to the radio. Rush hour traffic dragged out the trip, but soon they were home and climbing the steps to her second-floor apartment.

Noah still hadn't said a word.

She let them in and dropped her purse to the kitchen counter, then turned to find Noah sagging back against the door. He crossed his arms, let his head fall backward, and closed his eyes.

The man looked so freaking weary that it broke her heart. She couldn't help but go to him.

Kristina awkwardly hugged him, her hands going as far around him as she could with his arms folded across his chest. She rested her forehead against his sternum. For a long moment, they stood like that.

"Everything...everything is different now," he finally said, voice tight and gravelly. "So much that I used to take for granted is just gone for me, and it...it just—"

The sound of him swallowing thickly reached her ears, but she stayed silent to let him finish. Because he'd never before talked to her about what he was feeling, and she didn't want him to stop.

But he did. Kristina lifted her face to his—and found his dark brown eyes blazing down at her. "You'll get through this, Noah. I'll help you."

"I'm no good right now, Kristina," he said in a low voice.

She shook her head. "That's not true. You've been through something horrible. And you're still recovering. Still hurting. That's all understandable—"

"I am fucked in the head. You saw it yourself. Twice," he said, his voice suddenly loud, bitter. Under her hands, his muscles tensed.

"You are not fucked in the head," she said, anger and determination gathering deep in her belly. Not anger at Noah, but irrational anger for him. She hated that things had happened to him that left him feeling this way. So out of control, so sad, so unlike himself. "Sure, you have things you're dealing with. And you *will* get a handle on them—"

"No," he said, shaking her off and pacing in the narrow space behind the door. "You don't understand. I'm..." His hands squeezed into fists at his sides. "...so goddamned angry. All the time. It feels like I could tear the world to pieces. And I want to." He whirled on her. "Because the perfection of everything around me makes me feel so much more wrecked inside that I can barely breathe."

Oh, God.

Tears pricked at the backs of her eyes, but she wouldn't let them fall. She wouldn't let *herself* fall apart. Not now. Not in front of him. Not when Noah needed to lean on her so damn badly. "The world around you is not perfect, Noah. It's an illusion. And you are not wrecked—"

"I am." He got right up in her face.

Kristina held her ground. "You're not—"

"I am!"

"Noah—"

He grabbed her by the arms, not so much that it hurt, but with enough force that it surprised her. "Here's your proof. I want to fuck you, Kristina. I want to bury myself in you and stay there forever. Just lose myself in you until I don't know who I am anymore. I've been fantasizing about it, dreaming about it, imagining it. Having you is all I can fucking think about. Do you understand what I'm saying?"

Noah's words unleashed a flash fire in Kristina's blood. Her heart tripped into a sprint. Her breathing shallowed out. Heat roared across her skin. One heartbeat. Two. And Kristina knew what she had to do.

Acting on instinct, she pulled out of Noah's grip and stepped backward. Away from his confession. Away from him.

CHAPTER ELEVEN

"THAT'S WHAT I THOUGHT," Noah said, a rock lodging in his gut. He'd really gone and done it now, hadn't he? Opened his mouth and spewed his poison at one of the most important people in his life. And tonight was supposed to be all about making amends.

Goddamnit, the minute he came out of that flashback he should've gotten the hell away from her. He'd just been so shell-shocked by how realistic it had seemed. The anti-aircraft fire. The crashing Blackhawk. The screaming chaos.

He'd been even more stunned that Kristina had kissed him to pull him back—and that it had worked.

He shook his head, ignoring the fuck out of the wave of dizziness that threatened, and grabbed the doorknob. "I'll go."

"*No*," she said, her voice stern. Frowning, he dragged his gaze to her to see her fingers working at the knot in her dress's belt. She pulled it apart and let the fabric fall. The dress swung open, baring her all down the front. "You need me. Have me."

He blinked, once, twice, and his jaw fell open.

Jesus. She was beautiful, gorgeous, a fucking fantasy of soft, feminine curves. His pulse beat so hard he could feel it beneath his skin. Everywhere.

Noah gripped the doorknob harder, anchoring him in the moment. Keeping him from taking something that wasn't his to take. No matter how much he might want it. "Kris—"

"Have me, Noah." She shrugged the dress off her shoulders. It fell to the floor in a soft rush, leaving Kristina standing there in a pair of strappy silver sandals and a matching pale blue and white satin bra-and-panty set.

He couldn't do this. Not to her, not to them.

But his brain seemed to be the only part of him riding the do-the-right-thing train. Because his heart *wanted*. And his cock fucking *needed*. He licked his lips and shook his head, feeling solid ground slide out from beneath his feet with every breath. "I'm a fucking wreck, Kristina."

"Then be *my* fucking wreck." She shrugged and shifted her feet, and Noah studied these small movements, trying to decipher what they meant. "Just for tonight."

"Just for tonight?" He tried out the words—and their meaning. Could he really let himself have her...just this once?

The idea that he could escape all the bullshit in his head—just for one night, the idea that he could work out this crazy desire for her...and maybe get it out of his system. It was all so damn tempting. *She* was so damn tempting. When had that happened? Why was he seeing her so differently? And did any of that even matter?

"I don't want to use you," he said, his thoughts flying and tearing him in two.

She stepped closer. Heat flashed over Noah's skin. God, she was brave. So much braver than him.

"You wouldn't," Kristina said. "Because I...I *want* you to fuck me, Noah. You think you're the only one dreaming of that? Imagining it? Fantasizing about it? I wake up from those dreams and you're not there...and it *hurts*. It feels like there's a fire inside me that only you can cool. So maybe, maybe if we do this, if we give in, just this once..."

Her words resonated inside him, so deep it was like she was speaking his mind. "What?" he asked, his heart a runaway train in his chest.

"Maybe it will get rid of this tension between us." She hugged herself, plumping those beautiful breasts and making waves of soft blond fall around her shoulders.

He let go of the doorknob, but forced his feet to remain planted right where they were. Because if he got any closer to her, his brain was going to be off the hook for the rest of the night. "So this would be...just sex?" he asked, his chest rising and falling heavily.

Nodding, she looked him right in the eye. "Just sex. Just this one night."

He swallowed. Hard. He was so damn hungry for her, and that made him hesitate when all he wanted to do was give in. "I'm strung so tight right now, Kristina. I don't know if I can be gentle." He shook his head and forced his fists to unclench, but aggression was a living beast within him. "That wouldn't be right. That wouldn't be—"

"I don't want gentle, Noah." The smile she gave him was so confident, so sexy. When had she become so goddamned amazing? Or had she always been? "I just want you, however you are."

One second he was standing at the door, the next he was all over her. Hands in her hair, forcing her head back and her mouth open to him. Lips sliding over hers, claiming, sucking, tongue penetrating. Body fused to hers, pushing her back, one stumbling step after another, and trying to get closer. And closer. And closer.

"Oh God," Kristina moaned, her hands clutching at his neck, his shoulders, his hair.

"One night," he said, lifting her and wrapping her thighs around his hips. Her ass felt so lush in his hands he couldn't help squeezing.

"One night. I need you. Now. Here. Anywhere."

Sucking and licking at her throat, he stalked down the hall toward her bedroom. "No. I want you under me." In her room, he went right for her big bed with all its pretty blue and yellow covers and pillows. Standing beside the bed, he laid her out, the weight of his upper body coming down on top of her and making him grind right against the delicious heat between her legs.

"Oh, yes," Kristina said, her hips thrusting against his.

Nearly frantic, he fumbled at the buttons to his jeans. "Need in you."

"Yeah."

"Promise I'll take care of you." He shoved his jeans down around his thighs, freeing his cock against the satin of her panties.

Kristina moaned. "I know you will."

"Fuck, need you. Need you so much." He tugged her panties off, then took himself in hand. Standing between her spread thighs, he rubbed his head against her entrance, feeling her wetness, spreading it around. He wished he could go slower, savor, linger. She braced her feet against the edge of the bed and pushed, trying to impale herself on him. "Shit. Condom," he said. Resisting the urge to plunge forward was almost painful.

"On birth control. Now, Noah."

On a groan, he was inside her, sinking deep, finding home. Fucking hot and tight and perfect. And then he was all the way there, buried deep, as deep as he could go. Just like he'd been yearning for. Only the reality was worlds better than anything his imagination had been able to conjure. It was so good it sent him flying.

He came down over her as much as the position allowed, his hands curling around her shoulders.

She cried out, her hands clawing at his back. "Holy shit, you're big."

"You okay?" he asked, the comment making his balls heavy and sending an urgent demand to move down his spine.

"So much more than okay," Kristina said in a breathy, awed voice.

"Then hold on," he said, hips moving as he anchored himself to her. Slower at first, but quickly faster, deeper, harder. He could've roared out at the goodness of it. But it wasn't enough.

Going upright again, he tore off his shirt, then braced his fists snug against her sides, holding her hips as he gave her everything he had. She grasped his wrists and held tight, arching her back on each sharp thrust, making his mouth water for her breasts. The room filled with the sounds of sex—the slap of skin on skin, rasping breaths, needful moans.

"So fucking pretty," he rasped. And God, she was. So beautiful beneath him, open to him, accepting him into her heat.

"Noah," she cried, her hands squeezing his wrists tighter.

Hips flying, grinding, surging against her, he swallowed hard, loving the sound of his name on her lips. "What, baby?"

"Need you." Her head thrashed, blond hair sprawled out all around her. Like a fucking angel of mercy.

"What do you need?" He pulled a hand free from hers and circled his fingers between her legs. "This?"

Kristina almost came up off the bed. "Yes."

Hips flying, he moved his fingers harder, flicking them over her sensitive nub until he found just the thing that made her cry out the loudest, that made her stomach muscles clench the hardest. "Yeah," he said. Except watching her chase her pleasure squeezed at his balls. It had been too long. And he needed her too much. And she felt too goddamned good. "Fuck, Kristina. Not gonna be able to hold back."

"Don't," she whispered. Heavy-lidded and heated, her blues eyes looked straight inside him. "Don't hold back with me."

Her words were what did it. Heat lanced through him and then his orgasm was kicking him in the back, driving him into her even harder. He gripped her hips, lifted them off the bed, and brought their bodies together once, twice, three times.

Noah came inside her on a deep-throated groan. "Fuck, fuck, fuck," he said as his release rocked through him. His body stilled as the squeezing pulses ended, and he held himself all the way inside her.

"God, that was so good," Kristina said, a flush on her cheeks.

Pulse rushing behind his ears and under his skin, Noah stroked his fingers from her knees to her core, and from there up to her breasts. And back again.

"It was, but it was only the beginning, Kristina. From here on out, it's gonna be all about you."

***

KRISTINA SWALLOWED HARD. She was breathless, boneless, and overwhelmed by the reality of what was happening. She might've suggested it—pushed for it, even—but that didn't make it any less mind-blowing.

She just had sex with Noah Cortez.

And it was freaking amazing. *He* was freaking amazing. The way he moved. The way he filled her. That incredible expression on his face when he came, like he was shattered and put back together again all at the same time.

"All about me?" she asked.

Nodding, Noah withdrew from her, and she missed his presence inside her immediately. "If I only get one night, I want to learn everything I can about you. What makes you moan. What makes you writhe. What makes you come the hardest."

His words rushed heat over her body. It pooled between her legs, where arousal still had her wet and needy.

"This time, I want to start at the beginning," he said, pulling her into a sitting position at the edge of the bed and taking her face in his hands. Noah kissed her, softer this time, but every bit as deep, and maybe even more intense for the slow intimacy of it.

His tongue probed and explored, twining with hers. His hands wandered over her warm skin, stripping off her bra and lingering over her breasts, her nipples. He shifted closer, and she stroked her hands down the outside of his thighs, making her realize his jeans still hung around his legs. Feeling the roughness of the denim was when it really hit Kristina that neither of them had gotten all the way undressed before he'd gotten inside her. And for some reason she found that so freaking hot.

Noah ran worshipful kisses and playful nips along her jaw to the soft spot behind her ear, the spot that always made her melt and moan.

"Mmm, I'll have to remember this," he said, his breath caressing her ear and making goosebumps spring up all down her neck. He nipped along her neck to the tendon that sloped down her shoulder, his fingers plucking at her nipples, making her gasp and squirm. "This, too."

Kristina shivered at the sensual promise of his words. But a part of her ached, too, because he wouldn't need to remember the list of things that made her hot and wet if they weren't going to do this again, would he?

No. No thinking. If this is all there will be, live in the moment and memorize every second of it.

Yes. Live in the moment. That's exactly what she'd do.

"Want to feel all of you," he whispered against her throat. "Want to taste all of you."

How would she *ever* unhear him saying things like that? His lips chased the question away as they found her nipple and sucked it into his mouth. He held her there with his teeth and drove her mad with a series of hard, fast flicks of his tongue that had her gasping and whimpering. "God, Noah."

"Say it again," he said.

She stroked at his hair, and then gave in to the urge to press kisses there. "Noah." *Kiss.* "Noah." *Kiss.* "Noah." His hair was soft against her mouth and smelled like soap and sunshine.

"Fuck, yeah," he groaned, kissing down her belly. He stepped out of his jeans and lowered himself to his knees, then ran his hands roughly from her breasts down her belly to her thighs.

All the pain she'd seen in his dark eyes earlier was gone now, replaced by a sexy determination that had her stomach flipping and her heart panging in her chest. He pressed on her stomach, and she reclined a little.

Noah pushed her knees apart and stroked soft, teasing fingertips down the insides of her thighs, and Kristina was one hundred percent sure she'd never seen anything sexier than Noah on his knees between her legs. His gaze dragged down her body like a physical caress. His hands ran upward again and skated over her core, his thumbs dragging lazily over her clit where they met in the middle.

Kristina gasped at the too-brief contact. "Oh, God," she whispered.

"I want my mouth on you. You good with that?" The look he gave her was so damn sexy. Hungry. Daring her to say no.

Of which there was absolutely no chance. She'd only had one boyfriend who seemed to enjoy giving oral sex enough to allow her to enjoy it, too, so her heart was a freight train in her chest just imagining Noah's mouth. On her. She nodded. "I dreamed of you doing it."

"Did you now?" He scooted closer, a smug smirk played around his lips. "And how was it?"

"I woke up before you—"

Noah licked her, just one swipe of the flatness of his tongue over the top of her sex.

"Oh, Jesus," she said, her breath exploding out of her.

"Tell me what you like," he whispered, running hard flicks of his tongue all around her lips, making her flinch and thrust her hips. His arm clamped down around her lower belly, and his fingers opened her to him further.

"Anything," she rasped. "Because it's you." The words were out of her mouth before she really thought about how they might sound.

It's just sex. Just sex. Just sex.

But Noah only made a small sound of satisfaction in the back of his throat, and then ran more of those firm, flat licks over her clit. Kristina's eyelids wanted to fall shut to let her bask in the riot of sensations his mouth was causing, but *seeing him* between her thighs, his mouth on her pussy, was too erotic to look away from for even a single second.

And Noah gave her no reason to question whether he enjoyed doing this. He absolutely feasted on her. Sucking. Flicking. Licking. The wet sounds of his mouth combined with these crazy sexy little moans of pleasure he made to form a soundtrack she would no doubt hear in her dreams for a long, long time to come.

"Oh, God, Noah. Oh, God." Kristina couldn't control the little whimpers spilling out of her throat, the increasing volume of her breathing, the strain of her leg and hip muscles trying to push herself against his mouth.

In a sudden movement, Noah lifted her thighs over his shoulders and hiked her hips off the edge of the bed, and then he clasped his hands around her lower belly, making her core a prisoner to his mouth. He sucked her clit into his mouth and then flicked his tongue against it in a relentless demand that she come. His dark eyes stared up her body and bored into hers, the silent command so freaking loud that her head was spinning and her heart was hammering and sensation was whirling lower and lower in her body, collecting, building, until—

Kristina cried out as her orgasm crashed into her in wave after wave of pulsing, bone-melting pleasure unlike anything she'd ever felt before. She fisted her hands in the blanket beneath her and arched her back, her body utterly at the mercy of Noah's mouth.

"Stop, stop, I'm gonna die," she rasped. Absolutely sure of it. But not at all unhappy that this was the way she'd go. Receiving pleasure from the man she—from Noah.

He released her, and even that made her whimper and writhe. "I'm gonna hear you do that again and again before this night is over," he said, his voice full of gravel.

She wasn't sure she'd survive it. Body or heart.

CHAPTER TWELVE

KRISTINA CLAMPED DOWN HARD on the concern about her heart. She was having fun. *So* much fun. And she was fine. They were fine.

Noah pressed kisses against her inner thighs that made her laugh, then he slowly eased her legs off his shoulders and slid back up her body, dropping more kisses here and there as he moved. It was so damn sweet and affectionate that it shot warmth through her chest. Kristina pushed that reaction aside, which was easier to do when she felt the hard length of his cock drag against her thigh and settle between her legs.

She reached down and wrapped her hand around him. "Mmm, look what I found."

"What's that, baby?" he said, nuzzling her breasts, her neck, her lips.

Gah! Baby! There was that term of endearment again. Did he even realize he said it?

He kissed her, chasing the question away, and the taste of herself on his lips was so damn sexy. Really, what could be sexier than a big strong man willing to get down on his knees to give a woman pleasure?

"Your cock," she whispered, the word sending shivers over her skin. She stroked him, root to tip, root to tip, enjoying the little catches in his breath and flinches of his stomach muscles. "All hard again."

"Your fault," he said, his expression playful and full of challenge.

"Aw," she said. "Well maybe I should help you out with this little problem."

His brows slashed down. "Little?"

Kristina laughed. "I already complimented you on your size."

He smirked. "That shit doesn't get old."

"Good to know." She smiled, a new desire blooming deep inside her. "Well, given how *big* it is, I have to wonder whether I could take all of it in my mouth."

Noah's eyes flashed red hot. "Fuck, hearing you say things like that..." He shook his head.

"You might like seeing me do it even more." She waggled her eyebrows as his gaze narrowed. "Lay down," she said, patting the bed next to her.

He devoured her in a deep, slow, needful kiss, then slid off of her and rolled onto his back.

Kristina shifted to her knees and paused for a moment, just *looking* at Noah Cortez lying totally naked and mouth-wateringly aroused on her bed. He was all warm, olive skin with cut muscles and dark hair. Beautiful. Sexy. So damn masculine. Every inch of him.

Never had she thought she'd see this. And she refused to let herself waste one moment of their time together worrying about it coming to an end. She felt a little like Cinderella at the ball— she knew the clock would strike midnight and her beautiful glass carriage would turn back into a pumpkin—which meant she had to cherish every second of her prince while she had him.

Noah scooted up on the bed, and Kristina crawled to kneel between his thighs. Scars marked his skin here and there, and she didn't want to imagine all the things that had caused them, all the things that had hurt him. Because tonight was about pleasure—not hurt, not worry, not tomorrow.

Gently, Kristina grasped the hard muscle of Noah's thighs. She ran her hands down to his calves, staying away from his feet because she knew he was deathly ticklish there, and then she stroked upward, passing by his twitching cock to smooth her palms over his abs, his chest, his throat. The change in her position had her stretching over his groin and her nipples dragging over his length. Noah groaned and his hands cupped her breasts. She peered down, loving the look of his big hands massaging her. She leaned down further, causing his cock to nestle into her cleavage. She used her hands to press his together, inviting him to squeeze her flesh around his length.

"Fuck, Kristina," he rasped. His hips jerked in shallow pumps, and the feeling and sight of his cock sliding between her breasts had her instantly wet again.

She bowed her head as far as she could and stuck out her tongue, swiping it against his head on each upward pump.

Noah groaned at the contact, which made Kristina need him in her mouth right then. She pulled herself free from his grasp and slid back, dragging her tongue down his whole length as she moved. Kneeling, she fisted her hand around his thickness and bathed him with her tongue, getting him good and wet, loving the feel of him getting even harder in her grip.

"Looks so good," he rasped.

She cut her eyes to him and swirled her tongue around his head. His face was a mask of pleasure and anticipation, and Kristina didn't want to make either of them wait another second. Her eyes on his face, she opened her mouth and sucked him in deep.

"Jesus Christ," Noah bit out, his head jerking back. A hot thrill shot through Kristina's belly, driving her to take him deeper, and deeper still. He folded an arm behind his head, making it so he could watch her, and that drove her on, too. She settled into a rhythm that alternated slow and deep sucks that buried him as far into the back of her throat as she could take him with faster bobs of her head that she matched with the stroking of her hand.

Noah's fingers petted her hair, sometimes soft and encouraging, sometimes pushing her to go faster or take him deeper. She loved the feeling of him guiding her, showing her what he liked. Soon, his hips were moving in an almost desperate way and deep, guttural sounds spilled from his throat. "Stop, stop," he rasped. "Don't wanna come like this."

"Why?" she asked, already anticipating drinking him down.

He waved her toward him. "Want you to ride me, baby."

There that was again. It was funny that Kristina had possibly never adored a nickname more given that, when they were younger, she despised it any time Noah would boast or brag about being two years older. But, *baby*. Yeah, she freaking loved hearing him say that. To her.

Pang.

Stop it.

Kristina released his cock and crawled up him, and Noah helped her shift her legs to the outside of his hips. Butterflies whipped through her belly at the feeling of his cock nudging against her core again, but it was different this time. Gone was the urgent rush of their first time. Now, it was like Noah wanted to study every moment, savor it, draw it out. He gripped her hips and pressed her down, forcing her to grind against his cock.

She cried out as her wetness coated him and their tight press and shift created the most delicious friction.

"You look so good over me," he said in a voice so low it was almost a whisper, his gaze flickering from her face to her swaying breasts to where his cock slid between her lower lips. "Knew you would."

Oh, God. She loved and hated that he'd said that. Loved it because it was freaking hot and not a little sweet. Hated it because how was she supposed to keep this about just sex when he said things like that?

His hand reached between her legs, urging her up. He gripped and centered himself beneath her opening, then guided her down with a hand on her hip.

Kristina took him inside her on a moan, loving the overwhelming feeling of him filling her, stretching her, invading her. When she'd taken him all, she braced her palms on the firm plane of his stomach and slowly lifted herself back up again. Just long, slow strokes that made both of them moan and pant.

Noah stroked his hands over her thighs, her belly, her breasts.

"I want you to use my body to get off," he said, cupping his hand behind her neck and pulling her in for a wet, claiming kiss. "Whatever you like, however fast or slow, I want you to come on my cock."

His words licked over her skin like a blow torch. "God, Noah. You feel so good," she said, her hips shifting so that her clit dragged against where they were joined.

"That's it, baby. Use me." One hand still holding her neck, the other gripped her hip again, helping her move. They were so close that she felt his breath on her face, and his gaze absolutely blazed up at her.

Looking at Noah, it was almost as if she'd never had sex before. Because staring into the eyes of the man who knew her better than any other, with whom she had a nearly life-long history, while she took him inside her body—it was the most intimate and intense experience of her entire life.

Heat and emotion rushed through her in equal measure. Affection. Red-hot desire. And maybe something more. Something she couldn't let herself think about right now. Wouldn't.

"Oh, God," she cried, throwing back her head and breaking that suddenly too-close connection. Lifting and lowering, she moved faster and grinded herself against him harder. Her breasts bounced, and Noah shoved her closer to the edge by pinching and sucking at her nipples.

She was totally and utterly overwhelmed, overloaded, overcome by sensation. By everything. By Noah. And then she was right there, hanging on the edge until she could barely breathe.

"Oh, I...I'm gonna—"

The orgasm shattered her. Just ripped her into a million floating pieces.

"Fuck, yes," Noah said, suddenly lifting her hips enough that he could hammer up into her.

Dizzy, Kristina collapsed forward, her arms bracing her above Noah as he fucked her through the clenching spasms of her orgasm.

He banded an arm around her back and flipped them over. And then he pinned her legs open with his thick arms and her body down with his tall frame and his greater weight and fucked her so hard and so fast that all she could do was hold on and take everything he gave her. And it was so freaking good that she came once more almost immediately. She cried out into his ear, and he turned and pressed a wet kiss against her cheek.

"Can't get close enough," he rasped, his hips flying, his arms slipping free of her legs and curling under her shoulders.

The sentiment behind those words, the needful, yearning tone, the relentless, demanding friction of his hips...Kristina came again, a longer, drawn-out release that stole her breath and made her clutch her arms and legs around him.

"Don't want it to end," he rasped. "But you feel too fucking good."

Kristina's brain was in a whirl. From the orgasms. From the frenzy of Noah's body. From the fact that she just thought she heard him say that she didn't want it to end.

Did that mean...?

What did that mean?

"Fuck!" Noah shouted, his grip tightening, his hips slamming into hers on a series of mind-numbing punctuated thrusts.

Kristina pushed the thoughts away and turned her face to his. "Come in me," she whispered into his good ear.

Noah pressed his face to hers and yelled his release, his big body shuddering in her embrace. She held onto him with everything she had, loving the feeling of his cock jerking deep inside her, loving knowing that she'd made him fall apart every bit as much as he'd made her.

Words rushed to the tip of Kristina's tongue. About how good they were together. About how right they felt together. About how she'd never experienced anything as meaningful as being with him.

"Fuck," Noah rasped. He blew out a long breath, then pressed a kiss against her cheek.

She shifted to look at his face in the now-dim room, and he looked so damn...at ease. If she let any of those words loose, would she mess that up for him? Because it was the last thing she wanted to do, no matter that her heart felt too big to remain inside her chest.

"Food. Water. Sustenance," he said.

Kristina chuckled, following his lead and keeping the tone light. "I did promise to make you dinner."

"You totally promised to make me dinner." He lifted off of her, and she immediately missed his heat, his presence inside her. "Let's go eat ice cream while I watch you cook."

Despite the mess in her head—or her heart—that made her laugh, and she smacked his arm. "Ass."

Noah slid off the bed and headed for the door. "You need an anatomy class." He pointed to his exceedingly fine backside as he kept walking. "*This* is my ass."

She forced herself to get up as she heard him close the bathroom door.

Keep it light. Keep it fun. Just sex.

Right. She could do this. She *was* doing this.

Clicking on the bedside lamp, she saw Noah's black T-shirt discarded on the floor. She slipped it on and glanced at herself in the mirror. Lips swollen. Cheeks flushed. Hair a mess. Wearing a shirt miles too big.

She was a wreck, even if she secretly loved that it was Noah that had made her look this way. Except, then, why was her throat getting tight? She turned away.

When she heard Noah come out of the bathroom, she made her way there, grinning at the gob-smacked look on his face as he noticed what she was wearing. In the privacy of the bathroom, she cleaned herself up and then once again looked at her reflection in the mirror, intent on bolstering her resolve.

"It's just sex, Kristina," she whispered to herself. "No matter what, you'll always have this. Don't fuck it up." She nodded and took a deep breath, and then she put on a playful smile, made her way to the kitchen where she found him eating from the carton of Chocolate Chip Cookie Dough ice cream wearing only a pair of unbuttoned jeans, and ate dinner with him, just like she'd done a thousand other times.

CHAPTER THIRTEEN

Noah wasn't sure what had awakened him, only that—for once—it hadn't been a nightmare. He suspected he'd only been asleep a short while, despite the fact that he felt more rested and more peaceful than he had in a long time.

Staring into the darkness, he wondered what time it was, but he was too tired and comfortable to even thinking about moving to find out. Not to mention that he didn't want to disturb Kristina, whose heat blazed all down his back where she pressed up against him.

Kristina. They'd had sex three more times after dinner—once in the shower—and then Noah had used his mouth on her to see how many times in a row he could make her come on his tongue. It turned out the answer was four, and even then he only stopped because she was afraid the neighbors would call the cops from her inability to stop moaning and screaming.

Best sounds he'd ever heard.

A hollow ache took up residence in his chest. Because they were also the worst.

How would he go on without ever hearing her come again?

Even worse to contemplate, how would he be able to stand the thought of any *other* man making her make those sounds?

And she had that fucking date coming up soon. God, he didn't want her to go. Maybe he should ask her not to. But, then, there'd have to be a good reason to do that, wouldn't there? He couldn't ask her not to date if he wasn't planning on stepping up to be with her himself. That would just make him a selfish prick.

Except, how realistic was it to think he could actually have a relationship right now? Half the time he couldn't sleep or eat. There were times when paranoia and anxiety plagued him for no good reason. There were days when finding the motivation to simply get out of bed was beyond his reach. Christ, he could barely take care of himself these days, so how could he be a part of taking care of someone else? At least, the way she deserved.

And Kristina deserved *everything*.

Shit, Noah didn't even have a job—or even a firm idea of what the hell he wanted to do. He lived on freaking disability checks and his savings. And despite the fact that *seven months* had passed since his discharge from the Marines, some of his symptoms seemed to be getting *worse* lately, not better. Like those fucking flashbacks. It was as if the fireworks had opened some kind of twisted Pandora's Box in his brain that he couldn't get closed again.

Sonofabitch.

A few amazing hours aside, the truth was that Noah *was* a wreck right now. No matter what he did or how much he improved, he would always be a partially blind, partially deaf man who suffered at least some of the consequences of a traumatic brain injury.

He'd heard what his docs had said and read enough online to know that, for most people with TBIs like his, the consequences were life-long. You could learn to manage them— though he was a long fucking way from that—but the reality was you would *have* to live with them. Because there wasn't any other choice.

Intellectually, Noah knew he was lucky or, at least, luckier than a lot of other guys had been. Because others had head trauma and ended up in long-term care facilities learning to talk and feed themselves again. But it sure as hell didn't feel that way. And, on top of it all, feeling sorry for himself made him feel about a million times worse. Fuck.

How had he gone from that peaceful ease when he'd first woken up to the shit storm now whirling through his head?

But that was his reality, wasn't it? That's who and what he was. At least for right now. At least for the foreseeable future. And maybe forever.

Noah shifted and stretched his neck, then heaved a deep breath. The change in the position of his head lifted his good ear from being pressed against the pillow, which was the only reason he heard it. Kristina, talking in her sleep.

He turned his head a little more, trying to bring his ear closer to where she lay behind him. And then he heard his name.

"Noah."

He froze, listening hard for anything else. She said it again, and it made him remember demanding that she repeat his name as he'd kissed down her body. He'd wanted her to know that it was him kissing her, pleasing her, worshipping her. No one else. *Him.* And he had to admit, he liked hearing her say it in her sleep, too. It meant Kristina was thinking of him, dreaming of him, keeping him close even when she was asleep.

Low murmurs continued to spill from her lips every few minutes, and almost had him smiling into the darkness. He was totally going to tease her about this in the morning—

"But Noah," she said a little louder, a little clearer. Prickles ran over his scalp and he nearly held his breath to see if she'd say anything else. And then she did. "You're everything to me…"

For a moment, silence rang loudly in the room.

And then Noah's heart was thundering so hard that the beat of his pulse in his ears was all he could hear.

Everything? He was *everything* to her?

How the fuck could that be, when he felt like so much…nothing?

His chest tightened. Restlessness flooded through him. His skin flashed hot. His quickened pulse had him breathing faster, and faster, until a sweat broke out on his forehead.

Suddenly, an aching in his knuckles made him realize that he was fisting his hands so hard that his fingers were falling asleep.

His chest got tighter. A ringing started in his ear. Pain bloomed behind his eyes.

Fuck. A goddamned panic attack. Because she'd revealed, unconsciously or not, just how much she cared.

Did you really need her to say the words to know?

You're everything to me.

Running the words through his mind again made his gut go sour. The words *hurt*. Because friends didn't let friends fall for a broken wreck of a man. And that's exactly what Noah was. And it didn't matter that her kiss had pulled him out of the flashback or that being with her tonight had soothed him, because there was no fucking way he was going to expect Kristina to make him better. It wouldn't be fair to burden her with that kind of responsibility.

And it wasn't realistic either. Because despite all she'd done for him tonight, here he was again, right back at the beginning—fighting for a deep breath, fighting the urge to strike out at the unfairness of the world, fighting for normal.

And losing.

It took everything he had to move slowly, but Noah eased himself away from her and to the edge of the bed. He rose and immediately listed to the side as the world went topsy-turvy due to a moment of perfectly timed disorientation. As if he needed the additional evidence of his failings to bolster his resolve.

He'd left his phone on her nightstand earlier, and he used the light from its screen to collect his clothes. He carried everything into the bathroom and made sure not to look in the mirror as he dressed. If he did, he was likely to punch his reflection in the face. Really, the only downside to that was that it would wake her up. And seeing Kristina when he felt like this was the absolute last thing she or Noah needed.

He stole out of the apartment, making sure the door was locked behind him. Down the stairs, out onto the sidewalk, into the parking lot. Which was when he remembered for the first fucking time that he didn't have his car.

He could've screamed. He could've railed. He could've sank to his knees and just declared himself *done*.

Instead, he tore his cell out of his pocket. 5:12 AM. He opened the Uber app, hoping there was a car somewhere nearby at this hour. Closest was eight minutes out. He glanced over his shoulder at the windows to Kristina's apartment. Since he'd have to wait for a pick-up, he didn't want there to be any chance she'd catch him standing out here. So he started walking, and only when he was three buildings over did he call for a car.

And then all there was to do was wait.

KRISTINA CAME AWAKE ON A STRETCH, and the movement revealed that *all kinds* of places on her were deliciously sore.

So worth it.

The feeling and the thought had her opening her eyes and looking for Noah in the bed next to her—

Empty.

"Noah?" she called, pushing herself into a sitting position. The clock on the nightstand read 6:01. She reached over and turned off the alarm, set to ring in another fourteen minutes.

She swung her feet over the edge of the bed, and immediately noticed that her bra, panties, and sandals were the only clothes still scattered over the floor. Noah's clothes were gone. And his phone was no longer on the nightstand. Her stomach squeezed.

Maybe he was just out in the kitchen. Kristina got out of bed, wrapped her robe around her, and went looking, calling his name again as she went. But her apartment was small. It only took ten seconds to determine that she was all alone.

He'd left without saying good-bye. She found herself searching the kitchen counter, the table, the coffee table, her dresser—looking for a note to explain why he'd gone. Nothing. *My cell phone!* She unplugged it from the charger in her room and thumbed into her messages, but the last one he'd sent was from the morning before.

She sat heavily on the edge of her bed, her robe pooling around her.

Granted, they'd agreed the sex would just be for one night, so it wasn't like he owed her anything. But it wasn't like him to leave without a word, was it? And it wasn't like they were the traditional one-night stand, either.

For a long moment, she stared at the blank text box, and then she typed, *Are you okay?* She hit *Send* and waited, but ten minutes later, he still hadn't responded.

"Okay, don't jump to any conclusions," she said to herself. The words sounded loud in the otherwise empty room. "There could be a hundred reasonable explanations. Or at least a dozen.

Or a couple." She rolled her eyes at her ridiculous solo conversation and tossed the phone to the bed.

But as she showered and dressed for her day, Kristina couldn't help but worry that she wasn't going to like his reasons for leaving the way he had. Like, that he regretted sleeping with her. For one.

Which of course had her worrying about their friendship. Which then had her getting mad at herself for even suggesting the whole "just sex" for "just one night" thing because *Idiot!*

How the hell had she thought that made sense? Or that it was even possible for her to share so much of herself without her emotions getting involved.

Because, *oh baby*, they were involved, all right. All the freaking way.

But in the heat of the moment—a moment during which he'd radiated pain so intensely that it'd nearly been a physical force in the room—the only thing she'd cared about was making it better.

Standing at the bathroom sink, she applied the last of her mascara and then gave herself a good long look in the mirror. Had she made it better? She didn't know. But there was something she did know...

I love him.

The admission lodged a jagged knot in her throat. Kristina pressed a hand to her mouth and fought against everything inside her not to let loose the emotion attempting to rip up her throat.

I love him and he left.

She shook her head and squeezed her eyes shut, knowing she was smudging her mascara but not caring.

Dropping her hands, she shook them out, as if she were suddenly filled with a restless energy that needed to be exorcised. "Okay, okay," she said. "Stop freaking out. Everything will be fine."

Of course it would be. This was them. Noah and Kristina.

Right.

She fixed her make-up and, even though she told herself not to, checked her phone for messages again. Nothing.

Still nothing by the time the school day had ended.

Sitting on the edge of her bed that night, she texted him again. She typed out and deleted about a half a dozen things before settling on the all-purpose, *Hey.*

Casual. Friendly. No big deal.

Even though his silence felt like a really big fucking deal.

Maybe it wasn't supposed to matter that they had sex five freaking times. Or that he'd given her so many orgasms that she'd lost track of the number of them. Or that he'd called her *baby.*

But it did.

And even if none of those mattered, their friendship should've been more than enough to warrant a freaking *Hey* in return.

She typed again, *This is where you say Hey back.*

But by the morning, he still hadn't. She actually debated swinging by his place on her way to work to make sure he was okay, but he was probably fine and she'd end up seeming desperate and clingy. Sighing, Kristina shot off a new text, to Kate this time. *You around tonight?*

For YOU, always, she replied quickly, a lifeline Kristina didn't realize she'd needed so desperately until she had it.

Breathing a sigh of relief, she responded, *You are the literal best.*

Of course I am!

If was the first thing that eked a smile out of Kristina since she'd awakened alone.

Kate agreed to stop by after a work dinner, which was perfect because Kristina really didn't want to describe what had happened out in public. Not knowing Kate the way she did. When Kate arrived a little after nine, Noah still hadn't responded. And she'd sent another text and tried calling him once, too.

"Uh oh," Kate said, taking one look at Kristina as she walked in the door. Kate wore a form-fitting black suit and a pair of killer black heels. "What happened?"

"Want a glass of wine?" Kristina asked.

"I better not. I had two at dinner. But I think you definitely should." She kicked off her heels and settled onto the couch.

"Ha, well, I had two already, too, but another one can't hurt." Kristina poured herself a glass of white and grabbed a Diet Coke for Kate.

"You have dark circles under your eyes," Kate said as she accepted the can of soda. Kristina dropped on the couch next to her. "The only other time I think I've seen that was that time junior year when your dad disappeared and the police found him five days later wandering the streets in L.A."

God, Kristina remembered that. He'd believed someone was trying to harm him, and that he had to get far away as quickly as he could. So he'd taken a taxi to the airport and purchased a ticket on the first flight that would take him far away, to L.A. The only reason he hadn't left the country was because he hadn't taken his passport. But for five days she and her mom had no idea where he'd gone or if he was even alive.

"Well, this isn't about my dad," she said. He'd been doing much better for the past year so, the result of a new combination of medications. Well enough that he was now selling the beautiful furniture he'd always loved to make by hand. "It's about Noah."

"After what you revealed at dinner the other night, I

thought it might be." Kate took a drink of her soda, and Kristina recounted what'd happened. She hadn't gotten any further than telling about their just-sex/just-for-one-night agreement, when Kate interrupted. "Oh, honey."

"Yeah."

"Did you really think that would work?" Kate asked.

"Honestly, at the time, part of me thought it *could* work and part of me didn't care. He needed me, and he wanted me, and I wanted him, too. So I decided it was worth the risk and I just... went for it." Kristina pulled a pillow into her lap and hugged it against her stomach.

Kate's gaze narrowed, but after a moment, she nodded. "Okay, fair enough. And?"

"And the short version is that we had sex five times, had a fun dinner together, and fell asleep together. And when I woke up in the morning, he was gone. And now he's not responding to any of my messages." Tears threatened, clogging her throat and pricking at the backs of her eyes.

"You know at some point I'm going to want all the sexy details," Kate said, her expression sympathetic. For some reason, Kate taking this so seriously made the pull of those tears even greater.

"Yeah, I know," Kristina said, her voice strained. She'd been resisting the urge to cry since she'd woken up alone yesterday morning, telling herself over and over again not to jump to conclusions.

But two days had passed, and now the pressure was building up inside her, and she wasn't sure what *other* conclusion to come to other than he wasn't responding on purpose. Because she knew for a fact that the Cortezes would've called her if he'd been in an accident or something. Heck, after Josh, she was the second person Mrs. Cortez had called when they'd learned what'd happened to Noah in Iraq.

Kate scooted closer, close enough that their knees touched, and she placed her hand on top of Kristina's. "First of all, I get to call him a bastard for doing this to you. So, *fucking bastard*."

Kristina gave a watery laugh.

"Second of all," Kate said, squeezing her hand, "tell me where *you're* at. Are you just upset that you two slept together and then he went back to the avoidance routine he's been pulling the past few months, or is it more than that?"

Looking down at her lap, Kristina swallowed around that lump. And then tried again. But it was getting thicker and thicker. Tears spilled from the corner of her eyes. She forced a deep breath and shook her head, and then she managed a whisper. "I..." She shrugged. "Love him."

Saying the words opened a flood gate inside her, and Kristina couldn't fight the tears anymore. They fell no matter how many times she wiped them away. And no matter how hard she fought for composure, her breathing shuddered and hitched.

"Kristina," Kate said. "You've loved Noah Cortez since the day I met you."

And that was when Kristina really lost it. She curled around the pillow, and Kate put an arm around her and pulled her in.

Long minutes later, Kristina managed to calm herself down again, and she dried her face with the long hem of her top. "Okay," she said blowing out a long breath. "Okay." She sat back into the corner of the couch.

Kate braced her head on her hand. "Am I right?" she asked quietly.

"Maybe. I don't know. Yes," Kristina said, admitting what felt so obvious now, but what had eluded her before this moment. "I mean, he's been my best friend since I was five years old, so I knew that I loved him. But somewhere along the way, I fell *in love* with him. I can't even pinpoint exactly when it happened," Kristina said, thinking over the past days and months. "But it was before we slept together, for sure. And now that we did that *and* I know how I really feel, I don't know what to do."

"Yes, you do," Kate said, giving her a no-nonsense look.

Kristina's stomach fell. "I have to tell him?"

Kate nodded. "You do. You owe it to yourself *and* to him. And if he can't handle that or doesn't reciprocate, you need to know that, too."

"But what if I just...I don't know, played it cool? See how things are between us? See if things progress naturally?" She picked at the white fringe on the edge of the pillow.

"Do you really want to put on an act for the man who has been your best friend all these years and who is the man you now love?"

Well, when she put it like that, it didn't sound nearly as rational. "No, of course not, but—"

"Look, Kris, I said this the other night. There's no going back. There's only going forward. And you can't do that based on lies. Right?"

Kristina's shoulders fell, but this straight talk was exactly why she'd needed to see Kate. "Yeah."

Kate gave her hand another squeeze. "Then it sounds like you need to see him as soon as you can. You won't know anything 'til you do."

"Tomorrow's the last day of school," Kristina said, thinking out loud. "I could head over to his place as soon as I finish cleaning out my classroom." It was a half day, and the teachers and staff usually stayed around for a lunchtime party. She could leave right after that.

"Sounds like a plan," Kate said.

But whether it was a *good* plan remained to be seen.

CHAPTER FOURTEEN

KRISTINA STEPPED up to Noah's apartment door full of determination. Part of which had been fueled by Kate, who'd been sending her encouraging texts all morning. Things like,

Stop waiting for Prince Charming. Go find him. The poor idiot may be stuck up in a tree or something.

COURAGE: Do one brave thing today...then run like hell.

Just chuck it in the fuck it bucket and move on!

Stay stroganoff. Which she quickly followed up with, *Bahahaha! Best autocorrect ever!*

Kristina knocked on the door. After about a minute, she did it again. Glancing out at the parking lot, she reconfirmed that Noah's car was here. She waited another minute or two, and knocked a third time, this time with her fist instead of her knuckles.

She pulled out her cell and texted him, *I'm not leaving until you open your door.*

Twin reactions coursed through her—irritation at his continued avoidance, and worry that maybe there was a reason he wasn't answering.

She texted again, *I'm using my key to come in.*

At that, she dropped her phone in her purse and dug out her keys, which included the one he gave her last weekend. She slid the key in the lock and opened the door.

Inside, everything was quiet and dim, all the slats on the blinds pulled shut. "Noah?"

She dropped her purse on the coffee table and passed through the big open living area to the hall that led toward his bedroom, the bathroom, and the office. Something crunched underfoot.

Frowning, Kristina reached into the bathroom and flicked on the light switch. The bathroom mirror was shattered in a giant spider web of cracks that radiated out from a single, central break.

Kristina rushed toward the bedroom and pushed through the mostly closed bedroom door.

Noah was sprawled on his stomach wearing only a pair of black boxers, most of the sheets, blankets, and pillows knocked to the ground. Blood stains streaked across the top of the sheets. Kristina's stomach fell to the floor and she was on the bed in an instant, grasping his shoulder as gently as she could in her growing panic. "Noah." She shook him.

He came awake on a holler and flipped over, pinning her to the mattress with his forearm high across her chest. The movement was so fast and so unexpected that it'd happened before she fully realized what he was doing.

She should've known better than to scare him awake like that. "Noah, it's Kristina!"

"Kris?" He flew back off of her onto his knees and kept on going, stumbling off the edge of the bed and backing into the chest of drawers beyond it. "What? What are..." He shook his head, then dropped it into his hand on a groan.

"I'm sorry I scared you," she said, her heart racing in her chest. "You weren't answering your door and then I saw the broken glass and the blood." And now that she was regaining her wits about her, she noticed something else. A sickly sour smell. Sitting up, she saw a plastic trash can pulled to the side of the bed, something watery sitting in the bottom of it. "You got sick?" she asked, looking back to him again. "Jesus, Noah, what happened?"

He staggered to the edge of the bed and sank down onto it, his back toward her. He braced his elbows on his knees and stared down at the ground. "Please go," he said.

"What? No. You need me," she said, standing up.

"No. No, I don't. I want you to go."

"Well, that's too damn bad." She turned on the bedside lamp.

Noah groaned.

"Let me see your hand," she said, coming around to his side of the bed.

"It's fine." He blocked whatever injuries he had with his good hand.

"The sheets look like it bled a lot. You could need stitches."

"I don't." He spoke without looking at her.

Sighing, Kristina turned away, grabbed the trash can, and carried it into the bathroom.

"Don't go in there," Noah called.

Ignoring him, she tried to step around the broken glass, most of which covered the sink and vanity, and dumped the contents of the bucket into the toilet. She flushed on a grimace, then put the bucket under the bathtub faucet and filled it halfway up to rinse it out.

Standing in the bedroom doorway, she saw he hadn't moved from where she'd left him. "When was the last time you ate?"

"I don't want you here, Kristina," he said, shoulders rounded and down.

"Too bad." She pushed away the hurt his words caused,

because she could only imagine how much he'd hate anyone seeing him this way. But none of that mattered right now. Not why she'd come or what she'd wanted to tell him or what might or might not be going on between them. Not when he was in such bad shape. "I'll sweep up the bathroom floor and then make you something to eat. Then maybe you could take a shower."

"Don't touch a piece of that glass," he said, heaving himself to his feet. He turned to her, and holy crap, his abdomen looked noticeably leaner since she'd seen him three days ago, and his face appeared almost gaunt. He came around the end of the bed.

Kristina stepped right in his way. "Listen to me, Marine. You've been puking and you're bleeding all over the place, so I'm giving the orders and I'm telling you to sit your stubborn ass down and give me five freaking minutes to take care of you." She jabbed her finger toward the bed.

He glared at her for a long minute, then sat wearily, like even that took some effort.

Satisfied that he was going to cooperate, at least for the near future, she found the broom and dustpan tucked into the gap beside the refrigerator. She finished rinsing out the trash can and then cleaned all the broken glass off the sink and vanity into it.

"I hate that you're doing that," he said from the other room, his tone full of frustration.

"I know," she called back. What had made him punch the mirror? Between this, the weight loss, and getting sick, something bad had been happening to him the past few days. That much was clear.

The tile in the bathroom and the hardwoods in the hall made sweeping what had fallen to the floor fairly easy, but it took it a few minutes to wipe up all the little tiny slivers. When she was done, she spread out a big towel on the floor of the bathroom just in case she'd missed anything.

"Bathroom's all yours," she said.

Then she went on a hunting and gathering mission in his kitchen, where she was hoping to find— Yup. At least *some* things didn't change. Among the boxes of cereal and protein bars, he had a whole stack of instant cup of noodles soup. For some reason, he'd always loved the stuff.

Down the hall, the bathroom door clicked shut. A moment later, the beat of the shower water sounded out.

She nuked a big cup of water, spending the time wondering what had happened to him while she'd been fretting about him not calling. Guilt settled on her shoulders like a wet woolen blanket. She should've come sooner.

The microwave dinged and she poured the near-boiling water into the soup's Styrofoam container. By the time the noodles were soft, the shower water was off again.

She set everything on the table and sat down to wait.

A few minutes later, Noah emerged wearing a pair of old black sweat pants and a gray T-shirt with water droplets showing through the cotton where he hadn't bothered to dry off. And, God, he was beautiful to her even when he was so torn apart. He sat heavily in the chair beside her. "Kristina—"

"Eat first, talk second."

He grumbled under his breath but picked up his spoon and dug into the broth. Noah ate slowly at first, but then much quicker, like he was so hungry he couldn't get the food in fast enough. Band-Aids covered four places on his knuckles and fingers, and the bruising looked worse this time than when he'd gone head-to-head with the shower tiles. Without asking, she made him a second container of soup. He ate that one slower, but finished every last bit of it.

"When did you last eat?" she asked.

"I can talk now?" He gave her a look.

She gave him one right back.

"I'm not sure," he said. "What, uh, what day is it?"

The question was like a sucker punch to the gut. She nearly gasped. "It's Friday afternoon," she managed.

"Uh, then, yesterday morning. I think. I had some cereal."

And she'd seen what had become of that.

"What's going on with you?" Everything inside her wanted to reach out to him, touch him, comfort him, but he was radiating a desire for space so loudly that it nearly hurt her ears.

Staring down at the table, he shook his head. "Not in a good place right now. Had another flashback. Flipped out over it, and then I felt so drained all I wanted to do was sleep. So that's what I did."

An ache bloomed inside her chest. "What made you get sick?"

"My equilibrium was all fucked up and it made me nauseous." God, his voice sounded so flat.

"Is it better now? Do you need me to drive you to your doctor?"

He lifted his eyes to her, and they were flat, too. "Why are you doing this?"

"Why am I—" She shook her head and bit her tongue, taking a moment to rein in the anger his question caused. "You *know* why I'm doing this, Noah."

He didn't say anything for a long minute.

She rose and started clearing his place. He gently grabbed her hand. "Stop. Just stop."

Kristina sank back into her chair. And for possibly the first time in her life, she had absolutely no idea what to say to Noah Cortez.

No way was she sharing her feelings when he was like this. But asking questions didn't seem to be helping him. And it felt like they were two sentences away from an argument she had no interest in having.

"I texted you," she finally said. "I was...worried."

He gave a tight nod. "I saw a few, but then my battery died. I'm not even sure where my phone is right now."

"Why didn't you respond?" she asked, working hard to keep her tone neutral. Because she really didn't want to fight with him.

A long pause. "I didn't know what to say."

The echo of her own thoughts from a moment ago made her heart feel like it was about to break in half. "Anything would've been better than nothing."

He chuffed out a humorless laugh. "Nothing." He shook his head. "You're right. Anything would be better than nothing. But neither would be as much as *everything*."

Huh? She frowned as she replayed his words. "You've lost me."

"Yeah," he said. "I guess I have." He stacked his soup cups inside one another, gathered the remains of his lunch into his hands, and carried it all over to the trash and sink. After a moment, he turned around and braced his hands on the counter on either side of his hips. "I'm sorry that I didn't respond. And that I made you worry. And that you had to come over here to...all this."

Kristina stood and leaned against the breakfast bar opposite Noah. "I'm only sorry I didn't come sooner."

"I'm not," he said.

"Are you *trying* to push me away?" she blurted. She couldn't believe she'd just asked that, but this cold, distant, unfeeling routine was crawling under her skin and making her crazy.

He cocked his head and stared at her, and then he nodded. "Maybe."

With that one word, it was like he reached inside her chest

and squeezed his hand around her heart. For a few seconds after he spoke, she found it hard to draw in a breath.

"Wow," she finally said, finding it nearly inconceivable that they'd come to this...this *emptiness*. How had the best sex of her life broken them into so many pieces? "I'm going to leave now." She nailed him with a stare. "Not because you've succeeded in pushing me away, but because I think it's best to give you the space you so obviously want before you do."

Kristina went to leave, and then she quickly turned back, stepped up to him, and pecked a kiss against his cheek. Everything inside of her wanted to linger there against him, breathing him in and holding him tight. She wanted that so much that pulling away was almost painful.

But she made herself walk away. She collected her purse and stepped to the door, conflicted words and thoughts tumbling through her mind. "I'm here for you, Noah. All you have to do is ask."

She didn't wait for him to reply.

CHAPTER FIFTEEN

NOAH HADN'T SLEPT a fucking wink all night long. He supposed that was only fair since he'd slept most of the three days before. Lying in bed, he stared at the white walls, watching how the early morning sun moved streams of light across the floor, the walls, the bedding that covered his legs.

He was so numb that he could almost convince himself that he wasn't actually present in the world. Like he'd been in a state of such excruciating pain and mind-boiling rage that he'd totally flamed out.

That was fair, too, given what he'd done to Kristina.

Taking the amazingly intimate gifts she'd offered him without offering a word of kindness or gratitude in return. Stealing away in the dark of night like a thief—or a coward. Definitely a coward. Avoiding her, after all they'd shared. And coming at her with all kinds of attitude when she'd interrupted her day to make sure he was okay.

For God's sake, she cleaned up his fucking vomit.

And, Jesus, on top of everything else, he'd actually admitted to trying to push her away.

He wasn't sure he'd *ever* seen her expression as devastated as it'd been after those words spilled from his lips. Sure, she'd schooled her reaction pretty damn fast, but after nearly twenty years as her best friend, even when she didn't want him to know what was going on in that pretty head, he could read her like an open book.

It was just that, *he* was devastated, too. Devastated to realize how much he wanted someone that he had no damn right to want—not when he didn't have the ability to take care of her the way she deserved.

Hell, as much as he'd hated her seeing him yesterday—covered in sweat and filth and blood—part of him was almost glad she'd come. Because watching her clean up his puke and the debris of his rage and worry over him like a little mother hen, her face all pinched with concern, drove home his fucking beliefs in spades.

He was no good right now. And that certainly included being no good for Kristina Moore.

It didn't matter that he wanted her, cared for her...maybe even loved her.

Maybe? Really, Cortez? Now you're lying to yourself, too?
Fuck.

Problem was, how he felt didn't really even matter. Because Noah wanted *everything* for Kristina. And his definition of everything didn't include playing nursemaid to him. He might be partially disabled and old before his time, but he had absolutely no intention of putting her in that same position. She was twenty-five—her life and career just blooming. Full of possibilities and optimism. And he was none of those things.

He was nothing.

On a frustrated growl, Noah threw off the covers and pulled his sorry ass out of bed. He made a stop in the bathroom, where he was relieved *not* to be able to see his reflection despite the disaster that made that possible. He put on some coffee and choked down a bowl of dry cereal, not sure his stomach could handle anything more. The only decent thing about this day so far was that the vertigo seemed to have gone away. Thank fuck for small favors.

When he was done eating, he grabbed his cell off the charger. He'd finally found it yesterday afternoon underneath the edge of his bed, and it'd rebooted to reveal fifteen missed texts—mostly from Kristina, but also two from Josh and one from his dad—the latter revealing that Kristina had contacted his parents after she'd left here yesterday.

Kristina said you've been sick. Need anything? Give us a call, his dad had written. And though Noah was a little irritated that Kristina had brought his parents into it, he also respected the hell out of her for doing it—after the way he'd treated her, no one would've blamed her for forgetting all about him the moment she'd walked out the door.

Noah also had two voicemail messages, one from Kristina and one from the Art Factory reminding him that the mask class started this morning.

Fucking hell.

He was nowhere near being in the mood. Someone asked him to decorate a mask right now and he was liable to smash it to pieces with a goddamned hammer and call it a masterpiece. It sure as fuck would represent how he was feeling, so there was that.

Noah tossed his cell to the breakfast bar and leaned back against the wall. He scrubbed his hands over his face, wondering what the hell to do with himself.

You need some way to let this out, Noah.

The memory of his dad's voice encouraging him to take the art class. To take as many art classes as it took. At the time, Noah had almost been relieved at the idea that maybe something from that course catalog could help release the pressure inside him, even if only a little bit.

Buzz.

Noah glanced down at the cell phone's screen. *Enjoy the class, son. Hope you're feeling better. Give me a call after.*

If Noah had it in him to chuckle, he might've just then. *Okay, universe. I hear you.* Guilt souring the cereal and coffee in his gut, he shot off a quick reply to his father: *Feeling better. Thanks.*

What the hell. Maybe he'd go after all. He could always leave early if it wasn't working for him. And it wasn't like he had anything better to do. And in a twisted way, he felt like he owed it to Kristina.

So, fine. Maybe, just maybe, the class would allow him to get his head screwed back on right enough to have a rational conversation with Kristina. And tell her why what happened between them could never happen again.

THE ART FACTORY was located on the waterfront in Old Town Alexandria, right along the promenade where the previous week Noah and Kristina had walked eating their ice creams. It was a big cement-and-glass structure, and had actually been a munitions factory during the world wars.

As Noah walked in the front doors, he spied a glass case filled with historical photographs, including one with a group of men posing with a large torpedo painted with stars and stripes. The caption read, "The final torpedo made at the Naval Torpedo Station, Alexandria, 1945."

He chuffed out a laugh, because there was a certain poetry in a former Explosive Ordnance Disposal Technician coming to a former torpedo factory to try to recover from all the damage that repeated blast waves had done to his brain.

The long hallways were glass-filled, allowing him to see into the many classrooms and studios that filled the big building. He found his classroom nearly all the way at the end of one of them.

He hovered outside the door for a long moment, and then he found his balls and walked into the damn room.

Noah had come about three minutes before the class was scheduled to begin, and the room was more full than he'd expected. Fifteen people sat on stools at high tables around the room, and two men in wheelchairs sat at a low table in the front. Only three seats remained open, and they were all at tables where other people already sat.

Noah joined a big Mack truck of a guy with a bald head, shirt-straining biceps, and a thick neck at one of the tables toward the back, because if *that* guy was okay being here, then Noah should have nothing to say.

The man turned to him and extended his dark brown hand. "Moses Griffin. Everyone calls me Mo. I was First Ranger Battalion, mostly in Afghanistan, but a little bit of everywhere else, too."

Noah returned the shake. "Noah Cortez. I was in the Corps, Second Combat Engineer Battalion."

Mo nodded and smiled, and it was one of those grins that was so full of good humor that you couldn't help but smile in return. "First timer?" he asked.

"That obvious?" Noah asked, glancing around the room. The students were about half men and half women—young and old, white, black, Hispanic, and Asian, including several people with prosthetic limbs.

"Yeah, you got that newbie *what-the-fuck-am-I-doing-here* expression on your face." Mo winked. "It's all good, though.

Jarvis is a kick-ass instructor and all around good human. He'll ease you into it."

Turned out Mo was right. Jack Jarvis was a former Navy clinical psychologist who now had a private practice and a prominent reputation in the field of art therapy for veterans. He was tall and thin with salt-and-pepper hair and an easy, no-nonsense demeanor matched by the jeans and white button-down shirt he wore.

Everything the man said about his goals for the class resonated with Noah and alleviated his concerns that this experience was going to involve anything akin to sitting in a circle weaving flower chains while sharing their feelings. In fact, Jarvis made it clear that no one was expected to speak about anything beyond artistic procedures and techniques if they didn't want to.

Which had Noah sitting more comfortably on his stool.

There was one other exception about the speaking bit—Jarvis had them go around the room and introduce themselves to whatever extent they were comfortable. And hearing about the military backgrounds of the others in the room eased even more of Noah's discomfort. There were officers and enlisted. Vets from all of the services. Even a couple of other guys from the Corps. After seven months of being out of the military, it was a relief to be around others who'd had the same experience, who knew what it meant, who knew what sacrifices it required.

"Okay," Jarvis said when they all finished. "There are four parts to this workshop. Today, you'll write down a list of words that describe how you feel, in general and about yourself. You might also write down how you feel about your service, your injuries, and your discharge. There are no wrong answers here and you don't have to share the list if you don't want to. But this will give you a jumping off point for figuring out how to use the mask to represent those feelings." He unbuttoned his shirt sleeves and rolled both of them up his forearms. "You'll make the basic form of your mask using plastic facial molds—" He held up a smooth white oval generically shaped like a face. "— and molding clay. Once that's done, you'll create the actual mask out of *papier-mache* formed over the mold you make. The *papier-mache* will need to dry, so that's where we'll stop for today."

Jarvis walked down the side of the classroom and handed out enough paper, pencils, boxes of clay, and plastic forms for the people in each row. Noah found himself staring into that totally blank facial mold and wondering what the hell he was going to make.

"Start with the list of words," Jarvis said as he finished handing out the materials. "Then Mo and I will come around and help you get started."

Noah's gaze cut to the big man beside him.

The guy winked and gestured to himself. "Repeat offender."

"You've taken this class before?" Noah asked, surprised.

"Fifth time in as many years," Mo said, his expression almost serene. "These masks make a great benchmark for how the shit in my head is progressing. Know what I mean?"

Noah nodded because, even though he couldn't relate to the idea of progress—not at all, the very fact that Mo felt that he was making progress *and* could see an actual, tangible representation of it in these masks all of a sudden had Noah looking at the facial form in a whole new way.

After a moment of hesitation, he pulled the paper and pencil in front of himself. Noah felt ridiculously exposed even contemplating putting this particular list to paper, despite the fact that no one would see it if he didn't want them to. Out of the corner of his eye, he spied others already getting to work, so he picked up his pencil and wrote the first thing that came to mind.

Nothing

It soured his gut to see that word in black and white, but it definitely was at the very top of the list of how he felt about himself. He thought about the other things on which Jarvis had asked them to reflect, and jotted down a few more words:

Proud (of service)

Embarrassed (by weakness)

Noah tapped his pencil against his bottom lip, then continued writing.

In pain

Partial

Off center

Broken

Wrecked

His pencil moved faster and faster until it was almost an exercise in stream of consciousness.

Blind

Deaf

Muted

Fake

Uncertain

Adrift

Sad

His heart was beating harder now, and tension was settling into his shoulders, his arms, his fingers where they gripped the pencil.

FUCKING ANGRY

Noah underlined those two words so hard he broke the point off his pencil. He dropped his head into his hand and sighed.

"Here, use mine. I'm done," Mo said.

"Thanks," Noah managed, pressure building inside his chest.

Re-reading the list, Noah had prickles running over his scalp and an uncomfortable, hollow ache ballooning behind his sternum. Because, holy fucking shit, he'd just admitted more in the two minutes it'd taken him to write that list than he had to any doctor—any person, period—since the IED explosion that had caused his injuries almost a year ago.

Noah pressed a hand against his chest and heaved a deep breath. Christ, he was going to have a panic attack. Right here in front of all these people.

Mo slid out of his chair, stepped behind Noah, and gave him a single, solid squeeze on the back of the neck. Without a word or even a look, the big guy headed to the front of the room to help one of the students who was getting started with her clay.

And that single touch was filled with so much fundamental understanding that it pulled Noah back from the edge.

In that moment, despite the crush of bullshit in his head, Noah tossed aside his ignorance about the potential usefulness of an outlet like art and opened up to the possibility that this process—and these people—might actually help him start to get better.

At least, it had to be better than the nothing he'd been doing.

Jarvis interrupted them to explain the basics of using the molding clay, showing a short video tutorial on the screen at the front of the room to demonstrate the process. Afterward, Noah dumped the soft, colorful rectangular blocks out onto the table. The colors didn't matter, since this was just the base on which the actual *papier-mache* mask would be made, but Noah still found himself gravitating to the red and blue clays nonetheless.

He squeezed the cool material in his hands, making it go pliable, as his gaze skimmed over his list of words again. Broken, wrecked, blind, deaf, and muted jumped out at him, and ideas started coming to mind.

The room was mostly quiet as everyone got to work. Noah pressed the clay thin and began to lay it out flat all around the face. Whatever he did was going to reflect his reduced hearing and sight on his left side, which made him realize he needed to shape a little clay on the right side—and only on the right side—for an ear.

Hmm. He wasn't entirely sure how to do that. And that wasn't the only place where he wasn't sure how to get the clay to do what he wanted it to do. Because he felt like the side of the skull on the left side also needed to be misshapen or cracked or maybe in pieces. Somehow.

Which made him realize he needed to ask for help. It was suddenly very important that he get this right, that he use it to reveal his truth. Because maybe he could start finding himself again if he could just stop running from the wreckage in his head.

Noah had been working at the clay for a few minutes when Jarvis stopped at his table. "Jack Jarvis," he said, holding out his hand.

"Noah Cortez," Noah said, returning the shake. "So, I have a couple questions about how to do some things."

Jarvis stepped around the table to his side. "Shoot."

It took everything Noah had to resist the urge to flip his list face-down. "Okay, well. I want to create an ear on this side, and I'm not sure how to do that. And, uh, I think I want the skull up here by the temple and forehead to be cracked or broken." He spoke quietly and swallowed around a lump in his throat, working hard to ignore the embarrassment spreading heat across his face as he spoke. "And I was thinking that I only want the lips to be raised on one half of the mouth. Can we, uh..." He shrugged as an uncomfortable idea came to mind, but then he thought, *To hell with it,* and gave it a voice. "Can we maybe decorate the finished mask with something like duct tape? Because I'm seeing something like that on the one side."

Jarvis nodded thoughtfully, his gaze on the mask. And Noah appreciated the hell out of that because he wasn't sure he could handle eye contact right now. Not when just asking those questions felt a whole helluva lot like he'd just flayed off some of his skin. "Absolutely on the duct tape. Any detail work you want will be done at the *papier-mache* stage. So if you wanted to do cracks in the surface, for example, those can be carved in with an X-Acto knife when the *mache* is dried. But if you wanted to do some that was irregular or bumpy, you would do it now with the clay. Just build it up along this side however you want."

Ideas raced through Noah's head as the other man spoke. He liked the idea of carving cracks into the mask. "And the ear? Because this looks like Mr. Potato Head," he said, pointing to one of his attempts.

Jarvis laughed. "What about something like this?" The guy had magic fingers, apparently, because within a few minutes he created something that was exactly the right size, shape, and proportion for the mask.

"Yeah," Noah said. "Thank you."

"You got it," Jarvis said. "Holler if you need me. For anything," he added. And that time he not only made eye contact, but communicated in one quick look that he got what Noah was going through, even though he hadn't asked why Noah wanted to disfigure half the face or only put an ear on one side.

Noah glanced around the room at all these people. People with feelings and challenges not so different from his own. Teaching a class like this probably meant Jarvis had a lot of experience working with vets like Noah.

For the next hour, Noah was laser-focused on shaping the clay for his mask. When he finally got the clay how he wanted it, he coated it with petroleum jelly to keep the *papier-mache* from sticking. And then came the messy part—dipping strips of blue shop paper towels into a gooey mixture of plaster, school glue, and vinegar to make what would become the actual mask.

Sitting next to him again as he worked on his own mask, Mo showed Noah how to use small bits of paper towel to make textures, lines, and other details, so Noah used that knowledge to make the left half of the mask rough, where the skin on the right was smooth and unwrinkled.

As Noah worked, twin reactions coursed through him. On the one hand, he was almost enjoying the feeling of doing something, of being productive, of being able to concentrate. On the other, the more and more this mask started to come to life—with the left side of the face so utterly wrecked and broken, the more those panic attack symptoms started making themselves known again.

His chest went tight as his heart raced. His scalp prickled as it got harder to breathe. Tension settled into his muscles until he was a rubber band pulled taut and ready to break.

Because it was like looking into that fucking bathroom mirror—and actually *seeing* what he'd been feeling for all these long months.

Suddenly, the room closed in on him and there wasn't enough air. Noah reared back off his stool and stumbled into the table behind him. And then he scrambled for the door. All he knew was the urgent need to escape, to pull in a deep fucking breath.

As opposed to earlier, the halls were busy with people browsing the studios and studying the displays, and it left him feeling trapped.

He turned—

The bathroom.

He shot into the men's room and paced, his fists tight, his adrenaline on overload, his head all wrecked again.

God, when would he ever get control of this? Of himself? When would he ever get to his new version of normal? And would it be a version with which he could live? Because this was fucking miserable.

He stalked. Paced. Growled his frustration.

Fuck! I have to let this out before it eats me alive.

He turned, targeted the paper towel dispenser, and reared back his fist.

Someone grabbed his arm and hauled him around.

Mo.

"What the fuck?" Noah yelled.

Completely unfazed by Noah's aggression, Mo shook his head. "Abusing yourself ain't gonna help you none, son. But I know what will."

Noah glared, his hands fisted, his body still jangling with all this bullshit. "Why do you care?" he bit out, knowing he was being an asshole but unable to rein it in.

"Because I've been right where you are," Mo said. "Why else you think I'd be here making another fucking mask?" The question was serious, but there was a hint of humor around the man's eyes. But then they went solemn. "You ever feel like the only way you'd feel better is if you could destroy everything around you?"

Taken aback by the insightfulness of the question, Noah could only stare.

"Ever pull some stupid-ass move like punching a wall?" Mo asked, pointing to Noah's beat-up knuckles. "But it makes you feel a shit ton better afterward."

"Yeah," Noah said, his voice gravelly.

"That's what I thought," the big man said. "What you're doing here, in this class, it will help you. But if you don't have any plans tonight, then you should come out with me and meet some of my friends. Guys I suspect are just like you."

"Just like me?" Noah asked, frowning.

Mo nodded. "Yeah. Guys with anger and transition problems. Guys for whom fighting and training provide exactly the kind of outlet and therapy they need to deal with those problems."

Some of Noah's angst bled away. "There's therapy like that?"

"Yeah there is," Mo said. "It's called Warrior Fight Club."

CHAPTER SIXTEEN

NOAH COULDN'T REMEMBER the last time he'd actually looked forward to doing something. Dressed in his workout gear, he stepped out of his apartment psyched to meet up with Mo to check out this Warrior Fight Club.

After Mo had intercepted Noah from further mangling his fists, the man had explained more about WFC. The basic idea was to use the discipline and physical outlet of mixed martial arts training to help veterans struggling with anger management issues, PTSD, and other problems transitioning to civilian life.

Check, check, and check. All of that was Noah in a nutshell.

The other interesting thing about WFC—it was only open to active-duty service members and veterans. And given that Noah's panic attack in the art therapy class this morning was received with nothing but understanding and encouragement, knowing he'd be training with others like him gave him at least some confidence that they'd get it if he lost it again.

Baby steps, man. But he'd fucking take 'em.

Noah started down the stairs and nearly had a damn spring in his step. After months of feeling so down, this small sliver of excitement at the prospect of finally finding something that could make a difference nearly felt euphoric. Which showed just how down he'd been.

Footsteps sounded out below, and Noah moved to the side as a guy with longish brown hair and lots of ink rounded the landing and came jogging up.

"Hey, man," the guy said.

At some point, Noah would have to work on actually meeting his neighbors, wouldn't he? For now, though, he just nodded. "Hey."

"Oh," the guy said from where he stood up above him now. Noah turned. "Sorry to hold you up, but I wondered if you were the guy who just moved in." He came back down the steps, and that's when Noah noticed he carried a flower in his hand. A single pink rose.

"Yeah, that's me." Noah extended his hand and introduced himself.

The guy returned the shake, an easy-going smile on his face. "Ethan. Ethan Black."

For a moment, Noah couldn't figure out why the name sounded so familiar, and then he heard Kristina's voice from last weekend. *His name is Ethan and he's a bartender...*

Holy. Fucking. Hell. It was Ethan the Dickhead Neighbor. "You're the bartender," he managed.

Confusion painted the other man's face. "Yeah. How'd you know?"

"Kristina." Tension squeezed the muscles of Noah's neck so hard that a headache bloomed all down the back of his head. This. *This* was the guy she was going out with tonight. *This* was the guy she thought was hot.

"Oh, right," Ethan said, that easy-going smile returning. He looked down at the rose in his hand and blushed. Which almost certainly meant the rose was for Kristina. "You're her friend..." He kept on chatting, but Noah's brain tuned him out.

Because something about hearing another man label them as friends had Noah grinding his teeth. Especially another man taking his girl out on a date. Made no difference to the man underneath all the bullshit that Kristina wasn't actually his. Not as he looked at Mr. Happy-Go-Lucky-Hottie-McDickhead-Neighbor standing there with a fucking rose. And a pink one, at that.

Kristina was going to like that. Because it wouldn't be the presumptuous overkill of red, but it would be sweet and thoughtful all the same.

And Kristina would like sweet and thoughtful. Hell, she deserved it. And maybe Noah shouldn't resent that this guy was apparently capable of giving it to her, but he did. He resented it with every pissed-off fiber of his being.

Ethan didn't seem to have registered that Noah was on a DEFCON-5-level meltdown, because he asked, "Hey, what kind of stuff is she into? I really dig your friend," he said with a sheepishly charming shrug, "so I'd appreciate any pointers you could give me."

Snark and sabotage rushed to the front of Noah's brain. With some effort, he forced himself to resist the urge to tell him where to stick those pointers or to sabotage his chances with Kristina by suggesting he take her out for sushi, which she hated, or to order for her without asking, which she thought was a ridiculous thing for anyone to do ever.

Finally, Noah shook his head. "Just ask her. She's very laid-back and down-to-earth." Kristina deserved that much from him.

"All right, man. Well, thanks. I'll tell her we ran in to each other." Ethan gave a wave and started up the steps again. "Have a good night."

Noah couldn't return the sentiment. Because the idea of what might make Ethan's night good had Noah's blood boiling in his veins. His skin was suddenly hot and too tight. He stalked to his SUV and then sat there. Stewing and churning. Full of regret.

He had his phone out of his pocket and open to his messages with Kristina in an instant. His fingers hovered over the keys. Saying anything to her about this date was probably a bad idea. No, it was most definitely a bad idea. Which was probably why his fingers started in on the hunting and pecking.

Don't go on your date tonight, he sent to her, his gut tossing.

Why? Did something happen? came back at him almost immediately.

How easy it would be to tell her he needed her instead, that he wasn't doing well. But Noah couldn't do it. It already made him enough of an asshole to ask her not to go out with Ethan in the first place. He knew it did.

No. Everything's fine. Just don't go.

A long pause. And then, *I don't understand, Noah. Why not?*

He gritted his teeth, and that too-hot/too-tight feeling crawled over him again. *Because I'm asking.*

Tell me WHY you don't want me to go and I'll consider it.

Problem was, he couldn't tell her why. What would he say? That he was jealous? That the thought that another man might touch her was like shrapnel to the gut? That the thought that she might fall for that guy broke what was left of his fucking heart?

All those things were true, but he couldn't say a goddamned one of them to her. Because they would tell her too much. And they would give her hope that *he* wanted her for himself.

And he did. He really fucking did. With every-fucked-up-thing he was. But that didn't mean he could have her. *Because* of every fucked-up thing he was.

"Fuck," he bit out, dropping his head back against the headrest.

His phone dinged again, and he read her newest message.
Tell me why Noah.

But there wasn't a damn thing he could say. And that left him only two options—go silent and say nothing, or give her his blessing. Not that she needed it.

He stared at the screen until her words went blurry, and then he started typing.

Never mind. Have a good time.

The minute he hit *Send*, Noah turned his phone off. He didn't want to know how she might respond. Or whether she'd respond at all.

By the time he got to the Full Contact MMA Training Center in the U Street/Shaw neighborhood of downtown DC, Noah was more than ready to pound the shit out of something.

Taking his time—a necessity given the blind spot caused by his partial vision loss—he parallel parked in a street space in front of a block of red-brick row-houses, then made his way back up the block to the Center, which appeared to take up the first couple of floors in a newer-looking yellow-brick building.

Noah found Mo standing in the bright, modern reception area of the club. The big man had changed into a pair of black and blue athletic shorts and a form-fitting black tank with the club's name on it. Cases of trophies and ribbons filled one wall by the front desk, and a display of work-out gear for sale ran along the other.

"Glad you came," Mo said. "Sign in on that clipboard over there and I'll take you to meet the coach."

Noah walked up to the shiny steel counter and added his

name to a list of thirteen other people. And then he was following Mo down one level, to a large rectangular gym space. Blue mats covered much of the open floor, and two eight-sided practice cages filled the far end of the room. People were spread out across the mats doing stretches and shooting the shit, but Mo led Noah past them to where three men stood near a set of benches at the side of the space.

Mo greeted the men and then gestured to Noah. "This is Noah Cortez, a prospective new member. Noah, this is Coach Mack, Hawk, and Colby."

"John McPherson," a fortyish man with dark hair and eyes said. He had full tattoo sleeves down both arms. "Everyone calls me Mack. Glad to have you here."

"Glad to be here," Noah said, returning the man's shake. Next, he exchanged introductions with the other two men, Leo Hawkins and Colby Richmond, long-time members who apparently assisted Mack with the coaching. Despite the black tattoos around his biceps that gave him a harder edge, Leo's blond hair, blue eyes, and tanned skin gave him a surfer-dude look. Colby had light brown skin and eyes and close-trimmed black hair.

Everyone was friendly and welcoming, helping ease some of the tension flowing through Noah's muscles.

"Take over warm-ups," Mack said to Hawk and Colby, "while I get Noah oriented." The two men nodded and took off for the mats. "Have a seat," Mack said. They cleared a spot among everyone's belongings. "Tell me a little about yourself. What brings you here?" the older man asked, expression open and relaxed.

Heaving a deep breath, Noah wished he could be as laid-back. "Served five years in the Marine Corps with the 2nd Combat Engineer Battalion. Discharged last fall after an IED gave me a TBI that stole the hearing in my left ear and some of the vision in my left eye. I met Mo today at another class and he, uh, told me about the club."

Mack nodded. "Are you still receiving treatment?"

"I have monthly check-ups with a neurologist and primary care doc for the TBI, but otherwise, no." He understood that Mack probably needed to make sure he was healthy enough to participate, but that didn't mean he loved sharing these details. He squeezed the bench with his hands.

"Are you working with a mental health professional?" Mack asked.

Noah dropped his gaze to the floor between his feet. "Not regularly. Talking..." He shook his head as discomfort slinked into his gut.

"Doesn't help?" Mack offered.

Cutting his gaze to Mack, Noah nodded. "Yeah. Makes it worse, actually."

"I feel ya. That's the same thing that brought a lot of other people here, Noah. Hell, same reason I started this club in the first place." Mack gave him a solid, supportive look, then grabbed some paperwork from a folder. "Okay, here's the deal. I'd like you to complete this quick-and-dirty member profile and questionnaire before you join in today, and sign this release. But before you can become a formal member, I'm going to need a doc to sign off on a physical. Standard operating procedure. So you can participate in the technical training today, but no sparring."

Noah's stomach fell as Mack secured the stapled pages to a clipboard. What if the doctor wouldn't clear him for this?

Mack must've seen something on his face, because the man squeezed his shoulder. "Lots of people here have dealt with head trauma, and we have precautions we can put in place for people who've maybe already been dropped on their heads one too many times." He gave a wicked grin. "So don't worry, okay?

Oh, and if you flip to the last page, you'll see a strength-training and conditioning program I recommend. A bunch of us work out together when we can. You're welcome to join."

"Sounds great. Thanks," Noah said, the reassurance helping. Mack left him to complete the paperwork. For a moment, Noah watched the group over on the mats working through a series of stretches, then his gaze dropped back to the forms.

On the one hand, he felt more of that excitement from earlier—before running in to Ethan had left him feeling like shit again. On the other, not being able to spar tonight had his shoulders dropping in disappointment. Some part of him had been counting on fighting to release some of the stress and anger that always seemed to be ballooning inside him.

On the first page, Noah completed the profile sheet which gathered basic contact information, military service data, and the specifics of any injuries. On the second, he found the questionnaire, which got more personal—asking a whole series of questions about state of mind of the applicant.

Noah found himself thinking of his list from the art class this morning as he circled how much he agreed or disagreed with statements like, *I often feel emotionally out of control*, or *I often feel irrationally angry or anger that is out of proportion to its cause*. He found himself strongly agreeing across the board.

The third page asked him to detail his experience with various forms of martial arts. He had a lot of experience with boxing from the Corps, where he'd also picked up some kickboxing. And he'd been a wrestler in high school and college. But he had no familiarity with some of the other disciplines used in mixed martial arts fighting, like Jiu-Jitsu, Judo, Karate, Muay Thai, and Taekwondo—all of which he was looking forward to learning more about.

At the back of the packet, Noah found the training and conditioning regimen Mack had mentioned and an equipment checklist. He had a cup and mouth guard with him, but he'd have to pick up the right clothing, hand wraps, gloves, head gear, knee pads, and shin guards before the next class.

He supposed that not having all the gear he needed was another good reason not to actually spar tonight, which led him to the physical form he'd have to get his doc to sign off on. Noah wasn't thrilled about that because he loathed going to the doctor. It forced him to confront shit he'd rather not. But it would be worth it to have a chance at something that might actually help.

"All set?" Mack asked, walking up to him a few minutes later.

"Yeah." Noah rose and toed off his shoes.

"Then head out for the warm-up and I'll look this over." Mack took the clipboard from him.

Out on the mats, Noah found a space at the back of the group and joined right in on the standing quad stretches. They moved on to standing hamstrings, hip flexor, and calf stretches next. Hawk and Colby were at the front of the group demonstrating each of the moves, and then they both went down to their knees.

"We've got two prospective members here tonight," Hawk said. "Tara Hunter." A woman wearing her long brown hair up in a ponytail gave a wave. "And Noah Cortez."

Noah gave a single nod as some of the others turned to look at him. He was glad he wasn't the only newbie here, although Tara made him look at the group anew to see that she wasn't the only female student. A dark-skinned woman with shoulder-length curls sat toward the front of the group and another woman with jet black hair in an intricate-looking braid knelt at the far side.

"For the sake of our prospective students, I'm going to move a little slower through the yoga positions tonight," Hawk said. "Colby will come around to check you."

Yoga? That was about the last thing Noah expected at MMA training.

Hawk's gaze scanned the group. "The first position is called child's pose. Lower your head as you sit on your heels. Breathe out as you stretch your arms forward on the floor, trying to stretch as far forward as you can while keeping your butt on your heels."

Noah did as the man said, feeling kinda self-conscious even though the position offered a stretch all down his lats and back that felt good.

"We do yoga because your mind is your most important piece of equipment, and the peacefulness, mindfulness, and discipline of yoga can help you regain control of nervous systems that have been stressed and are on edge," Hawk continued, his voice even, calm. "Concentrate on your breathing, on taking long breaths in and out."

Colby came around and offered some guidance as Hawk worked them through a few other poses. With the lack of appetite and sleep, Noah hadn't been particularly kind to his body these past months, and he was definitely feeling that as they finished the warm-up.

"Okay," Colby said. "If you don't have gloves, you can grab a pair from the bin. Otherwise, our technical skills session today is going to focus on striking patterns."

Noah and Tara were the only two who needed to borrow gloves, and they met up over at the benches.

"Hey," she said, wearing a friendly smile. She was way shorter than him and had a prominent scar that circled part of her neck. Noah couldn't help but wonder what'd caused it. "I'm glad I'm not the only new person here."

"Me, too," Noah said, trying on a pair of thick fingerless gloves. "I was in the Corps. You?"

"Navy," she said, pulling off one pair and trying on another. She punched her hands together. "These work. Nice to meet you."

"You, too," Noah said as they rejoined the group.

"Okay," Colby said, standing at the front of the class. "A couple of things to remember about striking. You want to pop in and out quick, which reduces the opportunity for your opponent to strike. And you don't want to be predictable, so mix up your striking pattern and the pacing of your strikes." The man demonstrated a quick attack with a punching combo and sprung straight back out, and then he showed some variations where he came back at angles. "Give it a try."

Noah got in the correct stance and brought up his hands, muscle memory kicking in from his years of boxing. Even though he wasn't in peak shape, there was almost a freedom to the feeling of moving—his body fast on the attack, his arms delivering jabs, hooks, and combinations of punches to an invisible foe, his weight shifting between his feet as he moved. The sound of huffing breaths and feet squeaking against the mats filled the otherwise quiet room.

Working through the moves made it clear just how much he'd changed, though, because he now had a massive blindspot on his left side that he hadn't had when he'd last boxed. His peripheral vision was non-existent on his left, which meant in an actual competition, he'd have to turn his head to compensate, losing some of his peripheral on the right as he did.

Goddamnit. Why did everything have to illustrate just how much he'd lost?

"Nice, Noah," Mack said, pulling Noah from the defeatist thoughts. "Tuck that back elbow in against your ribs more. You don't want any daylight showing through there or you open yourself up to a liver kick." Noah made the adjustment. Mack stood watching a moment longer and nodded. "Good. Now vary it up further by ducking and turning out."

Noah changed it up again. Instead of popping out of the attack standing straight up, he crouched down on his retreat, as if avoiding a hook. On his next attack, he pivoted and turned out, which set him up for—

All of a sudden, the room spun, the quickness of his movement throwing his equilibrium off.

"Whoa, big guy," Mack said, catching him by the shoulder. "How long has it been since you've done any kind of regular workouts?"

Frustrated, Noah sighed. "A while. I've managed to keep up with strength training and some occasional runs, but I haven't figured out how to get the equilibrium issues under control." He was glad he'd included it on his injury profile and hadn't tried to hide it.

Mack gave his shoulder a squeeze, then released him as Noah got his legs back under him again. "It's not always about controlling our weaknesses. It's about finding ways to mitigate them. It may be that certain moves always exacerbate the issue, but you can find strength in knowing which ones do and then strategizing alternate and equally effective moves."

Noah nodded, liking that idea a lot. He often worried about what would happen if he could *never* fix his weaknesses, when maybe he'd been asking the wrong question. Maybe he should've been asking how he could work around them instead.

"There are many right ways to arrive at the same destination, Noah," Mack said, giving him a pointed look.

Bolstered, Noah threw himself back into the striking pattern exercises.

Quick attack in. Right jab, left jab, right hook. Straight

back out.

Quick attack in. Fast right jab, left fake, right hook. Duck out and to the right.

Quick attack in. Left, right, left combo. Skip out and to the left.

And damn if using his muscles, exerting himself, and feeling the promise of his strength didn't make him feel a little different, more focused yet less trapped inside his head.

They worked on those moves for a few more minutes, and then they paired off to practice choke hold and joint lock positions for grappling on the ground.

"Billy Parrish," his partner said by way of introduction. With short dark blond hair, dark eyes, and a stubble-covered jaw, the guy probably had five or more years on Noah, but the hard cut of his arm and shoulder muscles and the speed with which he'd moved during the striking pattern exercises made it clear that age wouldn't be an immediate advantage.

They tapped gloves. "Noah Cortez."

"The purpose of choke holds and joint locks is to achieve submission, or the inability to escape a hold and make your opponent tap out," Mack said. "The fighter on top is the mount, and the mount's goal is to ground and pound his opponent until he can put him in a hold and finish the fight. The fighter on bottom is the guard, who's looking to escape the holds and pass the guard, or reverse his position with his opponent. We'll show you the positions, and then each of you will try."

Colby and Hawk got on the ground and first took turns demonstrating a series of different joint locks, many of which came from Jiu Jitsu—new territory for Noah.

Part-way through their demonstration, a guy rushed through the gym door and made quick working of joining the group. "Sorry Coach," he called, running a hand through his dark hair.

"Got caught at work." He took a place on the mats toward the far side.

"Run through your warm-up, Riddick," Mack said.

The guy gave a tight nod and started in on the stretches they'd done earlier. "Miss me, Dani?" he asked a woman sitting near him in almost a taunting voice.

"I'm sorry, who are you?" the woman said. Noah's gaze cut from the demonstration up front to where Riddick grinned and the black-haired woman glared back at him.

"Don't mind them," Billy said. "Driving each other batshit is their favorite pastime. Okay, we're up. Why don't you go first."

They started with an ankle lock, both of them sitting on the floor facing each other. Noah pinned Billy's ankle under his arm pit, clasped his hands together around the lower shin, and bent his elbows back toward his ribs to trap the man's foot there.

"That's pretty good," Billy said. "Try trapping the joint with the middle of your forearm instead of the wrist though. Because you've got a gap there." He pointed to the crook of Noah's elbow. "That I can yank out of, especially when we're sweaty."

Noah tried again. "That feels better," he said. "Tighter."

Billy nodded. "Gives you more control and power."

"Have you been doing this long?" Noah asked, adjusting his hold again.

"Been a member for a little over eighteen months. Medically discharged from the Rangers about three years ago." He lifted his shirt up his ribs, revealing a large swath of twisted and mottled scarring. Billy dropped the shirt again and gestured for Noah's ankle so he could try the hold. "Total snafu. Ended up with second and third-degree burns over forty per cent of my body." He wrapped his arms around Noah's ankle. "Tap when it starts to hurt," he said.

His opponent turned on the power and started to lean back. Noah tapped his hand against the mat. "Shit."

"Right?" Billy winked. "See the difference?"

"Yeah," Noah said. "Do that again." Billy pinned him in the lock quick and tight, and then Noah tried it again, feeling like he had even more power and control this time.

"So what's your damage?" Billy asked.

The casual way Billy had showed his scars and shared his story encouraged Noah to do the same. "IED caused a severe TBI which took my hearing and most of my sight on this side," he said, pointing to his head.

"Shit. Life's a goddamned full-contact sport, ain't it?"

"Roger that," Noah said, feeling more and more comfortable here *despite* the talking and sharing he'd done.

The rest of the choke hold and joint lock session went that way, with Billy giving him pointers and the two of them chatting. The guy had apparently parlayed his military career into private investigating, which had Noah wondering how to translate his skills into something in the civilian world. One thing at a time, though. Right?

"Okay," Coach Mack said a while later. "One team at a time will go into the rings for sparring matches refereed by Hawk and Colby. The rest of you will divide into two teams for a grappling match drill. Hunter and Cortez, you'll need to watch these from the sidelines until you get your memberships finalized."

"Good working with you," Billy said as he rose. They tapped gloves again.

"You, too," Noah said, frustrated at being benched even though he understood why.

And that frustration only grew as, for the next forty-five minutes, he was forced to cool his heels while others competed in the grappling match or sparred in the rings. He thought about leaving, but he didn't want to come off as throwing some kind of temper tantrum. Besides, he knew enough from years of wrestling to know you could learn a lot by studying other fighters.

Still, sitting there made him restless and anxious, and soon he felt that pressure growing inside his chest again. It didn't help that the earlier exercises already had his adrenaline pumping.

By the time class was over, he was itching to get out of there. Because he liked everyone he'd met so far, and no way did he want to make anything but a good impression. He wasn't pulling another public meltdown. Not in front of these guys, fuck you very much.

As Noah was jamming his feet back into his sneakers, Mack came up to him. "So, what did you think of your first time?"

"Liked it," Noah said. "Made me feel...more focused than I have in a while."

"That's what I like to hear," Mack said, smiling. They clasped hands. "I'll see you on Tuesday then?"

Noah nodded, antsy to get out of there even though he liked Mack a lot. "Yeah. With my paperwork ready to go."

"Good man." Mack made his way through the group to Tara.

"Hey," someone said tapping his arm. Noah turned to find Mo towering over him—not something he was used to experiencing. "Want to come grab a drink? A group of us usually goes out after class."

The tightness in Noah's chest had him worried about chancing it. "Not sure I'm up for it tonight," Noah said. "Next time, though, count me in."

"You got it," Mo said. They clasped hands and the big guy pulled him in for a quick, one-shouldered embrace. "You opened yourself up a lot today, Noah. Don't be surprised if that throws you off center a little bit." Mo handed him a card. "You need anything—even to talk—before Tuesday's class, don't hesitate to call."

Frowning, Noah nodded. Throw him off, as in even more? For fuck's sake. "Thanks, Mo."

The car ride was quiet and solitary. He'd been around people way more than usual today, and that made him feel even more alone than he normally did. A heaviness settled over him as he approached his apartment complex, and all he could think about was grabbing a quick shower and falling into bed. It was as if the whole day—the classes, the panic attack, sharing parts of himself he normally didn't—had overloaded his mind and the only fix was to reboot by going to sleep.

As a soft rain started to fall, Noah parked and got out of the Explorer, and then found himself doing a double take. Because he was parked right next to Kristina's car. Hope surged through him. She hadn't gone on the date, after all. So glad he hadn't gone out with the club, he glanced up toward his apartment. The lights were all dark...

Confused, he frowned. And then dread snaked down Noah's spine.

No.

Noah ran up to his apartment and burst through the door. "Kristina?" He slammed through the space, turning on lights and searching behind doors.

But it didn't take long to know for certain she wasn't there.

Which left only one possibility. Kristina had come home with Ethan.

And Noah saw fucking red.

CHAPTER SEVENTEEN

KRISTINA SAT on Ethan's couch laughing and joking with him as *Hot Tub Time Machine* played on the TV. Just before their desserts had arrived, a waitress had spilled a whole pitcher of beer down Ethan's back, so they'd shelved their plans for checking out a band at a local club in favor of watching movies back at Ethan's so he could shower and change.

Ethan laughed as on screen the characters spilled the time machine's fuel over its controls, opening a massive temporal vortex. "God, I think I still smell like beer," he said.

Kristina chuckled. "No, you don't. I still say you were way better of a sport about that than I would've been." They sat close enough for it to be more than casual, but not so close they were touching. And despite how cute Ethan was, Kristina couldn't decide if she *wanted* them to touch. She smoothed her hands over the snug teal skirt of her dress.

He shrugged and scrubbed his hands through his hair, bringing her attention to the ink that covered his arms. "I think the waitress was more traumatized than me. I couldn't stand to see her cry."

"Well, it was sweet how nice you were about it," she said.

And it was true. All night, Ethan had been sweet and charming and funny. He had a million humorous stories from bartending and they'd laughed a lot together. Not only that, but he was hot *and* thoughtful, having brought her a pink rose.

He was a genuinely good guy.

So why aren't you more interested?

"Since we never got any dessert, would you like something now?" Ethan asked, pausing the movie. "I have a couple different kinds of ice cream."

Kristina ignored the question she'd asked herself as her stomach squeezed. Did it have to be ice cream? "Uh, sure. That sounds great."

"Awesome," he said with a cute smile. "Come tell me which you want and I'll get to scooping." She followed him into the kitchen, noting again how the layout was the mirror image of Noah's place.

Which had her thinking of him—and their strange text message exchange—for probably the tenth time tonight. Why had he asked her not to go? Kristina's gut told her Noah didn't want her seeing anyone else because he wanted her all to himself. But her heart told her that was probably just wishful thinking and she was reading into Noah's admittedly erratic behavior what she wanted to see.

Especially since, on top of everything else—on top of his constant backing off from what was happening between them, on top of him disappearing from her bed in the middle of the night without saying a word, and on top of him telling her he was maybe pushing her away—he hadn't responded to the last text message she'd sent tonight.

I don't want to have a good time, Noah. I just want you.

Just thinking about the fact that she'd sent him those words still made her stomach flip.

But he hadn't responded. Once again, he was avoiding her.

"Okay," Ethan said, pulling pints and half gallons out of his freezer. "I have rocky road, pistachio, cherry, and chocolate chip cookie dough. Pick your poison."

Kristina looked from Ethan's cute, playful expression to the cartons laid out on the counter. She didn't like marshmallow so rocky road was out. Pistachio was just gross—whoever thought of that anyway? And cherry wasn't one of her favorites. Which left... No. No way was she eating cookie dough ice cream. Like she wasn't having enough difficulties blocking Noah Cortez from her mind.

"I'll take cherry," she said.

He scooped it out and nudged the bowl her way, and then he scooped himself...cookie dough. Kristina could've banged her head against a cabinet.

As Ethan put everything away again, Kristina watched him work. He'd changed into a pair of jeans and a worn black band T-shirt, and his feet were bare. His hair, his tats, his smile, everything about him—Ethan Black was as sexy as they came.

She *should* be wanting to jump him...

"Wanna eat out on the couch?" Ethan asked.

"Yep." Kristina returned to where she'd sat during the movie, which was almost over now.

Ethan sat closer this time, his thigh almost touching hers. It made Kristina's stomach do a loop-the-loop, but not because it excited her. She suddenly found that she was nervous, despite how easy-going and friendly Ethan was.

They chatted about the end of the movie as they ate, and then Ethan grabbed the remote. "Want to watch something else?" he asked.

Kristina shrugged and gave him a small smile. "No, that's okay."

Ethan turned off the TV. When they finished their ice cream, he placed their bowls on the coffee table, and then he shifted so that he was sitting facing her. "I had a good time tonight, beer shower aside," he said, giving her a playful, flirty smile.

"I did, too. I don't think I know anyone with as many good stories as you have," she said, and she meant it.

He chuckled. "Bartending may not provide many benefits, but good stories and good people watching are definitely among them."

"Yeah," she said, giving a small laugh.

Ethan gently brushed her hair back off the side of her face and tucked it behind her ear. Kristina's heart tripped into a sprint, because Ethan was looking at her like he was interested. Like he wanted her. "Can I kiss you, Kristina?" he asked in a low voice.

She froze for a long moment, her mind a whirlwind of contradictory thoughts and unending debates and competing desires. And a whirl of Noah. Always of Noah. Who maybe wanted to push her away. Yet, here was Ethan. Light, easy, open Ethan. Who maybe wanted to hold her tight.

Kristina wanted to want Ethan, but didn't. She wanted nothing more than...to be friends with him. Because he wasn't Noah.

"I don't think I should," she finally said, feeling horrible. The last thing she wanted to do was hurt Ethan's feelings.

"Not happening for you, huh?" he asked.

"I'm sorry," she said, meeting his eyes.

He shook his head. "I'm the sorry one," he said. "Because some guy sure is going to be lucky to have you."

The comment had her ducking her chin.

"Is it Noah?" he asked.

Her eyes went wide. "How...why...?"

"Well, that kinda just confirmed it," Ethan said, giving her a playful wink. "But I suspected that at least *he* felt more than friendly about you after talking to him today. Because I was left with the distinct impression that he wasn't happy I was taking you out."

"Oh." She wasn't sure what to make of that. "I really am sorry, though. Things are actually very strained between Noah and me right now, and I genuinely wanted this to work because you're pretty awesome."

He grinned and propped his head against his hand. "I am way more than *pretty* awesome."

Kristina chuckled. "You're right. You're the most awesomest *ever*."

"Well, now my ego feels a little better." Another playful wink. "Should I walk you out?" he asked.

"Sure," she said. She gathered her purse, and Ethan walked her to the door. Out on the open landing, she realized that it had started raining. Hard. "You don't have to walk me down to the lot," she said. "It's pouring and my car is right there."

"I really don't mind," he said.

She shook her head. "That's because you're the awesomest ever. But it's okay."

"*Most* awesomest," he said, grinning.

She rolled her eyes, but laughed. "Right. Thanks for everything, Ethan." She pressed a quick kiss to his cheek, and then turned away. As she started down the stairs, she heard the click of Ethan's door closing behind her. She rushed past Noah's floor, but then remembered that his car hadn't been here when she arrived. She hoped that meant he still wasn't here, because the last thing she wanted was a run-in with him when she was feeling quite so raw.

And she was. Because it was a helluva thing to realize how much in love you were with someone who probably didn't love you back. And even worse when that person was your lifelong best friend whose friendship might now be at risk.

When she got to the bottom floor, she stood just underneath the roof for a long moment, staring out into the dark downpour. She was going to have to make a run for it. One look at the deep puddles forming on the sidewalk and in the parking lot had her slipping off her high-heeled sandals and carrying them instead. And then she took off like a shot.

The cold temperature of the rain got a few choice curses out of her. She was immediately soaked through to the skin, her sexy turquoise dress with its deep V-neck, fluttery sleeves, and snug skirt that ran to mid-thigh instantly sodden. She hopped off the curb next to her car and into an ankle-deep puddle that made her shriek. When she lifted her keys to the door lock, her fingers were so wet that she dropped them.

"Shit," she said, fishing them out of the puddle. She stood up, and nearly screamed.

Noah was standing there, right next to the hood of her car. "I was calling you."

She heaved a deep breath that failed to calm. "Why?" she yelled back.

He waved her closer, and she wondered if the sharp lines on his face were just the result of shadows thrown by the rain and the darkness. Finally, she moved closer. "Come up," he said, gesturing to the building.

She shook her head. "It's late."

"Come up," he said more insistently. He stepped off the curb into the puddle, closing the distance between them. His whole face was set into a frown. It wasn't just the shadows.

"Noah—"

"Just come," he said.

Was it possible he wanted to talk about what she'd texted him? The thought made her belly flip, and she found herself agreeing despite her concerns. "Fine." She pushed around him, still carrying her shoes. Neither of them talking, Noah followed her up the steps to his door. He'd apparently left it unlocked, because he turned the knob and pushed it open, gesturing for her to go first. They were both dripping water all over the little square of slate tiles inside the door, which was exactly where she stayed lest she drag a trail of water all over his hardwoods.

Noah shut the door and turned on her, hands braced on his hips. Tension rolled off him, and Kristina was suddenly, totally, and completely sure coming up here had been a mistake.

"What?" she finally asked.

The ticking of the muscle on the side of his jaw wasn't the only sign that he was wound tight. His shoulders were bunched. His brows slashed down. His eyes were on fire with anger and desire—or maybe she was only imagining the latter.

Kristina hugged herself against the chill of the air conditioning. "*What*, Noah?"

He raked a hand through his wet hair and chuffed out a laugh that held no humor.

"For God's sake. Say something."

His gazed slashed to her face. "Did you screw him?"

She gasped. "*What?*"

"Just answer the question," he said, his voice going stern. "Did you screw him?"

White hot anger ripped through her. "I don't believe you," she said. How could he ask her that after the text she'd sent? After they'd just slept together a few days ago?

He stepped right up in front of her. Even in his anger, he was freaking gorgeous. Just then, she hated him for that. "Answer the question, Kristina. It's a simple yes or no."

She threw out her hands and lost her temper. "What if I did? Why would you freaking care?"

Pressing his mouth into a grim line, Noah glared at her, his agitation nearly a physical presence between them.

Kristina blew out a long breath and shook her head. "You know what? I'm not doing this again." She turned for the door.

Noah slammed his palm down flat against it, blocking her from opening it. His front was right up against her back, close enough to feel his rock-hard erection.

Her blood flashed hot despite the fight. "Move, Cortez. *Now.*"

"I can't, Kristina," he rasped in a tone so shattered that it suddenly put out the fire of her anger.

She turned inside the tight cage of his arm and his body, her heart a freight train in her chest.

He crouched down enough to look her eye to eye. "I. Can't."

"Stop fighting," she whispered, licking at rain drops rolling over her lips.

Burning brown eyes tracked the movement. He stared at her until she was trembling, or maybe that was just the chill from how wet she was.

But finally it was way too much to take for another second, and yet not nearly enough. "Noah," she whispered.

"Fuck," he said, dropping his forehead against hers.

The contact made Kristina go tense, because she didn't know whether to pull away or push for more. So she stood there, frozen and on edge and wanting a man possibly more than she'd ever wanted anything in her life.

No matter how damaged he was. And, oh, he was. She knew he was.

He braced his other hand against the door, fully boxing her in now, and dropped his head a little farther. The movement felt like he was nuzzling her, and it lured a soft whimper from her throat.

He groaned in answer, his nose rubbing along hers, his breath ghosting over her lips. "Tell me to stop," he rasped.

Kristina shivered, her body, mind, and heart in a three-way battle that didn't seem like it would end any time soon. That left only instinct, which told her to stop fighting against everything she so badly wanted. Stop fighting this desire.

"No," she said.

The word hung there for a long moment, and then Noah was on her. Mouth devouring her mouth. Hands dragging over her, as if he wanted to touch every part of her at once. Body pinning hers flush against the door, his cock grinding against her belly.

Noah tasted like sweet, sweet sin and felt even better, all hard and aggressive against her. And the sheer raw pleasure of it made it impossible to do anything but surrender.

He pulled down her V-neck and bra cups, freeing her breasts to his hands, his lips. His heat was all-consuming, such a stark contrast to the chill of her skin. She clutched at his wet hair as he worked his tongue and fingers over her until she was panting and moaning and shifting, but she couldn't escape. And didn't want to even if she could.

As he sucked and tongued at her nipples, his hands tugged up the snug skirt to her dress, leaving it to pool around her waist. He dragged her panties down to her knees, and they fell to the floor. Noah kicked her feet apart and raked his hands up the insides of her thighs. The feeling was so intense, she went up onto her toes on a whimper. He slanted his mouth over hers and cupped her between her legs. She moaned into the kiss, from the contact, from his heat, from the frantic intensity pinging between them.

His middle finger penetrated her, slow at first, and then faster. He'd pull all the way out, spread her wetness around, and sink deep again. On each penetration, he ground the heel of his hand against her clit until Kristina thrust her hips forward, chasing what she could already tell was going to be an explosive orgasm, despite the fact that he'd barely touched her.

"That's it, baby," he said around the edge of a kiss, his finger slicking in and out of her, his palm grinding so deliciously right where she needed him. And, *gah!*, there was that term of endearment again. "I want you to come."

"Yes," she whispered, clutching harder at his shoulders.

His hand moved faster, and faster still, battering her clit and shoving her quickly to the edge. "Say my name, Kristina. Say my name when you fucking come."

"Oh, God, Noah," she rasped, her whole body going tight. She hung on the edge, her muscles straining, and then Noah withdrew his fingers from inside her and flicked them hard and fast over her clit. Kristina screamed his name and her knees nearly buckled.

Noah caught her easily as the pulsing waves washed over her. He fumbled at his jeans for a moment, and then he was lifting her against the door, spreading her legs around his hips, and sliding his cock deep. "Fuck, yes," he growled, burying his face into the crook of her neck.

Kristina moaned, her body still sensitive from the orgasm. She clutched her arms around his neck and her legs around his hips and rode out the storm of him. He fucked her like he was possessed by need and chased by demons, hard and driving and relentless. The door rattled and banged in the jamb, and Kristina absently thought that someone passing by outside might hear. But she had no capacity to care about anything but the beautiful, damaged man between her thighs.

"Oh, Noah," she cried, pressing kisses against his cheek, his neck, the slope of his shoulder. "Oh, Noah."

His hips flew, hammering against hers and winding her body up again. With his hands under her knees, he spread her wider, his body curled around her, his hips occasionally rotating in the most delicious, maddening circles.

The build-up to her second orgasm had her holding her breath, and then she came so hard she couldn't speak and saw stars. All she could do was clutch tight to him and ride it out, even as her heart ripped wide open and twenty years of history, affection, and love came rushing forth.

She bit back the words—barely. But only because she wanted to look into his eyes as she said them for the very first time. "Oh, God, Noah. You're so good," she rasped, finding her voice again.

On a groan, he withdrew from her and lowered her feet to the ground. Rough, hurried hands spun her, pushing her chest against the body-warmed door and tilting her hips out enough to force her back to arch. And then Noah was pushing back into her, filling her, burying himself deep. His fullness felt so good, so essential, so much a part of herself that she felt the rightness of it into her very soul.

Her Noah.

His hands curled tightly around her shoulders and his fore-head fell against the back of her head as his hips pistoned against her. He held her so tight she was nearly immobile in his embrace, and it felt to her like he couldn't get close enough, or deep enough. And she felt that, too.

"Fuck, I'm gonna come," he said, his lips beside her ear.

She moaned and licked her lips. "Yes, Noah. I want to feel you inside me."

"Jesus," he rasped, his hips smacking against her rear on punctuated thrusts.

"Yes, yes, give me everything," she cried, her hands pressing against the door.

Noah shouted as his orgasm hit him. "Oh, Kristina. Oh,

fuck. Oh, God." He moved through it, more of those slow, deep thrusts that made her whimper and writhe.

When he finally stilled, Noah withdrew on a shudder, but he didn't let her go. He hugged her tight, his front to her back, her front still to the door. He let his head *thunk* against the solid surface, the sound of a thick swallow right in her ear.

"Noah?" He didn't answer, just continued to hold tight. "Noah, let me turn around."

Finally, he released her, and then she was the one clinging tight to him. She turned, pressed onto tiptoes, and threw her arms around his neck. One beat passed, then another, and then he finally returned the embrace, his arms going loosely around her back.

Now. Now she had to tell him. She had to lay it all out there and tell him exactly how she felt. No more "it's just sex" charades, no more delusions that they were just friends, no more holding back this beautiful, overwhelming feeling inside her.

She pulled away just enough to meet his eyes, and her hands slid down to cup both sides of his face. "I didn't sleep with Ethan, Noah," she said, shaking her head. "I left his apartment because I realized how much of a mistake it had been to go out with him at all. Because ... because you're the one I want. You're the one I've *always* wanted. You *are* my best friend, but you're also the man I've fallen in love with." The words came faster and faster, spilling out of her now. "I don't know when it happened. I don't know if it was two weeks ago when we kissed in your room or nineteen years ago when I fell off my bike and you rode over to ask me if I was okay." She shrugged, so full of emotion that her chest ached and tears pricked her eyes. "But it doesn't matter when it happened, only that it did. I love you, Noah. I love you so much."

CHAPTER EIGHTEEN

THE WORDS WERE like a slap to Noah's face, jarring him back to reality. They rang in his ears over and over—*I love you, Noah. I love you so much.*

All Noah could do was stare down at Kristina's pretty face, so filled with sweet affection. For him. Her damp hair was drying in messy waves, and her lovely chest heaved, still flush with the exertion of what they'd done. And it all made her the most beautiful person he'd ever seen. But as much as her words tempted him, as much as he wanted to be able to lay claim to them, he also heard three others echoing inside his brain.

Give me everything.

The fucking irony.

Because if tonight proved anything, it was that Noah had absolutely nothing to give. Despite knowing he shouldn't take what wasn't his to have, he'd done it again. Despite knowing—and even saying—that he wasn't capable of doing what she wanted, being what she wanted, giving what she wanted, he'd done what *he'd* wanted, ignoring what was best for her.

In the end, all he'd done was take and take and take—her affection, her body, her love. Jesus, he'd fucked Kristina up against the front door of his apartment, not even bothering to undress her, or warm her, or dry her off from the storm.

Gently, he grasped her hands in his and pulled them away from his face. No matter what he might or might not feel for her, he just didn't have it in him to take care of her the way she needed. The way she deserved.

That much was clear.

Because if he couldn't put her first when they were friends, no way would he be able to do so if they were lovers. When it would matter more. When the stakes would be higher. And the fact that he was still holding her hands, that he wasn't pushing her away like he should, was the problem in a nutshell.

What a fucking selfish bastard.

Worse, he hadn't been motivated by anything good when he'd chased her out into the rain. Instead, he'd been driven by a noxious cocktail of blinding jealousy, raw emotion, and utter frustration. The whole day had been such a build-up of stressors that he should've known better than to even try to talk to Kristina. Finding that she'd come home with Ethan had just been one stressor too many. The thought that she might be just a few feet away and falling into another man's arms, another man's bed, another man's heart...it had all been too fucking much.

Especially since he had absolutely no question in his mind or his heart. Noah loved Kristina. He was in love with her, too.

So he'd gone after her. And made everything worse.

In all his pathetic weakness, he'd done the exact thing he knew he should never do again.

Not *just* having sex with her, though that was bad enough. But leading her on and giving her hope, when he for sure had none of that to give.

"Say something," Kristina whispered, wide blue eyes peering up at him. Hopeful and wary in equal measure.

"I don't know what to say," he managed, hating himself as a flash of uncertainty passed across her pretty features.

She licked her lips, her eyes boring into his. "Say you'll give us a chance. Say you're with me in this. Say you..." She gave a small shrug that read as self-consciousness. "Say anything," she whispered.

Noah dropped her hands, fastened his jeans, and stepped back. It hurt him to put space between them, it really did. Because he knew that he was building a permanent wall between them, one he'd never get to cross again.

"I can't, Kristina. I told you that. I *told* you," he said, heat slinking into his tone, pain slicing through him, anger and grief clouding his brain.

"There's nothing stopping us from giving this a try. You can't deny that there's something here, because we keep ending up in this same place—falling into each other's arms and then wondering what it means, or if it should mean anything—"

"It doesn't." It couldn't. He gave a fast shake of his head, swallowing the sour bile rising at the back of his throat. "It doesn't mean anything except that I'm a weak motherfucker and a horrible friend."

Her expression fell and her shoulders dropped. She pulled up her dress to cover her breasts and tugged down her skirt. "I don't understand, Noah. You didn't want me to go out with Ethan. You were worried about me when I got hurt. You called me baby and said you didn't want it to end. Those are the words and actions of a man—"

"Who's really fucked up," he interrupted, the words tasting like bitter acid as they fell off his tongue. "Those were the words and actions of a man who's been using you, who put his selfish need to feel better, to feel *something*, above what you needed and deserved. Those were the words and actions of a man with some unforgivably piss poor impulse control."

"Stop trying to push me away," she said, her voice strained, eyes glassy. And the threat of her tears broke his fucking heart. But better for her to have a little pain now than to have major heartache later, because with the way he was right now, that's all he'd ever be good for.

Pain. Disappointment. Failure.

"I'm no good for you," he said, the shattered pieces of his heart cutting him up on the inside, leaving him broken and bleeding. "It's time for you to face it. I'm not the man I used to be. He's gone." The admission coiled his anger tighter, unleashing that uncomfortable pressure in his chest, the one that sooner or later would demand violent release. His hands fisted.

"That's not true," she said, hugging herself.

"It's the *only* thing that's true," he said quietly.

Dropping her gaze, she paced across the wet floor, confusion rolling off of her and washing regret through him. Finally, she leaned back against the door, her expression and posture so damn defeated as her blue eyes cut up to him. "Don't you understand that you're *everything* to me?" she asked. The question was like a steel shank to the gut, opening up a wound that was gory and messy and sure to leave him bleeding out. "No matter how fucked up you think you are, no matter what problems you're facing, you're already enough for me!"

"No," he said, not wanting to hear this, not able to face the temptation.

"Damnit, Noah. Yes," she said, her voice rising.

He got right up in her face, towering over her and caging her in with his hands against the door. "You're wrong," he bit out.

"No! You're scared," she said, her gaze looking too deep inside him, seeing too much.

Her words hit him like a lightning strike, going straight to his heart and triggering an explosion. Because he *was* scared.

Scared that he'd never get better. Scared that he couldn't continue to handle this pain. Scared that, someday, Kristina Moore would find a man who actually deserved her. That shit was just fact.

He slammed his open palm against the door beside her head and yelled, "I'm not fucking scared."

It was possible Noah had never loathed himself more than when he saw her flinch in fear of him.

And that just clinched it.

He took a big step back this time, big enough that he couldn't reach out and touch her. And damn if she didn't look small curled in on herself against that door. "I'm just realistic, Kristina. And I'm doing the right thing by you. Finally. I'm just sorry I didn't do it sooner."

"But I love you, Noah. Doesn't that count for something?" A single brutal tear rolled from the corner of one eye.

"No," he said, the falseness of the sentiment making him nauseous. Because her love was *everything*, maybe even the *only* thing. But there were some gifts you could never accept and never keep no matter how precious they were.

"Why?" she whispered.

Noah swallowed once, twice, the lie not coming as easily as he wanted it to, or needed it to. "Because I don't love you. Not like that."

For a long moment, Kristina couldn't breathe. The words were like a punch to the gut, setting off a sickening ache and making her want to curl into a ball. She stared at Noah, willing him to say more. But he didn't.

Which meant there was nothing left for her to say, either. Because she'd laid it all out there, and she'd pushed him, and she'd fought. But she couldn't make him love her, and she couldn't make him admit that he did if he insisted he didn't.

Without saying a word, she bent down and retrieved her long-forgotten sandals and purse from where she'd earlier dropped them on the floor. Mortified, she stuffed her discarded panties into her purse, too. And then she stood up and gave him one last look.

"I guess we're done here, then," she said. Kristina turned and walked out the door.

She texted Kate before she pulled out of Noah's parking lot, so she wasn't surprised when Kate's door flew open before Kristina even knocked.

"Oh, honey." Kate pulled Kristina inside the apartment and into her arms. The sympathy beckoned Kristina's tears again, and she sagged against her friend and let them come. "I'm so sorry," Kate said.

Kristina kept her face buried in Kate's shoulder until she regained control of her breathing, and then she let herself be led over to the big overstuffed couch. Kate's place was decorated in rich golds and browns, with deep red and purple accents. It was like walking into a lush, autumn forest, and Kristina always felt at home here.

They sat heavily on the couch, their knees drawn up toward one another.

"Did you tell him?" Kate asked carefully.

Kristina nodded. "Yeah. I told him everything."

"And...it didn't go over well?" Dressed in her sleep clothes, Kate wore a strappy royal blue camisole and a pair of satin sleep shorts. And even though Kristina was in a dress and heels, she felt rumpled next to Kate because of having gotten caught in the rain—twice. Not to mention being fucked up against a door while mostly still dressed.

Couldn't forget that. Wouldn't *ever* forget that.

"No," Kristina said. "He said he doesn't love me. Not like I love him. And he said he's no good for me, and that he never will be." Her breathing shuddered as she spoke, but she managed to get through the words without falling apart again, despite the fact that she was pretty sure someone had punched a hole through her chest and ripped out her heart.

"Well, shit, Kristina. I might have to agree with him. Because if he won't even give you two a chance after the marathon sex session the other night and all the other things he's initiated, then he isn't any good for you. In fact, he's a freaking bastard for doing this to you."

"There's more, too." Kristina tugged her skirt down her cold legs.

Kate groaned. "I can already see I'm not gonna like this. But before you tell me, do you want to change into some dry clothes? You can borrow some sweats."

"That sounds like heaven," Kristina managed. A few minutes later, they were situated back on the couch, except this time the dry clothes warmed her on the outside, even if she was stone cold on the inside.

"Okay, let's hear this 'more'," Kate said, her eyebrow arched.

Kristina blew out a long breath. "We slept together again."

Kate's brows cranked down. "Wait. Again? As in, tonight?" She slapped her hands against her thighs, and her eyes went wide. "Whoa. Wasn't your date with Ethan tonight?"

Nodding, Kristina said, "Yes, yes, and yes."

"Motherfucker. Tell me *you* initiated the sex," Kate said, her cheeks going flush like they always did when something wound her up. "Because if *he* initiated the sex *again*, and then told you there was no chance for anything more between you, that's some fucking bullshit."

"It was sorta both of us. We were fighting about Ethan and then one thing led to another and he had me pinned against his apartment door. He told me to tell him to stop, and I said I didn't want to. So he kissed me. And stuff."

"And stuff?" Kate gave her a droll stare. "Stuff being you two had sex up against his door?"

"Pretty much."

Her friend's gaze narrowed. "Explain the part about fighting with Ethan. And how did that go, anyway?"

"He was great, honestly. But..." Kristina shrugged. "...I'm too far into this with Noah, and I just couldn't get into him. I guess Noah saw me leaving Ethan's apartment and he followed me down to my car. We went back up to his place to talk and—" Kate was going to flip her shit at this part. "—He asked me if I'd screwed Ethan. That started the fight."

Kate threw out her hands. "Hold the damn phone. Noah *actually* asked you if you'd screwed the guy?" Kristina nodded. "I'm gonna freaking kill him. I swear to God."

"Well, that's how I felt, too. But somehow we ended up half naked with my thighs wrapped around his waist." She smoothed her hands over her borrowed sweatpants. Maybe it made her a glutton for punishment, but she didn't regret being with Noah again. She loved him too much for that, even if what they'd done hadn't exactly been making love.

"That shit's a shame because it's freaking hot, but then he went and ruined it."

"It *was* freaking hot," Kristina said. "But, yeah."

Kate grasped her hand. "I'm so sorry, honey. I really am. I know you've wanted this—him—for a long time now. But it sounds like maybe Noah's as fucked-up as he says he is. In which case, you can't fix him, you know?"

The thought of him being fucked-up...and unfixable...made Kristina's throat go tight. It just broke her heart, not because she couldn't have him, but because she hated that he was hurting. Even if he'd hurt her, too.

"No matter how magical your hooha is," Kate said with a grin and a wink.

Surprisingly, Kristina managed a small laugh. Then she shook her head. "I don't think I can go back. The thought of spending time with him but having to hold all this in, not being able to act on it or express it, not being able to touch him—just the idea of having to deny my emotions...it hurts. It hurts a lot."

"Yeah," Kate said, regret plain in her voice. "I get it."

More of that pricking sensation at the backs of her eyes. "But doesn't that mean I have to give him up completely? If he won't let us try to be something more and I can't go back to being just friends, what does that leave?"

Kate squeezed her hand. "It leaves almost twenty years of amazing memories that will never go away."

A small sob caught in the back of Kristina's throat. "I don't want it to be over."

"Aw, honey. I know."

"But it is whether or not I want it to be, isn't it?" Kristina asked, hugging herself against the sensation that her chest was splitting wide apart. Kate nodded. "Then I guess that's it. After all these years, I guess Noah and I are really over for good."

CHAPTER NINETEEN

If Noah thought he'd been a wreck *before* rejecting Kristina's love, it was nothing compared to how he felt after.

He had no appetite and didn't eat. He couldn't sleep without seeing the crushed look on her face when he'd lied about not loving her. Hell, he couldn't even tolerate being awake, because his brain wouldn't stop replaying her voice saying that they were done.

And every bit of it was his own damn fault.

He hadn't gotten out of bed for most of the past four days because he'd been too damn depressed. And when he hadn't been able to get an appointment with his doctor for a physical until Thursday afternoon, he'd seen no reason to go to fight club Tuesday night. And the appointment earlier this afternoon was the only reason he'd bothered to get out of bed today. Otherwise, he'd probably still be laying there in the dimness, stuck right on the edge of sleep but never actually falling, every so often waking up his phone to reread the last text message Kristina had sent him.

I don't want to have a good time, Noah. I just want you.

I just want you.

Jesus, those words were an agony.

Noah hadn't turned his phone back on to see them until after he'd fucked everything up. Not that seeing her text sooner probably would've made a difference to how that night had gone down or the piss-poor choices he'd made. Because even on his best of days, he was still too many shades of fucked up.

On top of all that, Noah's energy level was for shit, and getting to the doctor's office had taken way more effort than he had it in him to make. The only thing that kept him from bailing on fight club again was stepping on the scale during his physical...and finding that he'd lost sixteen pounds since his last appointment less than a month before.

Noah was well on his way to *actually* becoming nothing.

Which was why he'd driven directly from the medical park to the Full Contact MMA training center, only detouring enough to pick up some fast food, and then waited the two hours until class time. A part of him felt like he was walking a very fine line between still being able to pull himself back up the cliff he'd fallen down or just letting himself fall the rest of the way.

Falling would be so much fucking easier.

But he didn't want to be a coward, and he didn't want to be a fucking tragedy, either.

Finally, class time arrived, and Noah made his way down to the gym, paperwork in hand. Inside, he walked up to Mack, who gave him a big open smile.

"Welcome back, Cortez," he said.

"Thanks," Noah said, handing over his form. "All squared away."

"Good." Mack's dark eyes scanned over the sheet, and then cut back up to Noah. "You doing okay?"

Noah nodded. "I'm five by five." He wasn't actually doing good, but the numbness that had washed through him over the past few hours was so much better than the pain that had wracked him during the past few days that it didn't entirely feel like a lie.

One of Mack's eyebrows went up, just the littlest bit, but enough to reveal his skepticism. "All right, then," he finally said. "Head on out and start warming up."

Noah found a spot on the mats. He'd come to class earlier this time than last, so there were only about a half dozen people here so far.

The woman sitting closest to him turned and gave him a smile. "Hey, you were here on Saturday, right?" she asked. "I'm Daniela England. Everyone calls me Dani."

"Yeah," he said. "Noah Cortez."

The woman had long shiny black hair pulled back into a low pony tail, light brown skin, and striking big brown eyes. "Well, welcome, Noah. You'll like this place. It's a great group of people."

"Thanks," he said as more people joined them on the mat. He exchanged greetings with Billy, who introduced him to Sean Riddick, the guy who'd come in late the last time he'd been here. Sean was apparently former Navy and Dani a former Army nurse. Noah enjoyed learning how varied everyone's backgrounds were, yet they were all united by their service to country. And Billy was right about Sean and Dani making a sport of driving each other crazy, because they started in on it the minute Sean sat down.

"Look who's on time for once," Dani said, looking at Sean.

The guy shook his head. "Not in the mood, Daniela."

She glared. "Aw, poor boy."

He nailed her with a stare. "You're going down tonight."

She rolled her eyes. "Dream on."

"Wait for it," he said.

Mo sat down beside him, wearing that big open grin Noah

already associated with the guy. "Hey, man. Missed you on Tuesday."

"Yeah, sorry," Noah said. "I couldn't get in for a physical until today."

Mo's dark eyes narrowed. "You look like you've been under the weather."

Given Noah's habit of not paying attention to his own reflection, he wasn't sure what exactly might be giving Mo that impression. The beard that was coming in, maybe? Given the last few days, though, Noah supposed he wasn't too surprised. "That a nice way of saying I look like shit?"

Chuckling, Mo shook his head. "No, man. Just checking in."

"Okay, let's get started," Mack called from the front of the room.

For the next hour, they worked through their yoga warm-up, striking-pattern exercises, and kicking forms. And then came the sparring matches and tag-team grappling match drills that Noah had been forced to sit out the last time. Adrenaline already flowing, Noah was freaking ready to mix it up and work out some of the bullshit in his head.

He started out in the grappling match, on a team with Mo, Sean, Tara, and some others he hadn't yet met.

"Same rules as always," Mack said. "We're practicing groundwork here. Your turn ends either when you've been finished and tap out or you can get close enough to the edge of the mat for one of your teammates to touch you and tag you out. We'll do a five-second change over, and during that time and that time only it's okay for the tagging team to have two fighters on the mat both attacking their opponent. This is *just* about groundwork, no striking. Mo, Billy, you're up first."

The two men knelt facing one another about ten feet from the corner of the mat. Big as Billy was, Mo looked a mountain beside him, and Noah was almost glad he wouldn't have to face off with the guy. When Mack gave the signal, they tapped gloves and then grabbed each other around the backs of the head and shoulders, both of them throwing themselves into gaining advantage over the other.

Mo got into the mounting position pretty quickly, managing to get a hold on Billy around his chest and flip him over. But Billy demonstrated his agility, rolling his hips up so that he got close to a neck lock before their positions shifted again. They grappled for maybe another forty seconds until Mo rolled Billy close to their team's edge, close enough for Noah to reach Mo's foot.

Noah tapped Mo out and Mack started counting down from five.

Not wasting a second, Noah sprung out onto the mat, piling on top of Billy, who was face down. Then Mo was out and it was all Noah and Billy.

Eight years of wrestling training held Noah in good stead as he used every muscle group to dominate his opponent. He grabbed hold with his arms, worked to gain leverage with his legs, fought against getting pinned with his stomach and back. From the corner of the mat, Mack called out guidance and encouragements.

And though it felt *good* to exert himself, just as it had the other night, Noah couldn't ignore that he didn't feel anywhere near as strong as he had at Saturday's class. The energy it took to compete effectively against a much more practiced opponent was more than he had after nearly a week of neglecting himself, which was why within about a minute, Billy had them close enough to his team's sideline to get tapped out.

For a few seconds, his two opponents double teamed him, and then it was just Noah and a guy whose name he didn't know. The man was also skilled, though Noah fared better against him and ultimately gained the advantage, catching him in a half-nelson hold around his neck.

His opponent struggled against it, but Noah kept squeezing until the guy tapped out, his hand smacking against the mat.

One of his teammates joined him as Mack counted down from five, and then Noah's turn was over. Way too fucking fast. Because the adrenaline from competing for just those few minutes was a rush. And Noah wanted more of it.

Not to mention, those few minutes in the match were the first all week when something successfully distracted him from thinking about Kristina.

Kneeling on the sidelines again, Noah watched Sean take on one of their opponents, who managed to gain the advantage. Dani tagged her teammate, and then it was Sean and Dani on the mats.

"This ought to be interesting," Billy said from next to Noah.

And it was. Though Sean probably had a good fifty pounds on Dani, she was fast and held her own against him as they grappled and fought for domination. Sean managed to pin her, his knees between her legs, his arms winding around her neck and going for a D'Arce choke. But somehow Dani got one of her arms inside his and was able to break the choke, roll her hips, and lock her legs around his neck. She reached out a hand...and one of her teammates was just able to reach her. They tagged her out.

"What was that about going down?" she said as her teammate joined in against Sean.

"Oh, sweetheart," Sean said. "Revenge is going to be so sweet."

New competitors subbed in as fighters were called into the practice cages to spar, and Noah got another turn on the ground a few minutes later. He once again found himself immersed in the thrill of the fight, the distraction of exertion, the rush of competition.

He was up against Billy again, and this time he had no intentions of letting the guy best him, no matter how fatigued he was. They went at it hard, rolling and pushing and clutching, their efforts to grab hold becoming harder, more aggressive. Grunts and curses ripped into the air, and competitiveness gave way to anger and frustration in Noah's belly when Billy's glove caught him in the jaw.

"No striking in this drill," Mack called from the corner.

Reining himself in, Noah focused on working them closer and closer to his team's side. He was almost close enough to reach out a leg to get tagged when Billy flipped out around him and managed to pin Noah face down, arms around Noah's neck applying pressure against Noah's windpipe.

He struggled against the hold, twisting and pushing, but Billy just squeezed harder, and then the other man managed to get a leg over Noah's thighs, pinning them too.

Noah was done. Fuck. *Fuck*. He had no choice. He tapped out.

It was possible he'd never felt more angry to lose a match in his life. Because, damnit, he *needed* a fucking win.

"All right, good round. Noah, Billy, head over to Colby's cage," Mack said.

Billy let him go, And Noah shot off the floor. At least sparring would give him a way to focus the aggression flowing inside him, because right now Noah just wanted to break something with his bare hands.

I just want you.

Aw, fucking hell.

Thoughts of Kristina flooded in behind the memory of her voice. How was she doing? Had her workshop at the Art

Factory started yet? Was she thinking of Noah? Or had she written him off completely?

I guess we're done here.

That's what she'd said right after Noah uttered the filthy lie about not loving her, and it had been twisting like a knife in his gut all week long—a wound of his own making, of course. He got that.

Having not bought his own equipment yet, Noah suited up in some borrowed pads and guards from the club, including protective headgear—something Noah's doctor had insisted upon. The man had been familiar with fight training as therapy, but he'd still been hesitant about signing off on it for Noah.

In the end, though, it had been Noah's call—and to his mind, it was better to take the risk that he'd get hurt in the ring than live with the certainty that he'd die from all this pain.

He and Billy climbed into the ring.

Colby gave the signal, and then they were circling, assessing, planning their first strikes. Billy attacked with a punching combo which Noah easily defended. Noah counterattacked, striking in a series of quick punches, jabs, fades, and hooks. Billy came at him with a leg kick, pivoted out, and got in a backhand. As they fought, Colby called out guidance, and it quickly became clear that while Noah was a stronger boxer, Billy had a stronger kicking game. Something Noah would have to work on, then.

But just then, the deficit only added to Noah's frustration.

Noah pulled from deep inside and poured on a burst of energy, getting Billy in a clinch against the cage. Punch, punch, punch. Noah went at the guy like he was possessed. The more he fought, the more his anger consumed him, blinded him, took over his mind. He pinned Billy and nailed him with a spinning back elbow.

Billy went down against the cage, but the guy wasn't to be

underestimated, because he got his legs around Noah's knee and forced him down, too.

Landing half on top of the other man, the fight became all about the ground and pound. They grappled. Clutched. Flipped each other. Hit. Kicked.

Christ, I want Kristina. Punch, punch, punch. *Will I ever stop feeling like this?* A hard elbow to the ribs. *What is the fucking point of all of this without her?* Pound, pound, pound.

Noah got his thighs around Billy's neck and went to town on the man's unguarded ribs.

"Whoa! Noah! Noah, stop!" Colby called, grabbing his arms. Billy scrambled out from under him, going into a kneeling position a few feet away.

Blinking away the haze of red in his head, Noah looked from one man to the other.

"What the fuck, man?" Billy said, glaring at him. "I tapped out thirty seconds ago."

"Shit...I..." He shook his head. "I didn't realize."

"And you didn't hear me call it off?" Colby asked, a concerned expression on his face.

Fuck. "No."

Colby nodded, and took some notes on a clipboard. And then he started to give them some pointers based on what he'd seen of their fighting. Noah could barely hear the words the man spoke. Utter exhaustion flooded through his veins, a heaviness that almost made it impossible to lift off his pads and rise to his feet minutes later when Colby dismissed them.

"I'm sorry," Noah said to Billy outside of the cage.

Billy looked at him a long minute, and shook his head. "Don't worry about it. I see where you are right now, Noah. I recognize it because I was there. Better get a handle on it before it consumes you." He gave Noah a pointed look, and all Noah could do was nod.

Damn hard to hide the shit inside you when the person standing in front of you had once waded through it himself, wasn't it? Right in that moment, Noah didn't know if that was a relief or a curse.

When time was up, Mack asked Noah to hang out afterward. Noah was glad for the delay, because it gave him an easy excuse for not joining the guys for drinks after. He was pretty sure that the last thing he needed to be doing was adding alcohol to the fucked-up cocktail in his brain, although there was a certain temptation there, he had to admit.

And wasn't that a cheery goddamned thought.

Noah helped Mack stow the gear in a supply closet. Back out in the gym again, Mack turned to him. "What happened in the cage today?"

Shit. Guess he should've expected that. You never kept fighting after the bell rang, the round ended, or your opponent tapped out. "I lost focus," Noah said.

Mack's gaze narrowed on him. "You sure it wasn't more than that?"

Noah frowned, hating that this was one of the first impressions he was making on the guy. "I didn't do it on purpose."

"I didn't think that you did," Mack said. "Colby said you were really waling on Billy, and didn't hear either the tap out or Colby's voice. And that tells me that whatever's going on in your head was louder."

Shame ran a flush across Noah's skin.

"I was there, Noah. I know what it is. And all I have to do is look at you to know you've lost, what, a good eight or ten pounds since I last saw you?"

Noah dropped onto one of the benches, his elbows on his knees, his head hanging. "Yeah."

Mack sat down next to him. "You're not okay, and I'm worried about you. Did something happen?"

"Yeah," Noah said. "I was an asshole to someone I care about, and I'm pretty sure I've lost her." He almost surprised himself by saying this, but Mack got his bullshit on some fundamental level, and Noah was too tired, too overloaded to keep it all inside.

"Have you tried apologizing?" Mack asked.

"I haven't done anything at all since it happened." Noah turned his head to look at the other man.

"I see," Mack said, bracing his elbows on his knees. "Look, I'm not a doctor or a psychologist. But a couple of things seem important here. First, apologize. Right? You don't know where things stand until you do, and things might seem worse than what they really are. Depression does that. Makes everything seem worse than what it is. I know that first-hand."

Noah dropped his gaze to the floor again, and he fought against the knot suddenly in his throat and the sting at the backs of his eyes for all he was worth. Because his depression had never been this bad, not even right after his injury. And deep down he hated himself for not being stronger, for not just willing himself to get the fuck over it already.

Mack clapped his hand against the back of Noah's shoulder. "Second, you need to get some help, Noah. I'm telling you that you can't do it alone. Also from experience."

Noah looked to Mack again, relieved not to see any pity on the other man's face. Finally, he nodded. "Okay, Mack. I will."

CHAPTER TWENTY

By SEVEN O'CLOCK on Friday night, Kristina was already in her favorite nightgown—a pretty yellow little thing with blue ribbons under the bust, along the shoulders, and along the frilly bottom hem.

It was beyond pathetic.

This had been her first week of summer break, and she'd barely left the house except to teach her workshop at the Art Factory, which met on Tuesday and Thursday evenings. She'd actually been really glad for those classes, because they'd given her something fun and rewarding to think about, something to distract her from the ragged hole that existed right in the center of her chest.

The hole caused by removing Noah from her life.

And damn, it wasn't easy to do.

She couldn't stop thinking about him, no matter how much she tried to distract herself with TV or books or work for her class. And she occasionally unthinkingly reached for her phone to text him, not remembering until her fingers hit the keys that she couldn't. Or, at the very least, shouldn't.

Clearly, she had a long way to go.

For his part, Noah hadn't reached out to her, either. And frankly, that seemed to say quite a lot.

Oh, God, it hurts.

Sitting on the couch, laptop in her lap, she pressed a hand against her chest and tried to take a deep breath.

Knock, knock, knock.

Kristina frowned, then shifted everything off her lap and made for the door. Glancing down at herself, she decided her nightgown wasn't too revealing, so she pulled open the door just a little.

Her stomach plunged to the floor.

Noah.

She'd half thought it would be Kate, who'd been on a non-stop Kristina-watch ever since Saturday night, stopping by, texting, and sending her funny links at regular intervals to make sure she was okay and try to cheer her up.

"What are you doing here?" Kristina finally asked.

His expression fell and he shifted his feet, making her notice the blue cooler bag dangling from his one hand. Oh. My. God. He did *not* bring her ice cream.

"Um, well, can I come in?" he asked.

She was a hundred percent certain neither of them had ever had to ask the other one to be allowed in, and it hurt to hear him say those words because it revealed just how messed up they were now.

It hurt even worse to say, "No. Tell me why you're here."

He frowned, and the longer Kristina looked at him, the more she noticed that Noah...didn't look good. Dark circles marred the skin beneath flat, bloodshot eyes. His cheeks appeared hollow. And holy crap, even with a T-shirt and jeans on she would've sworn he'd lost weight since last weekend. Again.

"I wanted to talk to you." He shrugged. "Maybe hang out."

Her jaw dropped. "Hang out?"

"Yeah." He held up the cooler. "Reverse dinner?"

"Noah—"

"Please, Kristina," he said, stepping closer, close enough that all that separated them was the invisible plane where the door would be if she shut it. "At least let me apologize."

Almost sure that Kristina was going to regret it, she nodded, opened the door wider, and stepped out of Noah's way. He came in and dropped the cooler on the table, then turned toward her. His gaze raked over her nightgown, and Kristina hated the heat that rushed over her skin in its wake. But that reaction proved that her decision about their relationship had been the right one.

Noah held up his hands in a gesture of surrender. "I'm sorry," he said. "For so many things, Kristina. For the way I talked to you. For the way I've been treating you, all the way back to when I came home. I've just felt so bad about myself that I didn't want you to see it. But that's no excuse, I know." He stepped closer, sending Kristina's heart into a sprint. "And I'm sorry for hurting your feelings, for not responding better to what you had to say."

She frowned. For not responding better to what she had to say? Like what she'd said was just any old thing? Whatever.

"Okay, I accept your apology," she managed.

Fighting wouldn't serve any purpose, and the easier she made this for him the faster he would leave. At least, that's what she told herself.

Relief filled his expression, smoothing out the furrowed wrinkles on his forehead. He came toward her, arms lifted like he was going to hug her.

Kristina stepped back and raised a hand. "Don't. Please." She couldn't let him touch her because she didn't think she'd be strong enough if he made it in to something more.

Noah dragged a hand through his hair. "Oh. Okay. Sure.

Well, I brought your favorites." He started for the kitchen. "I'll grab some spoons and bowls."

What? "Noah, stop." She hugged herself. "What do you think is happening here right now?"

His brow furrowed again and he shrugged. "I, uh, thought we could hang out, eat ice cream, maybe grab dinner. You know, like old times."

Those words broke her heart. They really freaking did. He didn't get it, did he?

Kristina shook her head and nailed him with a stare. "No, we can't. We can't do any of that. Or, maybe I should say that *I* can't. Did you not hear me last weekend? I'm in love with you, Noah. And unless anything's changed, you made your position very clear." She pressed a hand to her mouth and willed herself not to cry. "It...hurts to hang out with you knowing you don't want me the way I want you. Just being in the same room with you right now, it hurts too much."

His brow rose toward his hairline as Noah closed the distance between them. This time, Kristina held her ground. "Are you...are you seriously saying we can't even be friends?"

Kristina shrugged, not out of a feeling of uncertainty, but because she felt so damn helpless. "It hurts, Noah."

His jaw ticked and his gaze narrowed. "So, what? You're giving me an ultimatum?"

Sadness had Kristina's chest throbbing. "No. I know you can't help how you feel. But I can't help how I feel, either. I can't be *just friends* with the man I love. Because I want to tell him that I love him and touch him and talk about the future with him. And if we're just friends, we can't do any of that. I can't pretend to feel something I don't any more than you can."

Something that looked like panic slid over his expression, and he gently grasped her by the shoulders. "Please don't do this."

She twisted out of his hold. "I'm not trying to do anything," she said, her voice sounding thick and strained to her own ears. "It just happened. It's not either of our faults."

"Kristina—"

"Go," she said, pressing a hand to her mouth again. A single tear tracked hotly down the side of her face, and she dashed it away. "Please just go."

Noah spun from her and paced into the living room, his hands scrubbing over his face. "Fuck. *Fuck*, Kristina, we've been friends for twenty goddamned years." He whirled on her, his eyes blazing.

Kristina walked to the door and opened it, and then she stood there waiting. "I know. And I will always, *always* cherish that." She dropped her gaze to an indistinct point between them.

His footsteps were heavy as they stalked toward her. For a long moment, he stood in front of her, but she couldn't bring herself to meet his eyes. And then he walked out the door. She quietly closed it behind him.

Then Kristina clapped her hands over her mouth, slid down against the inside of the door, and mourned those twenty years coming to an end. Her blurry gaze landed on his cooler full of ice cream, still sitting on the table.

And she'd thought she couldn't feel any worse than she already had.

SATURDAY MORNING, Noah didn't go to his art class. He didn't see the point in it.

Actually, he didn't see the point in much at all.

He'd sat on the couch all night, phone in his hand, wondering what the hell had happened to his life.

Because not only was he partially deaf and blind and no longer a Marine, but he'd lost Kristina. And the latter was his own damn fault.

Worse, overnight it had hit him—losing Kristina was far more catastrophic than losing the hearing and sight had ever been. *Those* he could compensate for, work around, figure out new ways to deal with.

But there was no way in hell to compensate for losing Kristina.

She was gone. That was it. And Noah was pretty sure he'd never before felt pain, because *nothing* had ever been this goddamned agonizing.

He looked down at his phone. He'd left Kristina about a million and a half voicemails and text messages over night. Apologizing. Begging her to reconsider. Asking to talk. She hadn't answered. Apparently, Noah was a glutton for punishment, though, because he'd been holding out hope that she hadn't answered because she'd been asleep. Once sunlight had slowly but surely poured between the slats of his blinds and filled his living room with its golden glow, he'd watched his phone non-stop, half holding his breath for the device to make a sound.

Now, the LED screen on his phone read 11:56.

No way was she still asleep. Which meant she was really done with him. For good.

Noah tossed the cell to the couch.

He must've nodded off at some point, because the next thing he knew his phone was ringing. Noah dove for it and pressed it to his ear. "Kristina?"

"Nope," came a deep voice. "It's Mo."

Noah's shoulders fell and he collapsed back against the couch. "Hey, Mo."

"You okay?"

Foot bouncing, Noah regretted answering the phone. He had no interest in talking to anybody but Kristina right now. "Yeah, sure."

"Well, huh. Why weren't you in class then?"

"Something came up," Noah said, rubbing his free hand hard against his thigh.

"Wanna know what I think? I'll tell you, just in case you don't ask," Mo said. "I think that's some bullshit. I can hear in your voice that something's wrong. So, should we start this conversation over from the beginning?"

"Fuck," Noah said, nearly groaning.

"Yeah, that's what I figured. Tell me where you live, Noah. I fucking hate talking on the phone."

"Mo—"

"I didn't ask, son. Tell me where you live."

"What are you, a drill sergeant?" Noah grumbled.

A quick, deep chuckle. "Nope. But I always thought I would've made a good one." Noah liked Mo and didn't have the energy to fight, so he gave him the address. "See you in fifteen." They hung up, the clock on his cell reading 4:15. Apparently, his body had decided to check out whether his mind wanted to or not.

Noah had just enough time to take a shower and change clothes when a knock sounded against the door. Sure enough, it was Mo.

"I like how you've decorated the place," Mo said, looking around at the completely blank walls. "Homey."

Noah actually managed something close to a laugh. "I just fucking moved in."

Mo chuckled as he took a seat on the couch. "Suuure you did."

Shaking his head, Noah sat down, too. "Why are you here, Mo?"

"I had this friend in the Rangers. His name was Sebastian Kalinsky, and everyone called him Bash." Mo leaned back, eased his legs up, and crossed them at the ankle, the heel of one mammoth boot resting on the coffee table. "Bash was a funny motherfucker. Always pulling pranks, had a nickname for everyone, just a super quick, dry wit. Bash was good at his job, too. If he had your six you always knew you were covered. Know what I mean?" Noah nodded. "Year before I got out of the Army, Bash stepped on a landmine. He lost most of his right leg, but he lived, and he was a lucky SOB to have survived, too. Everyone said so. When I got out, one of the first things I did was go visit Bash. He wasn't doing great adjusting to the amputation and civilian life, but he said he was hanging in, and I believed him. Three months later, he stuck a Glock in his mouth and pulled the trigger." Mo nailed Noah with a stare. "You remind me of Bash. A lot."

The words hung there for a long time.

Noah heaved a deep breath. "I'm sorry about your friend." He braced his elbows on his knees and scrubbed his hands over his face. For a long time, all Noah could do was look down at the floor. Finally, he said, "I don't want to end up like him."

Mo put his feet down one big boot at a time. "I know you don't. But sometimes, you need help to make sure that doesn't happen. Consider me your help."

Unsure what to say, Noah managed a nod. Emotion clogged his throat anyway, so he wasn't sure he could've talked if he wanted to.

"Now, you and me are gonna go grab some dinner, and then we're gonna go to Full Contact." Mo rose from the couch, then turned to Noah and raised an eyebrow.

Noah got up, threw some gym clothes in a bag, and followed Mo out the door.

Almost two hours later, they arrived at the gym, stuffed full of steak and eggs they'd gotten at Mo's favorite diner. Mo's company and no-nonsense directness had pulled Noah back from the edge of something almost too scary to contemplate.

Even though Noah had finally gotten some food in him, fight club turned out to be a disaster. His equilibrium was fucked all to hell, the vision in his good eye kept going wavy, and he was so exhausted that he actually asked Mack if he could sit out from sparring.

After class, Mack asked him to stay after again. Mo stayed, too.

"Talk to me, Noah," Mack said. The three of them sat on the benches at the side of the gym. "I know we haven't known each other long, but WFC is family. My family. And you're part of that now."

Problem was, Noah didn't know what to say. He was just so...lost. "I don't know what to do. I just know I don't want to feel like this anymore."

"Sometimes you have to hit rock bottom before you can decide you want to get back up again. Are you there?" Mack asked.

"God, if this isn't the bottom, I don't want to know what is," Noah said, looking from one man to the other.

"No, you don't," Mo said. "And I don't want you to find out, either."

"So what do I do?" Noah asked, genuinely wanting to know, entirely ready to do *anything*. "Because I've lost so much, and I don't know how to get any of it back."

"The first thing you do is choose to live, Noah. Embrace it. Fight for it. *That's* what fight club is about. And that means you have to be more responsible for your own mental health, because you can't fix anything else in your life until you fix yourself. It all starts with you. But you don't have to do it alone. We're your unit now, and we're fully invested. We'll fight with you every step of the way," Mack said. "You hear me?"

Noah nodded, not even embarrassed about the tears rolling down is face. Because it was entirely possible that these two men had just saved his life.

CHAPTER TWENTY-ONE

OVER THE NEXT NINE WEEKS, and with Mo's stuck-to-you-like-glue companionship, Noah threw himself into three activities—fight club, talk therapy, and finishing his mask.

He forced himself to eat three squares a day, even when he wasn't hungry. He went to every fight club meeting, even when he wasn't up to sparring, and worked out five days a week, often with Mack, Mo, or other guys from the club. Even though he hated talking, he forced himself to do it, seeing his psychologist at least twice a week, sometimes more back at the beginning. Maybe it was because he had other outlets now, too, but talking didn't make things worse the way it once had. At least, not most of the time.

Noah also came clean with his family on just how bad he was doing. He'd been home from overseas for nearly ten months, but opening up made him feel like he'd actually, and finally, reunited with them for the very first time.

And he thought of Kristina—of apologizing to her, thanking her, trying to rebuild...something with her—every minute of every day.

Sitting in his classroom at the Art Factory, Noah put the finishing touches on his mask. His second one, actually.

Two weeks ago, he'd belatedly joined another session of Jarvis's mask-making class after Noah's therapist had asked him to make another list like the one Jarvis had him write out back in June, and Noah was surprised to see that it had changed. Not entirely, but enough to see that Noah Cortez was now a man who had hope.

And that had given Noah the idea to make a second mask based on the new list.

The paint on the new one was still wet, which meant Noah wouldn't be taking it home with him today. But he didn't need it for another week, and it wasn't for him anyway.

Jarvis came up to Noah's table, his gaze going back and forth between the two masks. "You did good work on this, Noah," he said, looking at the new one.

It helped to be highly motivated. And for the first time in a long time, Noah was. Because this was his second chance. There were so many things he wanted, and he still had a long way to go—he had no illusions about that. "Thanks," Noah said, a little self-conscious at the praise.

"If you had to pick one thing that most brought about the changes between these masks, what would it be?" Jarvis asked.

"Warrior Fight Club," Noah said without hesitation. "But that actually means that the best decision I ever made was in coming to your class, because I wouldn't have met Mo without it."

And he had Kristina to thank for all of it, because he never even would've known about the class without her, but he didn't say any of that. Jarvis wasn't the one who needed to hear it.

His instructor grinned. "I have to say I absolutely love that you and Mo go from my art class to a mixed martial arts class every Saturday."

Noah chuckled. "Yeah. I guess they're two things you wouldn't necessarily put together, huh?"

"No," Jarvis said. "But it just goes to show why alternate therapies are so important. Come back to my class any time."

"Mo will make sure of it, no doubt," Noah said. And it was true. Mo didn't let Noah get away with anything, and he'd become one of the best friends Noah ever had.

Besides, Kristina, of course.

Which had Noah looking at his masks again.

They weren't so different that you'd describe one as night and the other as day, but if you were working on a gray scale, you might describe the first one as black and the new one as medium gray.

Baby steps, and damnit, he'd take 'em.

Over the last couple months, so many things had improved for Noah. He was eating regularly, sleeping most of the time, coping with stress and anxiety better, and making plans for his future. He'd even met with a career counselor that one of the fight club guys had recommended to him, and had an appointment with a head hunter that worked exclusively with ex-military this coming week. He still had nightmares, panic attacks, and migraines, but they were fewer and farther between. He still had equilibrium problems, but strength training and hours and hours of MMA training had made him much more competent, controlled, and formidable in the cage.

He still didn't have Kristina Moore.

But he wasn't sure there was anything he could do about that.

Still, he was trying, and he believed Mack was right. He couldn't fix anything with her until he worked to fix himself first.

It all starts with you. Words he now lived by.

Noah only hoped that he got far enough fast enough, before Kristina moved on with someone else.

That night at Full Contact, Noah walked into the gym to find a roomful of people he knew, and who knew him in return. He'd met Mack's wife and Mo's mama, and attended Hawk's wedding. Mack was right—they really were a family. He was privileged to be a part of it.

Hell, he was fucking lucky. Full stop.

Just like always, they worked through the warm-ups, striking pattern exercises, technical training, and grappling matches as usual, and then Noah found himself in the cage with Mo.

The man's chuckle could sound downright evil. It really could.

"I'm not afraid of you, Moses," Noah said as they knocked gloves.

"You should be," Mo said, giving him a wink.

Colby gave the signal, and then they were circling, punching, kicking, looking for the perfect takedown. Mo was bigger, though Noah had put on a good thirty pounds of muscle these past weeks and he was still faster on his feet. By a lot. Which meant Noah needed to wear Mo down, way down, before the fight moved to the ground.

Noah attacked with a whole string of fast-paced punching combos, got in a few liver kicks whenever Mo's bad habit of letting his elbow go loose from his side materialized, and was slowly but surely wearing the big guy down. Mo got in his hits, too, especially on the left side. Noah was still working on compensating for his lack of peripheral vision there.

So much about him was a work in progress.

And Noah was okay with that.

Noah nearly got caught in a clinch against the cage, but he poured on the power and twisted out of it, catching Mo by surprise and taking the man down. Hard. Before Mo regained his wits, Noah got behind him and caught him in a choke hold. Mo fought and twisted and tried to gain leverage. Holding on for everything he was worth, Noah managed to wrap one of his legs around one of Mo's, further immobilizing him. But the guy wouldn't stop fighting.

"Tap out, Mo," Noah gritted out, his muscles straining.

"Fuck. You." Mo's voice was raspy from the pressure of the choke.

Noah would've laughed if it wouldn't have stolen some of his strength. Instead, he squeezed tighter. "I can...do this...all day," he said.

Mo chuffed out something close to a laugh. "Like hell."

"Admit it...you're finished," Noah said, grinding his teeth together against the strain to hold the big guy. It was like wrestling a damn bull.

One moment passed. Then another.

Mo tapped out.

Elation absolutely flooded through Noah's veins. He let Mo go and sprung to his feet, hands in the air. And that's when Noah noticed that they had an audience. Most of the club had gathered around their cage, and they were now clapping and cheering.

For Noah.

It was the first time he'd ever beat Moses Griffin. And, for the first time in a long, long time, Noah felt like he was ten fucking feet tall.

He felt good. He felt good *enough*. Certainly for himself, and maybe even for Kristina.

And given how he'd felt not that many months ago, that was really something.

No, that was *everything*.

THE ABSOLUTE LAST thing that Kristina wanted to do was go to a wedding. Any wedding. But especially the wedding of Joshua Cortez.

Because that would mean seeing Noah again. And *that* would no doubt pick at the very thin scab that had been trying to form over her broken heart.

Kristina hadn't seen Noah since the night he'd walked out of her apartment. Or, more correctly, since the day she'd asked him to leave. Ten weeks ago. Okay, ten weeks and one day ago, but who was counting?

Still lying in bed, she pulled the covers over her head and wished it was acceptable for a twenty-five-year-old woman to hide from the world that way. But she couldn't do that to the Cortezes, who had been a surrogate family to her since she'd been a small child. More than that, because of the severity of her father's mental illness, they'd sometimes been more of a family to her than her own family had the capacity to be.

No way could she skip the wedding of their oldest son.

She faked a pitiful cough.

Nope. That wouldn't fly either.

"Stay stroganoff, Kris," she murmured to the empty room. Right. So. Okay.

On a groan, she threw off the covers and climbed out of bed.

Her gaze went right to the long bag hanging on the back of her closet door. Kate had insisted that Kristina needed armor to protect herself from *He who shall not be named*—Kate's newest nickname for Noah. Kristina supposed that was a step up from *the bastard* though possibly a step down from *that guy*, but either way, her armor of choice was made of crepe de Chine. She removed the bag covering the sleeveless, floral, asymmetrical maxi dress. A teal and yellow print, almost like a watercolor, ran over the white silk. Paired with some gorgeous yellow heels, Kristina felt like a million bucks wearing it.

And she was going to need that feeling to make it through this day. She was sure of it.

As she got ready, Kate sent her a steady stream of funny memes around the theme *You can do it.*

One read, *If Nicolas Cage can still get work, you can do anything!*

The next had a picture of a cat staring at itself in a mirror. The caption read, *Carl, you're going to get out there and do it. This time you're going to catch that red dot.*

Another had a particularly sexy picture of Ryan Gosling and said, *Hey girl, good luck today. I believe in you.* Kristina made that one the background on her phone.

All too soon, she was on her way to the church. Of course, when she wouldn't have minded a delay, she caught every green light and hit no traffic at all.

Talk about your bad luck.

"Okay," she murmured to herself, walking up to the church door. "Big girl panties are now *on.*"

Inside, the usher, a Cortez cousin Kristina knew, led her to one of the front rows with the Cortez family. Noah was nowhere to be seen yet. She distracted herself by skimming over the beautifully engraved program until a murmur passed over the guests. When she looked up, Josh was standing at the top of the aisle. And Noah stood right next to him.

Seeing him again stole her breath and brought rushing forth every single emotion she'd been trying to repress these past months. Love. Sadness. Desire. Grief. Worry.

But mostly love.

Noah found her in the crowd and their gazes collided. Then locked tight. Kristina couldn't force herself to look away. Seeing him after all this time was like water to a wanderer in the desert. Necessary. Life-giving. Absolutely and utterly undeniable.

The wedding march started, the warm, echoing tones of the

pipe organ filling the church. Everyone rose, breaking Kristina's connection with Noah. Kristina rose, too.

And, oh, Maria was such a beautiful bride. Not just because of the gorgeous beaded gown or the glittering jewelry or the hand-crafted lace on the veil, but because of the amazing joy radiating from her face.

The ceremony itself was a total blur.

Kristina was incapable of paying attention to anything besides Noah. And, holy crap, how he'd changed. He'd picked up weight, and the fine black fabric of the tuxedo jacket fit his noticeably bigger physique like a glove, the cut perfectly accentuating the breadth of his shoulders and the trimness of his waist. His face had filled out, and the dark circles were gone, replaced with a healthy-looking tan that said he'd spent time in the sun.

But it was his eyes where she most saw the change. They weren't flat anymore. They were bright and full of life.

Silently, she sent up a few words of thanks. Noah was doing better, and Kristina couldn't have been happier for that. Maybe she could finally let go of her worry, if not any of the other things she felt for him.

Another thought snuck in behind those—he'd gotten better without her. And that probably hurt more than it should.

When the ceremony ended, Kristina didn't think twice. She cut through the crowd to a side door and made her way to her car. No way in hell was she walking through the receiving line because the best man would undoubtedly be part of it.

Instead, she drove to the hotel where the reception was taking place and waited in the air conditioning of her car until other guests began arriving. Soon, cars poured into the lot and wedding attendees streamed into the hotel lobby, and Kristina finally joined them in the ballroom.

It was a lovely space. Big framed mirrors lined three walls, and the fourth was nearly floor to ceiling windows with occasional doors that opened onto what looked like gardens beyond. Jeweled chandeliers hung from the ceiling and towering floral centerpieces decorated the tables in shades of bright pink and dark orange and golden yellow.

It was beautiful. Magical. A space in which any bride would be happy to celebrate her wedding and the start of a new life with the man she loved. So of course Kristina found herself fighting back tears.

No. There would be no crying here. Armor. Big-girl panties. Ryan Gosling. Right.

Assigned seating placed her at Noah's parents' table, and Kristina resolved herself to be normal, to just get through it. At least the wedding party had its own table on a raised dais, which saved her from any chance of having to sit with Noah.

The meal was lovely, and Kristina enjoyed it and the Cortez's company as much as she could. Kristina smiled and clapped in all the right places. When the couple cut the cake. When Maria smeared icing on Josh's lips. When Maria and Josh shared their first dance. And when the couple danced with their parents. Each moment was special and joyous, but she didn't have to ask why each also set off a pang in her chest, just left of center.

Noah.

She tried to keep her eyes from straying his way, but every so often she found herself looking at him up at the head table. He was rugged masculinity personified, and more gorgeous than she even remembered. How that was possible, she didn't know. But it was true.

It was torture.

The minute they asked all the single ladies to come to the dance floor for the throwing of the bride's bouquet, Kristina excused herself for the bathroom.

Because. No.

No freaking way.

She hid out in there as long as she thought she could. But it wasn't long enough. Because when she walked out of the bathroom, she nearly walked right into Noah.

Who was clearly waiting for her.

"Noah," she said, her voice barely more than a whisper.

"Kristina. You look amazing. That dress..." He shook his head. "Gorgeous."

Up close, she could really tell how much bigger he was. God, he was stunning. "You look good, too."

"Will you take a walk with me?" he asked.

Alone? That seemed like a bad idea. A very very no good terribly bad idea. "Uh..."

"Please?" The vulnerability on his face made him impossible to resist.

"Sure," she finally said, both because a part of her really wanted to, and because there was no sense torturing herself by putting the inevitable reunion off for another minute.

He offered her his arm, and she threaded hers around. She almost sighed when he tucked her arm in close to his side, forcing her to walk even closer to him. And, damn it all, but nearly three months of being apart had done absolutely nothing to quell her desire for him. Touching him rushed heat through her veins, sending her heart flying and her pulse racing.

Noah guided her along the marble-floored hallway that ringed the ballroom and led to a set of glass doors opening onto the gardens. A warm breeze sent her skirt fluttering around her legs as Noah led them to a secluded spot where a white bench sat under a trellis heavy with fragrant lavender wisteria.

The utter romance of the secluded little spot turned her stomach inside out.

A wrapped gift sat on the bench.

"Sit with me?" Noah asked.

"Okay," she said, her voice shaky as she joined him on the narrow bench. Narrow enough that their thighs touched.

Noah held the deep rectangular box in his hands. Colorful whimsical wrapping paper with a cupcake design covered the gift, and a bright pink bow sat on top.

Anticipation built up inside her. Why had he brought her out here? And what was the present for? When he didn't say anything else, she fumbled for something to say herself. Their inability to communicate, the one thing she'd always taken for granted, broke another piece of her mangled heart.

"So, um—" she said.

"Kris—" he began at the same time.

They chuckled, the sound awkward and tense. Two words that had never once described them before.

Her shoulders fell. "How are you, Noah?"

He gave a single nod, the clean-cut profile of his face so freaking attractive she had to look away. "Actually, that's why I brought you out here. Here," he said, holding out the box. "This is for you."

For her? The last time he'd given her a present, it had been ice cream. And that had hurt so much that she'd left the cooler sitting untouched on her table until the smell of the long-melted confection necessitated that she throw the whole thing away. "Noah, I don't think I should—"

"Please, Kristina. It's not what you think."

She had no idea *what* she thought, so she took the box with shaking hands and carefully unwrapped it.

"I wrapped it myself," he said.

She glanced at him, and found just the hint of a smirk around his lips. "Shut up," she said. That brought out a little smile. And the echo of their old banter, and all the loss it represented, made her need to look away again.

Layers of white tissue paper filled the box. She set it on the ground, and pulled out the first solid-feeling object. Carefully, Kristina unwrapped it.

What she found in the middle rushed tears to her eyes.

Noah's mask.

"Oh, God, Noah. It's...amazing." And it was. But it was also the most heart-wrenching thing she'd ever seen.

Crisscrossing red slashes marred the left side of the face, and patches of duct tape covered the left eye, left side of the mouth, and wrapped around the left ear. The head on the left side was fragmented and broken, and in three places pieces of the "skull" were missing. He'd secured paper on the underside, and in each of those empty spots he'd written the word, "Gone."

Instinctively, Kristina grabbed Noah's hand and pulled it into her lap. She squeezed his fingers so tight she was probably hurting him, but she couldn't sit there and look at this tortured self-portrait without holding some part of him.

The right side of the face, the side on which Noah retained his sight and hearing, had a smooth surface, but the way he'd done the eye made it appear empty. Cracks from the broken side of the skull stretched across the forehead, thinner on the right side, but drawn as if they were threatening to break apart. The lips were a bluish-red, as if the mask had been deprived of oxygen. On the cheekbone was a small, rectangular tattoo—a black-and-white American flag.

She couldn't stop staring at the mask and trying to imagine exactly what emotions he felt inside that translated to *this*.

She clutched his hand against her heart. "I don't know what to say, Noah. Except that I am honored that you shared this with me."

A single tear drop escaped her eye. Noah caught it with the fingers of his free hand. "Don't cry." He reached in and drew something else out of the box, then handed it to her.

"Oh, God, there's more?" she asked, having to let his hand go to take the second item. Noah just nodded. She placed the first mask in her lap and began unwrapping.

Another mask.

A significantly *different* mask.

The slashes still covered the left side, but were much paler, as if they'd faded. The duct tape was gone from the mouth. The skull was broken and cracked as it had been in the first one, but a layer of gauze wrapped around it, as if the wound had been treated.

And was healing.

She heaved a shaky breath.

On the right side, the eye stared pointedly at her, the flatness gone. The lips were a normal, pale red all the way across. The tattoo remained below the eye, but another joined it.

Below the flag sat three block letters: WFC.

What that meant, she didn't know, but it was obviously important to Noah. Important enough that he saw it as defining him the same way the flag did.

Kristina placed both masks on top of the tissue sitting on her lap and looked at them side by side. Swallowing around the knot of emotion in her throat, she managed, "Both of these are you?"

"Yeah. I started this one the day I told you I didn't love you," he said, pointing to the first mask. Kristina's gaze cut to his face. "I was in such a low place that day, Kristina. Almost the lowest of my life. I *was* every bit as fucked-up as I said, and I told myself it wouldn't be right to burden you with that when I was completely sure it would never change. *That's* why I pushed you away, and I'm sorry for it. I regret it every single day."

"Noah—"

"Please let me finish," he said, his dark eyes serious and intense. She nodded. "My lowest point actually came a week later, after I came to your apartment that night to apologize. Do you remember?"

"Yes," she whispered, a shiver racing over her skin.

"That next day was the worst day of my life. And, in a way, the best. Because it was the day I decided I had to try to heal, or I would end up killing myself."

A sob tried to rip up Kristina's throat, but she forced it down, her breathing audibly catching. She grasped his hand again, wishing she had the power to hold him to this world with the sheer force of her will alone.

"I'm so sorry," she whispered, her gaze dropping to the first mask.

Fingers gently lifted her chin, forcing her to look at him. "Don't be. If you'd let me back into your life that night, I might've thought I could keep right on doing the same thing. It wasn't working then, and it never would've worked. *That's* why I kept falling apart. You saved my life, Kristina. You, and Moses and Mack from the fight club. Hell, you don't even know about the fight club, do you?"

She shook her head, just glad that he'd found something that'd helped him.

"I'll tell you. If you want, that is. But, for now, I just need you to know. You pushed me to examine myself and make a choice. And I chose to live, to fight. And that's what I've been doing the past couple of months."

Sadness and cautious hope rushed through her like a flash flood. The things he'd been going through all this time...

"And...how's it going?" she asked.

"Good. Slow. I'm a work in progress, of course. But I've been working hard, trying to get myself ready to see you today. Two weeks ago, I started on the second mask. Because I wanted you to know."

"That you've changed?"

"Yes, in part," he said. He gently pulled his hand free, stood up, and faced her.

One by one, he unbuttoned his dress shirt until he'd created a gap in the middle of the buttons. He pulled the left side open, exposing the absolutely cut muscle of his chest and abdomen.

A new tattoo sat across his heart.

IT ALL
STARTS
WITH YOU

He held out a hand, inviting her to stand. She carefully placed the masks on the bench and accepted his grasp. Noah pulled her closer until he pressed her palm flat over the ink. He held her hand there with his.

"This tattoo is about me, because I had to fix myself before I could do or have or be anything else. But this tattoo is also about you, because you were my reason, my inspiration, my hope against hope."

Kristina's heart suddenly thundered inside her chest. Her brain struggled to make sense of everything he was saying. And her heart wasn't the only one going a little crazy, because beneath her fingers, his drummed out a fast, hard beat. "Hope for what?"

His eyes went almost soft as he peered down at her. "You have every reason to hate me, every reason to want me to stay away. I'm not all better, and maybe I never will be. But if you could forgive me for the way I treated you or, God, I know this is hoping too much, but maybe even think of some way I might get to be a part of your life, even if infrequently, it would mean the world to me—"

"I don't hate you, Noah. I never hated you," she rushed out, her mind spinning. "And there's nothing to forgive. I'm proud of you. So proud of you. It takes a strong, strong person to do what you've done. I'm just..." She shook her head, emotion clogging her throat. "...really proud. And, as far as being in my life—"

"I know that I've hurt you. After using you and lashing out at you, I wouldn't disrespect you by hoping for more than friendship now. And God knows I don't want to do another thing to hurt you—"

Kristina cupped his face in her free hand. "Noah, what are you saying?" she asked, her head and heart a confused, hopeful, scared mess.

He pressed her hand more firmly to his skin. "I just wanted to apologize for the way I treated you. And thank you for your part in helping me get better. And...and to tell you that I lied. I lied that night when I told you I didn't love you. Jesus, every word out of my mouth during that conversation was a lie, and I'm so damn sorry. But I—"

"You lied?" she asked in a small voice. The whole world narrowed to the space between them.

He nodded, just once. "I'm sorry."

"What does that mean?" Because what she *thought* it meant was too freaking important to guess at.

Noah looked her right in the eye for a long moment, and then he said, "That I love you. That I'm *in love* with you. And I'm only sorry that I figured it all out too late."

"No," she said, shaking her head. Kristina couldn't hold back the sob when it threatened this time. She was trembling and a little dizzy and quite possibly dreaming, because the man she loved had just told her he loved her, too. "Oh, Noah."

"Oh, God, please don't cry. Damnit, I knew I was going to fuck this up." He gently grasped her face in both of his hands and swiped at her tears with his thumbs.

"Not...not too late," she finally whispered through her tears. "I still love you. I never stopped. I don't think I ever could."

Noah's eyes went wide as saucers. It would've been almost comical if the wonder on his face hadn't been so damn beautiful. "Wait. You still...love me? After everything?"

She pressed onto tiptoes and threaded her arms around his neck. "Noah, I will *always* love you."

"Aw, Jesus," he said, his arms banding around her tight and his forehead pressing against hers.

"I love you," she said as warm joy rushed over her and through her until she was nearly bursting with it.

"Oh, thank God," he said. And then he kissed her. Softly at first. Tentatively. Just a feather-light press of skin on skin. "Is this okay? Can I—"

"Yes. More than okay," she whispered, trembling in joy and need and more than a little disbelief.

He kissed her harder then, deeper, like he couldn't get enough of her. Kristina was absolutely okay with that, because he would never have to.

Long minutes passed, and then Noah broke the kiss. "I never expected..." He shook his head. "You love me." He said it with such aching wonder in his voice.

"Yes. No matter if you're wearing one of these masks or some other, my heart will always and only ever know yours. That's the way it's always been, and it's the only way I ever want it to be. I love you, Noah."

"I love you, too, baby," he whispered. "And I'll never get tired of hearing you say that." Those now bright dark eyes blazed with desire and devotion and love.

And, *God*, it was such a different look on him. This...utter lightness, this newfound happiness. He wasn't the old Noah, he was totally new. Scars and all, she loved him even more for all he'd gone through to come back to himself, back to her. "Good," she managed, her throat so tight with emotion.

"Damnit, I can't believe I'm getting to say all this. I never even dared to hope. But I love you and you own me, Kristina. You own every part of me. Everything I am or will be. *Everything* is yours."

She stroked her hand against his hair, her heart so full she was sure her chest couldn't contain it. "Then that's all I'll ever need. Because you're everything I've ever wanted. And I will fight this fight with you. Always."

"Always," he said, nodding. "And I'll never lie to you again, Kris. I promise you here and now. I'm going to have bad days. And I'm going to make mistakes. And I'm sure I'll still fuck things up from time to time." They both grinned, so caught up in this moment, this joy, each other. "But I'm in this with you. And I want you in this with me."

"I am. But I need you to know. I don't want perfect, Noah. I just want my best friend. I just want you. The rest we'll make up as we go."

"Better fucking believe it," Noah said, a smile so pure on his face that it was like the sun coming out from behind the clouds. Kristina laughed, so filled with awe about the way this evening had gone. She'd dreaded coming to Josh's wedding, dreaded seeing Noah.

Now, here she was with him, finding more than she ever thought possible, finding *everything*. And willing to fight through anything to make sure they never lost it again.

EPILOGUE

THE ROW of picnic tables was piled high with burgers and dogs, beer and soda, chips and salads. It was his parents' annual Labor Day party, and Noah was right in the middle of it.

Better yet, he had his girl at his side and his new friends from WFC and his art class all around him—Mo, Mack, Jarvis, Riddick, and about a half dozen others from the club.

Well, they didn't feel new anymore, not when they'd collectively been responsible for saving Noah's life. With some people, it was like that. You might not have known them long, but their impact was immediate, fundamental, and lasting.

Sitting on his good side, Kristina leaned in with a smile. "How you doing?"

He nuzzled her cheek, finding the solace in her company that he always did. Always had, even before he realized everything she meant to him. "Never better. At least, not in a long damn time."

"Yeah?" she whispered, heat slipping into her eyes. "Well maybe I could make you feel just a *little* better?"

"Mmm, tell me more," he said with a chuckle. For a

moment, he got lost in their sweet words and stolen touches until the madness around them all but faded away.

Something hit him in the head. "What the hell?" Noah said, startling as a hot dog bun rolled into his lap. The whole table erupted into laughter.

Mo sat there grinning like an idiot. "You weren't hearing me, son. Had to get your attention somehow."

Laughing, Noah gestured to his left side. "Deaf over here, remember?"

With a smirk, Mo shook his head. "You have two damn ears, *remember?* The real problem is that other organs are stealing all the blood meant for your brain." He winked at Kristina, who started chuckling, especially as the peanut gallery's commentary flew around the table. Damn lovable assholes.

"*You too*, baby? You're supposed to be on my side." He leaned toward her as she laughed, his mouth zeroing in on her neck. He knew attacking that spot on her had the power to make her *very* agreeable to his desires. A discovery he loved using to his advantage. Again and again.

Really, though, Noah didn't mind their friends' teasing. He hadn't realized how much he'd missed the camaraderie of the military until he hadn't had it anymore. Warrior Fight Club had given that back to him, along with so much else.

Kristina chuckled and squirmed. "Of course, I'm on your side. But that doesn't make the look on your face when that roll hit you any less funny."

"See, I knew I liked this girl," Mo said.

Noah scowled at the big guy. "You know I'm gonna take your ass down next time we're in the cage."

Mo looked totally unconcerned. "You can always try. Anyway, your dad was calling you."

Noah had just started to search for his father in the crowd when a hand settled on his shoulder. He looked up to find his father staring down at him. "Your friend Billy just arrived. He had to take a call, though, so he's using my office. Seemed like...I don't know, maybe he was a little upset."

"Thanks, Dad," Noah said, already rising. He gave Kristina's hand a squeeze. "Be right back. I'm gonna go check on him." He and Billy hadn't spent a lot of time together outside of Full Contact, in part because Billy's private investigation work meant he often kept odd hours, but they were frequent sparring partners because they were pretty evenly matched in skill and speed.

Elias nodded, his gaze full of pride and contentment as he took in the big, rowdy group of Noah's friends. It was the first time since he'd come home from war that Noah had brought people around. "Can I bring anyone anything else?" his dad asked.

As he rounded the table, Noah couldn't help but think how different his parents' Labor Day party was for him. Almost four months ago, he'd stood at the edge of their Memorial Day cookout. More observer than participant. More ghost than real.

No more. Now he had friends, a community, a closer relationship with his family than ever before. He had a new job starting in a few weeks working for the Transportation Security Administration as a bomb appraisal officer at Reagan National Airport. He had his health, which was getting better everyday.

And he had his girl. His Kristina. And some plans for her of the forever kind.

"Coming with you," Mo said, joining Noah as he made his way into the house. "Something's been bothering Parrish lately."

They found Billy sitting on the couch in Elias's study, his head in his hands. Noah and Mo exchanged a glance, and Noah closed the door behind them.

"Hey, man. Everything okay?" Noah asked.

Billy gave a shake of his head, then met their gazes for just a moment before he looked away. The man's eyes were glassy, and dread settled into Noah's gut. "Got some bad news."

Noah sat beside him, while Mo settled into the desk chair off to the side. "What's going on?" Mo asked in that deep, soft voice he had.

"Buddy of mine got hurt in an op two weeks ago. Didn't look good." Billy shook his head, his gaze trained out the window. "Just found out he didn't make it."

"Aw, hell, B," Mo said. A rock slid into Noah's gut. There wasn't a day that went by that he didn't think of the friends he'd lost.

Johnson. Kendrick. Martinez. Fender. Smythe. Khan. Stein…

And Noah knew how each and every loss took a little piece of you with it. They all did.

"I'm sorry to hear it, Billy. Someone you served with?" Noah asked.

Billy nodded. "Yeah. Came up through West Point together. A real smart-ass motherfucker." The chuckle he gave was full of memories and pain. "Do anything for anyone though, you know? Fuck."

Mo crossed the room to the other man and clasped him on the shoulder. "Come on. Won't do you no good being alone right now. Get some eats or at least a drink. Plus, Kristina's friend Kate is here and she's a cutie."

Making a visible effort to square himself away, Billy rose. "Yeah, well, I'm not sure how many cuties are in my immediate future, since on that call my asshole of a best friend also asked me to take in his baby sister for a few weeks 'til she finds a place of her own. And it's not like I can say no to one of my brothers, you know?"

"Dude, you definitely need a drink, then," Mo said.

"Maybe she'll be a cutie, too," Noah said, trying to help the guy out.

"Bite your tongue, Cortez. That girl has got to be, like, a hundred years younger than me and ten kinds of off limits," Billy said, humor starting to return to his voice. They laughed.

"Then Mo's right. Alcohol, stat," Noah said.

They headed out and rejoined the others. Food and beer and conversation flowed for hours, until the hanging lanterns came on and the sun set over the big back yard.

Boom. Poppoppop. Boom!

Noah flinched, caught off guard even though he'd known there would be fireworks tonight.

His heart beat triple-time as Kristina squeezed his hand. "Sure you want to stay?" she asked.

He heaved a breath and swallowed down the knee-jerk anxiety that tried to climb up his throat. Noise-canceling headphones had gotten him through the Fourth of July, but tonight, he'd wanted to try. He'd gained a shit-ton of insight into the way his mind worked now, and he'd come a million miles over the past few months. But he was still on the journey, and maybe always would be.

So instead of leaving, he focused on his breathing, on keeping himself grounded in the real world, on remaining in the here and now. With all these people who cared about him, and about whom he cared in return. "I think I've got this."

"I know you do," Kristina said, kissing him.

Everyone shifted in their seats to get good views of the bursts of color lighting up the September night.

Noah settled between Kristina's legs and rested his back against her front. She wrapped her arms around him, her firm embrace helping to hold him together when he couldn't quite manage it himself.

And that was the moment he knew the truth down into his very soul. "I want to stay right here," he said, peering up at her. "In your arms. Because this is right where I'm supposed to be."

THE WARRIOR FIGHT CLUB SERIES CONTINUES!

Fighting for What's His - Coming August 7, 2018

Order Now!

Resisting her only makes him want her more...

Private investigator Billy Parrish's is good at three things—fighting, investigating, and sex. MMA training with the other vets in the Warrior Fight Club keeps his war-borne demons at bay—mostly, and one night stands ensure no one gets too close. But then his best friend from the Army Rangers calls in a favor.

Shayna Curtis is new to town, fresh out of grad school, and full of hope for the future. With a new job starting in a month, she's grateful when her brother arranges a place for her to stay while she apartment hunts. But she never expected her roommate to be so brooding. Or so sexy.

Billy can't wait for Shay to leave—because the longer she's there, the more he wants her in his bed. To stay. He *can't* have her—that much he knows. But when fight club stops taking off the edge, Billy lets down his guard...and starts fighting for what's his.

Fighting the Fire - Coming Fall 2018

The more they fight, the more desire consumes them...

There's only one thing firefighter Sean Riddick doesn't like about Warrior Fight Club, and that's Daniela England, the sexiest, snarkiest, most irritating woman he's ever known. But MMA training keeps the Navy vet grounded, so Sean's not about to give it up, no matter how many times he goes toe to toe with Dani—or how bad he wants to take her to the mats.

A former Army nurse and the widow of a fallen soldier, Dani is done with the military *and* with military men. Fight club is the only thing that eases her nightmares, which means she *has* to put up with Riddick. He might be sex on a stick, but he's infuriating and everything she's vowed to avoid.

But when a crisis throws Sean and Dani together, all that fight bursts into a night of red-hot passion. Now they're addicted to the heat and must decide if the one person they've most resisted might be exactly what they've both been looking for.

Worth Fighting For - March 2019

A crossover story with Kristen Proby's Big Sky Series - now available for preorder!

Getting in deep has never felt this good...

Commercial diving instructor Tara Hunter nearly lost everything in an accident that resulted in her medical discharge from the navy. With the help of the Warrior Fight Club, she's fought to overcome her fears and get back in the water where she's always felt most at home. At work, she's tough, serious, and doesn't tolerate distractions. Which is why finding her gorgeous one-night stand on her new dive team is such a problem.

Former navy deep-sea diver Jesse Anderson just can't seem

to stop making mistakes—the latest being the hot-as-hell night he'd spent with his new partner. This job is his second chance, and Jesse knows he shouldn't mix business with pleasure. But spending every day with Tara's smart mouth and sexy curves makes her so damn hard to resist.

Joining a wounded warrior MMA training program seems like the perfect way to blow off steam—until Jesse finds that Tara belongs, too. Now they're getting in deep and taking each other down day and night, and even though it breaks all the rules, their inescapable attraction might just be the only thing truly worth fighting for.

ACKNOWLEDGMENTS

A lot of wonderful people helped bring *Fighting for Everything* to life. First, big shoutouts to Liz Berry, Jillian Stein, and Tessa Bailey for reading and loving an early version of this book. Their encouragement came right when I needed it most! Second, thanks to Lea Nolan, Christi Barth, and Stephanie Dray for cheerleading me through the writing, editing, and production of this book - you ladies know everything you've done for me and I appreciate it so much!

Next, I have to thank my agent, Kevan Lyon, for loving and believing in Noah and Kristina's story. Your support kept me going and bolstered my belief that these wounded warriors needed to have their stories told one way or the other! Thanks next to Franci Neill for making the story shine and helping me with all the little details that help launch a book into the world. Finally, thanks to KP Simmon, a friend and colleague I'm so lucky to have at my side and behind my books. And finally, thank you to my Original Heroes and Reader Girls for all the amazing support and encouragement - you guys rock!

Noah's story was most directly inspired by two real-world stories and a personal experience: First, the 2014 NPR story,

"First Rule of this Fight Club: You Must Be a Veteran," which detailed an organization called P.O.W., which stands for Pugilistic Offensive Warrior, a mixed martial arts training session that's free for veterans. And, second, a *National Geographic* story called "Behind the Masks: Revealing the Trauma of War," which displayed masks made by veterans in art therapist Melissa Walker's classes at Walter Reed (search for that title to see pictures of the masks). Both led me to thinking about how important alternate therapies are for veterans for whom more traditional talk therapy doesn't work. Additionally, I suffered a traumatic brain injury in 2008, and it's something I've explored in my characters several times. So from all of that, Noah's story in *Fighting for Everything* was born, as was the entire Warrior Fight Club series.

I hope these stories mean as much to you as they mean to me to write, and I thank you for taking my characters into your heart and letting tell my stories again and again. ~LK

ABOUT THE AUTHOR

Laura Kaye is the New York Times and USA Today bestselling author of over thirty books in contemporary romance and romantic suspense, including the Hard Ink, Raven Riders, Heroes, and Hearts in Darkness series. Her books have received numerous awards, including the RT Reviewers' Choice Award for Best Romantic Suspense for *Hard As You Can*. Laura grew up amid family lore involving angels, ghosts, and evil-eye curses, cementing her life-long fascination with storytelling and the supernatural. Laura lives in Maryland with her husband and two daughters, and appreciates her view of the Chesapeake Bay every day.

Learn more at LauraKayeAuthor.com

Join Laura's VIP Readers for Exclusives & More!

facebook.com/laurakayewrites

twitter.com/laurakayeauthor

instagram.com/laurakayeauthor

bookbub.com/profile/laura-kaye

ALSO BY LAURA KAYE

The Raven Riders Series

Brotherhood. Club. Family.

They live and ride by their own rules.

These are the Raven Riders . . .

Ride Hard (Raven Riders #1)

Raven Riders Motorcycle Club President Dare Kenyon rides hard and values loyalty above all else. He'll do anything to protect the brotherhood of bikers—the only family he's got—as well as those who can't defend themselves. So when beautiful but mistrustful Haven Randall lands on the club's doorstep scared that she's being hunted, Dare takes her in, swears to keep her safe, and pushes to learn the secrets overshadowing her pretty smile before it's too late.

Ride Rough (Raven Riders #2)

Alexa Harmon thought she had it all—the security of a good job, a beautiful home, and a powerful, charming fiancé who offered the life she never had growing up. But when her dream quickly turns into a nightmare, Alexa realizes she's fallen for a façade she can't escape— until her ex-boyfriend and Raven Riders MC vice-president Maverick Ryland offers her a way out. Forced together to keep Alexa safe, their powerful attraction reignites and Maverick determines to do whatever it takes to earn a second chance—one Alexa is tempted to give. But her ex-fiancé isn't going to let her go without a fight, one that will threaten everything they both hold dear.

Ride Wild (Raven Riders #3)

Wild with grief over the death of his wife, Sam "Slider" Evans merely lives for his two sons. Nothing holds his interest anymore—not even riding his bike or his membership in the Raven Riders Motorcycle Club. But then he hires Cora Campbell to be his nanny. Cora adores Slider's sweet boys, but never expected the red-hot attraction to their brooding, sexy father. If only he would notice her... Slider does see the beautiful, fun-loving woman he invited into his home. She makes him feel *too* much, and he both hates it and yearns for it. But when Cora witnesses something she shouldn't have, the new lives they've only just discovered are threatened. Now Slider must claim—and protect—what's his before it's too late.

Ride Dirty (Raven Riders #3.5)

Caine McKannon is all about rules. As the Raven Riders Sergeant-at-Arms, he prizes loyalty to his brothers and protection of his club. As a man, he takes pleasure wherever he can get it but allows no one close —because distance is the only way to ensure people can't hurt you. And he's had enough pain for a lifetime. But then he rescues a beautiful woman from an attack. Kids and school are kindergarten teacher Emma Kerry's whole life, so she's stunned to realize she has an enemy—and even more surprised to find a protector in the intimidating man who saved her. Tall, dark, and tattooed, Caine is unlike any man Emma's ever known, and she's as uncertain of him as she is attracted. As the danger escalates, Caine is in her house more and more – until one night of passion lands him in her bed. But breaking the rules comes at a price, forcing Caine to fight dirty to earn a chance at love.

The Hard Ink Series

Five dishonored soldiers

Former Special Forces

One last mission

These are the men of Hard Ink...

Hard As It Gets (Hard Ink #1)

Trouble just walked into Nicholas Rixey's tattoo parlor. Becca Merritt is warm, sexy, wholesome—pure temptation to a very jaded Nick. He's left his military life behind to become co-owner of Hard Ink Tattoo, but Becca is his ex-commander's daughter. Loyalty won't let him turn her away. Lust has plenty to do with it too. With her brother presumed kidnapped, Becca needs Nick. She just wasn't expecting to want him so much. As their investigation turns into all-out war with an organized crime ring, only Nick can protect her. And only Becca can heal the scars no one else sees.

Hard As You Can (Hard Ink #2)

Shane McCallan doesn't turn his back on a friend in need, especially a former Special Forces teammate running a dangerous, off-the-books operation. Nor can he walk away from Crystal, the gorgeous blonde waitress is hiding secrets she doesn't want him to uncover. Too bad. He's exactly the man she needs to protect her sister, her life, and her heart. All he has to do is convince her that when something feels this good, you hold on as hard as you can—and never let go.

Hard to Hold On To (Hard Ink #2.5)

Edward "Easy" Cantrell knows better than most the pain of not being able to save those he loves—which is why he is not going to let Jenna Dean, the woman he helped rescue from a gang, out of his sight. He may have just met her, but Jenna's the first person to make him feel alive since that devastating day in the desert more than a year ago. As the pair are thrust together while chaos reigns around them, they both know one thing: the things in life most worth having are the hardest to hold on to.

Hard to Come By (Hard Ink #3)

When a sexy stranger asks questions about her brother, Emilie Garza is torn between loyalty to the brother she once idolized and fear of the war-changed man he's become. Derek DiMarzio's easy smile and quiet strength tempt Emilie to open up, igniting the desire between them and leading Derek to crave a woman he shouldn't trust. Now, Derek and Emilie must prove where their loyalties lie before hearts are broken and lives are lost. Because love is too hard to come by to let slip away...

Hard to Be Good (Hard Ink #3.5)

Hard Ink Tattoo owner Jeremy Rixey has taken on his brother's stateside fight against the forces that nearly killed Nick and his Special Forces team a year before. Now, Jeremy's whole world has been turned upside down—not the least of which by kidnapping victim Charlie Merritt, a brilliant, quiet blond man who tempts Jeremy to settle down for the first time ever. With tragedy and chaos all around them, temptation flashes hot, and Jeremy and Charlie can't help but wonder why they're trying so hard to be good...

Hard to Let Go (Hard Ink #4)

Beckett Murda hates to dwell on the past. But his investigation into the ambush that killed half his Special Forces team and ended his Army career gives him little choice. Just when his team learns how powerful their enemies are, hard-ass Beckett encounters his biggest complication yet—his friend's younger sister, seductive, feisty Katherine Rixey. When Kat joins the fight, she lands straight in Beckett's sights . . . and in his arms. Not to mention their enemies' crosshairs. Now Beckett and Kat must set aside their differences to work together, because the only thing sweeter than justice is finding love and never letting go.

Hard As Steel (Hard Ink #4.5)

After identifying her employer's dangerous enemies, Jessica Jakes takes refuge at the compound of the Raven Riders Motorcycle Club. Fellow Hard Ink tattooist and Raven leader Ike Young promises to keep Jess safe for as long as it takes, which would be perfect if his close, personal, round-the-clock protection didn't make it so hard to hide just how much she wants him—and always has. The last thing Ike needs is alone time with the sexiest woman he's ever known, one he's purposely kept at a distance for years. Now, Ike's not sure he can keep his hands or his heart to himself—or that he even wants to anymore.

Hard Ever After (Hard Ink #5)

After a long battle to discover the truth, the men and women of Hard Ink have a lot to celebrate, especially the wedding of two of their own —Nick Rixey and Becca Merritt, whose hard-fought love deserves a happy ending. But an old menace they thought long gone reemerges, threatening the peace they've only just found. Now, for one last time, Nick and Becca must fight for their always and forever.

Hard to Serve (Hard Ink #5.5)

To protect and serve is all Detective Kyler Vance ever wanted to do, so when Internal Affairs investigates him as part of the new police commissioner's bid to oust corruption, everything is on the line. Which makes meeting smart, gorgeous submissive, Mia Breslin, at an exclusive play club the perfect distraction. Their scorching scenes lure them to play together again and again. But then Kyler runs into Mia at work and learns that he's been dominating the daughter of the hard-ass boss who has it in for him. Now Kyler must choose between life-long duty and forbidden desire before Mia finds another who's not so hard to serve.

The Hearts in Darkness Duet

Hearts in Darkness (Hearts in Darkness Duet #1)

Two strangers. Four hours. One pitch-black elevator. Makenna James thinks her day can't get any worse, until she finds herself stranded in a pitch-black elevator with a complete stranger. Caden Grayson is amused when a harried redhead dashes into his elevator fumbling her bags and cell phone, but his amusement turns to panic when the power fails. Despite his piercings, tats, and vicious scar, he's terrified of the dark and confined spaces. Now, he's trapped in his own worst nightmare. To fight fear, they must reach out and open up. With no preconceived notions based on looks to hold them back, they discover just how much they have in common. In the warming darkness, attraction grows and sparks fly, but will they feel the same when the lights come back on?

Love in the Light (Hearts in Darkness Duet #2)

Two hearts in the darkness...must fight for love in the light... Makenna James and Caden Grayson have been inseparable since the day they were trapped in a pitch-black elevator and found acceptance and love in the arms of a stranger. Makenna hopes that night put them on the path to forever—which can't happen until she introduces her tattooed, pierced, and scarred boyfriend to her father and three over-protective brothers. Haunted by a childhood tragedy and the loss of his family, Caden never thought he'd find the love he shares with Makenna. But the deeper he falls, the more he fears the devastation sure to come if he ever lost her, too. When meeting her family doesn't go smoothly, Caden questions whether Makenna deserves someone better, stronger, and just more...normal. Maybe they're just too different—and he's far too damaged—after all...

The Heroes Series

Her Forbidden Hero (Heroes #1)

Former Army Special Forces Sgt. Marco Vieri has never thought of Alyssa Scott as more than his best friend's little sister, but her return home changes that...and challenges him to keep his war-borne demons at bay. Marco's not the same person he was back when he protected Alyssa from her abusive father, and he's not about to let her see the mess he's become. But Alyssa's not looking for protection—not anymore. Now that she's back in his life, she's determined to heal her forbidden hero one touch at a time...

One Night with a Hero (Heroes #2)

After growing up with an abusive, alcoholic father, Army Special Forces Sgt. Brady Scott vowed never to marry or have kids. Sent stateside to get his head on straight—and his anger in check—Brady's looking for a distraction. He finds it in Joss Daniels, his beautiful new neighbor whose one-night-only offer for hot sex leads to more. Suddenly, Brady's not so sure he can stay away. But when Joss discovers she's pregnant, Brady's rejection leaves her feeling abandoned. Now, they must overcome their fears before they lose the love and security they've found in each other, but can they let go of the past to create a future together?

96033666R00141

Made in the USA
Columbia, SC
19 May 2018